OODLES OF POODLES

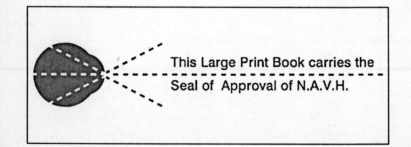

This Large Print Book carries the
Seal of Approval of N.A.V.H.

A PET RESCUE MYSTERY

OODLES OF POODLES

LINDA O. JOHNSTON

WHEELER PUBLISHING
A part of Gale, Cengage Learning

GALE
CENGAGE Learning·

Detroit • New York • San Francisco • New Haven, Conn • Waterville, Maine • London

GALE
CENGAGE Learning·

LIBRARY OF CONGRESS CATALOGING-IN-PUBLICATION DATA

Johnston, Linda O.
  Oodles of Poodles / By Linda O. Johnston. — Large Print edition.
    pages cm. — (A Pet Rescue Mystery.) (Wheeler Publishing Large Print
  Cozy Mystery.)
    ISBN 978-1-4104-6185-8 (softcover) — ISBN 1-4104-6185-8 (softcover)
  1. Animal welfare—Fiction. 2. Large type books. I. Title.
  PS3610.O387O53 2013
  813'.6—dc23   2013021307

Published in 2013 by arrangement with The Berkley Publishing Group,
a division of Penguin Group (USA)

Printed in the United States of America
1 2 3 4 5   17 16 15 14 13

ACKNOWLEDGMENTS

I want to thank the film industry and its usually fun depiction of animals — although, of course, there are always exceptions, and films and TV shows that don't earn the coveted "No Animals Were Harmed®" designation. I wanted *Oodles of Poodles* to show the industry at its best, at least in its love and care for animals.

I also want to thank Natalee Rosenstein, senior executive editor at Berkley Prime Crime, for suggesting the title of *Oodles of Poodles,* as well as for everything else she does for this wonderful imprint of Penguin Group (USA) Inc. And of course I thank my editor, Michelle Vega, who's an absolutely delightful editor in all respects.

Then there's my wonderful agent, Paige Wheeler, founding member of Folio Literary Management, LLC, without whom my career would be very different, and a lot less fun.

As always, this book is dedicated to my wonderful husband, Fred, who brainstorms with me and bears with my fretting over nearly everything as I write. I thank him, and I also thank my adorable pups Lexie and Mystie for always acting as my inspirations . . . and interruptions.

AUTHOR'S NOTE

Oodles of Poodles is completely fiction. However, it includes a lot of references to a wonderful organization called the American Humane Association that does, in fact, scrutinize movies and TV shows to make sure that all animals, from insects to elephants, are treated well. Only then will the production receive the coveted "No Animals Were Harmed®" designation. "No Animals Were Harmed®" is a registered trademark of American Humane. The designation of the Certified Animal Safety Representatives™ is also a trademark. I was fortunate enough to receive permission to refer to them in this book, thanks to the kindness of Jone Bouman, director of communications, American Humane Association Film and TV Unit, who also gave me a generous amount of her time, plus a lot of reading and viewing material, to help me learn about her excellent organization.

CHAPTER 1

I adore animals, and will do nearly anything not only to save them, but to make them happy, too.

That made it particularly hard to look through the chain-link fence at the end of the kennel run in the facility I was visiting and see that adorable, sad doggy face.

The white miniature poodle sat there, head cocked, eyes on mine as if begging me to get her out, hug her, find her the perfect new home.

"I'm sorry, Sheba," I said softly. "I can't do anything right now but it'll be all right. I promise."

I never make idle promises, but this one was especially true. Sheba wasn't just any sad little rescue dog like the ones I nurture at my excellent private shelter. In fact, although this sweet poodle had apparently gone through hell so far in her short life, it had turned to puppy perfection — or at least it ultimately would, even if she didn't know it.

At the moment, she was waiting for the next scene to be shot in the already touted major Hollywood movie about her fictional counterpart, also named Sheba. The film's name? *Sheba's Story.*

"She's one cute little girl, isn't she, Lauren?" said my good friend Dr. Carlie Stellan, who had come with me to the set this day. She and her veterinary staff had been there on many other days as well. "Sheba's bound to become a popular movie star, don't you think? She and all her similar-looking friends. How many are there?"

Like me, Carlie was dressed well in a nice pantsuit, hers blue and mine charcoal. She's a pretty blond and is used to being in front of the camera. She stars in her own reality TV show, *Pet Fitness,* on the Longevity Vision Channel.

I'm Lauren Vancouver, average looking, with green eyes and dark hair that I keep short so it doesn't get in the way as I take care of animals. I have no need to impress anyone with my appearance.

"There are four dogs that play Sheba that I know of so far," I responded. I hadn't realized it before I got involved in this filming, but each dog or other creature depicted on a movie screen might be a conglomeration of several similar-looking animals. Each lookalike would have a different specialty in action or reaction thanks to his training, or he may represent the star at different ages. Sometimes they even wore makeup to appear identical. They really were actors.

The forlorn dog here waiting for the latest scene to shoot, was the number one Sheba, both the actor and the real dog. Like the Shebas in the film, she'd had a miserable existence as a puppy but now all was good in her life. She had been discovered and was on her way to stardom.

Knowing that the filming process was one of hurry up and wait, I shouldn't have felt so antsy but I did. This poor dog shouldn't be kept waiting so long.

I looked around the pseudo-kennel area. It was actually a film set, one modeled somewhat on HotRescues, the private pet rescue facility where I'm the chief administrator. I'd given the director and a few members of the film crew a tour of Hot-Rescues to make sure they knew what an excellent shelter looked like.

This one was composed of several kennel runs, which were empty right now except for Sheba, all surrounded by filming equipment that included cameras on wheels, mechanical booms that could lift people wielding camera gear or just the cameras themselves, sound recording gadgetry, lots of lighting equipment, and items I couldn't begin to identify. Beyond were buildings that were the soundstages and administrative offices of Solario Studios in Woodland Hills, in the western part of L.A.'s San Fernando Valley.

I heard a lot of voices of people who remained beyond the set and out of my sight, probably discussing how to shoot the next scene. Or maybe they were just talking about the weather.

I decided it was time to take action, for Sheba's sake. There were two people I could talk to and try to get things moving.

One was Hans Marford. The renowned director was working on this movie. That helped with publicizing it even this early in the production process as a potential blockbuster and Hollywood awards contender.

The other was Grant Jefferly, the "Certified Animal Safety Representative" assigned to this film by the American Humane Association — the only group that can certify that "No Animals Were Harmed," which actually was a registered trademark of theirs. The designation "Certified Animal

Safety Representative" was also a trade-mark.

"Let's find out what's going on," I told Carlie and began walking out of the kennel area.

I first saw Hans at the edge of a crowd of people. He was talking, using his hands for emphasis, and everyone seemed to listen intently. Some were cast members, others were crew, and a few were dog handlers.

"This is a crucial scene," I heard him say as we got closer. "It's near the end, right where Millie makes the final decision that she'll adopt Sheba as her own. You ready for it, Millie?"

Hans was a tall, thin man with a mop of wavy gray hair, which he used to help him communicate. I'd seen him run his fingers through it in frustration and nod his head till his hair fluttered in the breeze he created. His nose was a long beak over straight, narrow lips, which he also sucked in to make a point, and he wore thick, dark-rimmed glasses.

"Let's run through it, Hans," said Lyanne Shroeder. Yes, *the* Lyanne Shroeder, the youthful actress who was emerging as one of Hollywood's top stars. A petite brunette with a winsome smile, she played the main human character in the film, Millie Roland, who ultimately rescued and adopted the Sheba character. "I'll show you how I think Millie would react."

Good. Something was about to occur that would at least give Sheba some attention. Even so, I edged through the now dissipating crowd toward Grant. He was a handsome guy, probably in his mid-forties — around my age. I wouldn't have been surprised to learn he had aspirations of stardom himself. Instead, he wore a vest with the AMERICAN HUMANE ASSOCIATION logo over his gray T-shirt. He was the person who would ascertain whether the coveted "No Animals Were Harmed" certification would ultimately be given to this film.

Carlie and I stopped beside him. "I know it's not cruelty, but poor Sheba — the real one — looks lonesome," I told him. "I'm glad the filming's going forward now."

He smiled at me, revealing even, gleaming white teeth. "Glad to have additional observers around on this set," he said. "But a little bit of downtime might actually be a good thing for our little Sheba. She's had a busy morning."

"She sure did," I acknowledged.

The three of us — Carlie, Grant, and I — stayed out of the way as the rest of the gang started prepping for their scene, then filming it. I watched as the Millie character walked by the kennel and stopped to look in at the sad little poodle inside, as I had. Maybe Sheba was even remembering what it felt like to be a stray.

A trainer I knew only as Cowan stood in the background. He gave a hand signal and Sheba stood on her hind legs, her front paws on the mesh gate of the kennel. Millie/ Lyanne unlatched the gate and stooped to let Sheba hop into her arms. I couldn't hear the dialogue, but I watched as Millie hugged Sheba, who licked her face in a way that suggested she was lapping up the human's tears. The scene made me just as emotional as the actress pretended to be.

"Cut!" I heard Hans shout. "Let's do it again, but that looked good."

Even so, he shot at least a half-dozen more takes. After that, he let the cast and crew dissipate, all but the assistants who were dog handlers. I'd met some of them, and the person who took charge of Sheba was one I'd spoken with — Jerry Amalon, a young, enthusiastic kid who immediately snapped a leash on Sheba's collar, gently roughhoused with her for a minute, gave her a treat, and led her off.

Just to be sure all was well, Carlie and I accompanied Grant to the area where the many other dogs that were part of the shoot were being kept.

No apparent worries there about how the animals were treated. A large, open area in one of the buildings had been converted into what could pass for a doggy hotel, with fluffy bedding in each of the kennels. They were separated by fencing on top of a laminate floor that resembled posh wood and was cleaned at least twice a day. No more than two dogs occupied each kennel, and some had the enclosures to themselves. Jerry and the other handlers took each dog for walks often to ensure they remained housebroken.

In addition to the five or so dogs that played the Sheba character, there were a bunch of additional poodles that represented her siblings, as well as others including mixed breeds that played dogs she met and interacted with, per the film's script.

There were enough dogs in the cast that American Humane had recommended a full-time vet. Carlie was there that day instead of one of her veterinary staff from The Fittest Pet Veterinary Hospital. She was too busy especially with her own TV show to commit to being there every day, but she'd been glad to help by assigning other vets in her office to come to the set. Even so, she, like I, enjoyed visiting from time to time.

Now, Carlie and I both played for a short while with some of the dogs until Grant motioned for the humans to join him. As we stood in the center of the kennel area, he began talking with the handlers and Cowan, the trainer, about some suggestions. On the whole, though, he sounded pretty pleased with how things were going so far.

One handler, a girl named Elena Derger whom I'd also met, came running inside with two poodles on a leash. She was panting and laughing. "Sorry," she said to no one in particular, since Grant had smiled and motioned to her to join the group. "These two have lots of energy." She proceeded to lead them to one of the empty kennels.

Before Grant could continue, though, one of Hans Marford's assistants joined us. "There's an all-hands meeting just starting about tomorrow's filming schedule," she said. "Hans would like all of you there."

I doubted she meant Carlie and me, but we followed anyway. The next day was a Tuesday. I'd spent more time today on the set than I'd intended so I wasn't planning to come to the filming. Even so, it would be interesting to hear what would be going on.

The cast and crew were gathered at an area that had probably been designed on the studio lot for such impromptu meetings, since it had a podium surrounded by wooden bleachers. Most people were seated, but Hans stood in the middle. He spoke loudly enough that no microphone was in his hands, which he waved and gesticulated with as if they were integral to his announcement.

"Thanks to excellent footwork by our production staff, we received a permit to film on some Valley streets tomorrow rather than having to wait any longer. We're therefore going to shoot some of the film's early scenes over the next week or two, including those where Sheba and her siblings escape from the nasty people who grabbed up her mother once the puppies were born. Refer to pages three through seven of the script, which describe this part and includes all their weaving through traffic to elude their former owners and get away. Lots of action here. That's what we'll be working on."

"It won't involve the dogs much and will be choreographed safely for them, the way we've already discussed, right?" called Grant. He had come from the kennel area with Carlie and me but now stood at the front of the bleachers.

"I'm sure you'll let us know if it isn't safe."
Hans shot him a glare. Because Grant had
interrupted him, or because he didn't like
the reminder that he had to protect the
animals while devising a scene to awe
moviegoers? I hoped it was the former. A
lot could be done digitally, I knew, so there
was no need to endanger the dogs.

The filming had started four weeks earlier.
I'd been there a few times, and had no
reason to believe that the idea of "No
Animals Were Harmed" had been, or ever
would be, violated. That would make no
sense at all for a movie of this kind, especially considering the way it was already being publicized.

But catching the way Grant and Hans now
glared at each other, I had to wonder.

CHAPTER 2

HotRescues is located in Grenada Hills, which isn't too far from Woodland Hills. Even so, this was L.A., so traffic kept me away from where I wanted to be for much longer than I'd hoped.

Eventually, though, I parked my Toyota Venza — the vehicle I'd bought because of its pet-friendly configuration and accessories — in the parking lot and entered the welcome area via the side door.

Fortunately, it wasn't very late so Nina Guzman, my assistant administrator, was still there. She sat behind the leopard-print reception desk working on her computer. Behind her were lots of recently updated photos of happy adopters and the former HotRescues inhabitants who were now part of their families, displaying well on the bright yellow walls. I loved to look at those pictures.

I was immediately greeted not only by

Nina, but also by Zoey, my own sweet Border collie–Australian shepherd mix. She was mostly black and white, with some merle gray thrown in.

"Hi, Nina," I said as I knelt to hug Zoey, who licked my face. "Hi, Zoey." Even though my tone was warm when I spoke to Nina, when I talked to Zoey I sounded even warmer. And no wonder: My kids were both away at college, so Zoey was my closest nearby family member.

"How'd it go?" Nina maneuvered from behind the desk. I smiled as I rose and looked at her. She of course wore a blue HotRescues knit shirt, as did all staff members while on duty, including me. Nina no longer looked as frazzled as when she initially began working at HotRescues — and had come fresh from an abusive marriage. Now, her attractive face was all smiles beneath long bangs of her straight brown hair. I'd gotten used to the fact that she was younger and prettier than me. She was an absolutely wonderful asset to HotRescues, and I relied on her.

"Fine," I said. "I'll tell you all about it in a bit — or tomorrow, if you'd rather, since it's getting late. I need to call Dante now. Have you heard from him?"

"Just a quick call early this afternoon. He

21

wanted to confirm that you were on the set. He asked for a report from you whenever possible."

"It's possible right now." Gesturing for Zoey to follow, I headed down the hall from the reception area to the first doorway, my office. I quickly sat behind my desk, an antique-looking L-shaped piece of furniture that I'd refinished once upon a time, though it wasn't as old as it seemed. I put my purse into a desk drawer as I looked toward the other side of my office. I used the pleasant conversation area across from me mostly to chat with potential adopters.

I grabbed the receiver for the landline on the desk and punched in Dante's number.

Dante DeFrancisco was HotRescues' benefactor. He's an incredibly wealthy man, thanks to making lots of money from his highly successful chain of HotPets stores, where he sells all kinds of pet-related foods and other items. He gives some of it back to the animals that made him rich, funding HotRescues and a wildlife sanctuary called, unsurprisingly, HotWildlife.

Now, he was also helping to call attention to abused and unwanted animals in another way. He was a co-producer of *Sheba's Story* — which meant he was throwing a lot of money into the production. That was partly because a good friend of his, Niall Cransley, was the screenplay writer and also a co-producer.

Dante's affiliation was why I, too, was involved.

"Hi, Lauren," he said, answering the phone almost immediately. I smiled as I watched Zoey jump onto the sofa in my conversation area and settle down to sleep. "How's the production going?"

"Fine, as far as a newbie like me can tell," I replied. I told him about all I'd seen on set. I'd been to the filming other times since it had begun but I'd stayed the longest today. "Carlie was there, too," I finished. "She temporarily had more time available than the other vets from her clinic."

"Sounds good," Dante said. "Any idea what's next?"

"Hans said that permits finally came through for shooting scenes on some Valley streets," I reported. "I can get more particulars if you'd like."

"Don't bother," Dante said. "I'll call Niall and make arrangements to meet him there. That sounds interesting enough to carve out some time to see. Thanks for the update."

"Anytime," I said. "Let me know when you'll be there. I'd enjoy seeing some of the street filming, too." I didn't mention to him the possible clash of wills between Hans and the American Humane representative, Grant. I might have misread their interaction, and even if I hadn't they'd surely work it out for the good of the production.

I hoped.

Dante and I didn't talk much longer; we both had things to do.

Mine was to take my last walk of the day through the HotRescues facility, one of my greatest pleasures.

When I stood, Zoey immediately rose and jumped off the couch. As usual, she accompanied me.

I loved our shelter, especially after it had been enlarged and remodeled last year. The kennels were all spacious and kept clean, including the first ones Zoey and I walked past once we got into the outside area. They were mostly on the left of the pathway since there was a building midway on the right. Outdoor portions of the kennels extended into small indoor areas so each dog could decide whether to stay in or out.

At the moment, the animals acted like they knew we were coming — which they probably did, considering their keen canine senses of hearing and smell. All dogs on both sides sat or stood at attention. A few barked, although the shelter staff and volunteers always discouraged it. Noisy pups are less likely to get adopted fast.

We kept pages slipped into a plastic folder near each kennel gate containing the history of each inhabitant. I was thrilled to be reminded by ADOPTION PENDING stickers that two of our longest-term residents, Dodi, a sheltie mix, and Hannibal, mostly Great Dane, were about to go home with their new families. As always, I wondered why some pets were snatched right up by adopters and others had to wait a long time till the right family came along. Sometimes, I supposed, it was obvious, depending on an animal's loving nature and cute looks and demeanor versus the pit bull syndrome, where people tend to avoid animals they assumed — often wrongly — could be aggressive. But Dodi and Hannibal were both sweet and adorable, and both had been here for many months.

Soon, though, they, too, would have new homes.

Zoey and I passed the building on the right, part of last year's remodel. The upstairs was now an apartment for our overnight security personnel.

My cell phone rang and I silently cursed myself for bringing it along. I pulled it out of my pocket.

The number that showed wasn't one I knew, but I answered anyway.

"Hi, Lauren. This is Grant Jefferly. I was just checking out the streets where the filming will be for the next few days, and it's right in your neighborhood. Care to join me?"

Northridge was, in fact, fairly near the HotRescues location in Granada Hills. It was definitely closer to us than to the Woodland Hills studio.

But it wasn't exactly in our neighborhood.

Even so, I was interested in learning what the American Humane representative thought of the area — not that I believed streets would be vastly different in one place from another. The filming was to occur both in commercial and residential areas.

No matter where they were located, busy shopping sites would have a lot of traffic. Like the American Humane folks and others connected with the movie, I'd read the screenplay. I knew that Sheba and her sibling poodles were supposed to be loose for part of the time in a location where there could be a lot of activity, both vehicle and pedestrian.

The plan was that, for the animals' safety, all genuine traffic would be halted in favor of pseudo-activity staged by actors and crew — and that cars would be dubbed in by animation. At least that was the way I understood it.

With Zoey along, I drove to the filming area. After parking in a shopping center lot, I spotted Grant walking toward us. He'd taken off his American Humane vest and wore just his gray T-shirt and jeans. He still wore rubber-soled shoes, and so did I, since crew and other people on the set were encouraged to use comfortable and safe footwear.

Grant's smile seemed even broader now that he was supposedly off duty. It made him look more human and less wannabe film star; or maybe he just appeared more like a regular, if quite handsome, guy when he wasn't near a currently operating set.

"Who's this?" He knelt to pet Zoey, who basked in the attention.

"That's Zoey," I said. "And no, she has no aspirations to become a film star — or at least she's never told me of any."

Grant laughed and rose again, then gestured around the area where we stood. "I visited here with Cowan before any filming started," he said, "when they first applied for the permits. The description of what they intended to do sounded acceptable, but I thought I'd visit again before the shoot to refresh my memory."

"Great. What will they do here?"

I looked around. A major shopping mall was just down the street, and I doubted that stores there would welcome the nearby road being shut down for any length of time for filming. On the other hand, this was March, not a huge shopping season, so maybe they'd like the publicity.

For the next half hour, Grant, Zoey, and I walked around. Grant pointed out the locations he'd understood would be the main filming areas.

"That's all subject to change," he said as we walked back to my car. "At least somewhat. Seeing it with one of the trainers is one thing, but having the director and others on the set can mean adapting to the reality of what happens. Some flexibility is okay, as long as the animals are, too. It will involve filming dogs and cars separately."

"I figured. Thanks for showing me. The filming starts here tomorrow?"

"That's right. Bright and early, at five A.M. It'll continue for about a week. Will you be here to watch?"

"Not sure," I said. I was definitely curious but had a lot to do at HotRescues. "I doubt there's anything I can do but gawk anyway.

There'll be a vet here from The Fittest Pet Veterinary Hospital, whether or not Carlie comes."

"Come and gawk anytime," Grant said. "You've got a perfect tie-in — your relationship with the producers." He glanced at his watch. "Care to grab dinner with me? There are a couple of places down the street with outdoor patios where Zoey would be welcome."

That wasn't asking me out on a date, or so I told myself. I was in a sort-of relationship with Matt Kingston, a really great captain with Los Angeles Animal Services who kept me informed about when particularly adoptable animals were in danger of being put down for lack of room at the public facilities. I didn't want to do anything to jeopardize that.

And, well, I really didn't want to do anything to jeopardize the personal nature of our relationship either. I'd been married once to a really wonderful man — the father of my kids — who'd died. I'd remarried to give them a new father, and that had been a huge mistake. Now, although I had no real commitment to Matt, I cared for him. A lot.

But even if handsome Grant thought having dinner with Zoey and me was a date, I could disabuse him of that while learning more about what he did to ensure that "No Animals Were Harmed" at movie and TV filmings.

All that was a long way of convincing myself that I did want to have dinner with this man.

It was a pleasant dinner, too, at a nearby family restaurant with an outdoor area, where we sat. Our conversation was filled with anecdotes about movies and TV shows I'd heard of, ones with animals that Grant had sometimes been called to observe even just the night before the shooting.

I laughed, a lot. Was I acting — or truly enjoying myself? Too much of the latter, I feared.

And even though I try to never second-guess myself, much later that night, when Zoey and I were home and getting ready for bed, I called Matt.

"It was quite a day," I told him, sitting on the fluffy blue upholstered sofa in my living room with my state-of-the-art TV — chosen by my son, Kevin — turned off. I recounted what I'd seen on the set of *Sheba's Story.*

"Any chance of my getting to watch a filming?" Matt asked.

"Not sure," I said. "I'm special only because Dante told me to get involved, be his extra set of eyes. There's already an American Humane representative present." I felt my face grow warm as I thought about getting together with Grant for dinner. "Plus a veterinarian, either Carlie or someone from her office. They might not like someone from Animal Services there, too."

"Oh." He sounded disappointed.

"I'll think about how to finesse it, though," I assured him. "I'd love to have you see how this works. It's time-consuming when they shoot scenes over and over, but it's so much fun to watch. I'm not sure when I'll go back — I know Dante wants to pop in sometime this week. But the next filming will be street scenes, so maybe I can figure something out. It may be easier than getting you on to a studio lot."

"Sounds good. So how are Zoey and you?" His tone had gotten warmer, which made me warmer, too — and not just because I felt a little guilty.

"We're fine. And Rex and you?" Rex was his black Lab mix.

"Why don't I give you an update in person? You free tomorrow night for dinner?"

"Yes," I said emphatically. That would definitely be a date, one I'd enjoy.

We made arrangements to get together at

my place, a good thing.
   They might even stay the night.

CHAPTER 3

I got up early to head to HotRescues because I'd spent so little time there yesterday. Since I'd run a marathon to benefit Hot-Rescues and other shelters a few months ago, I occasionally still took Zoey out for a morning run, but not today.

I was dressed in my HotRescues shirt and ready to head for the car when my smartphone rang.

Still standing near the kitchen table with Zoey looking up at me expectantly, I pulled my phone from my pocket and glanced at the ID. Dante.

"Good morning," I said as cheerfully as I could while waiting for some kind of shoe to drop. Dante didn't call this early for no reason. I eased myself onto a chair and leaned forward as tension clamped my insides.

Most of the time he caught me while I was at HotRescues — by design, since he often wanted me to look something up on the computer about finances or the supplies he sent from HotPets to feed our rescuees.

"Hi, Lauren. Sorry to call so early but I really want us to have a presence at the filming today and I'd like you to go. I told Niall I'd be there but I got a call in the middle of the night about an incident in one of my Midwest warehouses — a break-in. The cops caught some kids and I think everything's okay, but I need to go check it out. I'll be gone for a few days, though I hope I'll be back in time to catch some of the filming in Northridge. In case I don't, please take a lot of pictures. I've cleared that with Niall and let him know you'll be taking my place."

"Sure," I said, again trying to sound cheerful. I pulled a half-filled bottle of water toward me from where it sat on the table and took a quick drink, even as I heard Zoey lapping water from her bowl near the refrigerator. I've always considered myself a micromanager but believed that Dante was a lot better than me about delegating. Maybe he was. He was delegating to me, though, and not someone in his offices. "Is Kendra going with you?"

Kendra Ballantyne was Dante's lady friend, a lawyer and pet-sitter whom I'd got-

ten to know a bit because of her relationship with the HotRescues patron. She was
nice, if a bit offbeat at times. She considered
herself a murder magnet since she'd wound
up solving a bunch of crimes over the last
few years.

I'd begun to wonder if that was somehow
contagious, since I, too, had gotten involved
in situations where someone had died and
I'd needed to find the killer to clear the
primary suspect — who, in one instance,
happened to be me.

"No, she has a lot of pet-sitting and law-
yering going on. I've got to run to the
airport now" — where he would undoubtedly have a private jet waiting to sweep him
to his Midwest destination — "and I suspect
it would be good for you to head to
Northridge as soon as you can."

"Will do," I assured him. "I'll drive Zoey
to HotRescues and take a quick look
around, then head to the film shoot. I'll be
interested to hear more about that break-
in," I finished.

"Me, too."

He hung up, and I rose. "Come on, Zoey.
Sounds as if I'll need to channel Dante
today, and you can channel me."

I called Matt before I left home. I wasn't

sure in what capacity I'd be able to sneak him into the filming but decided to try.

He had a meeting scheduled that morning with members of SMART, the Specialized Mobile Animal Rescue Team which he supervised. It was a recent amalgamation of all the L.A. Animal Services teams he had previously headed, including the Small Animal Rescue Team, the Department Air Rescue Team and more. Once the meeting with SMART members was over, he promised to head for the filming site.

That would give me time to lay some groundwork for his appearance.

I kept my time at HotRescues brief — always difficult when I wanted to greet every one of our residents with hugs. Fortunately, our staff and usual early morning volunteers had begun to arrive, so I was certain all the animals would receive some loving even without me. I again left Zoey in the welcome area with Nina.

It was nearly nine thirty when I reached the parking lot where I'd been with Grant the night before. I had a hard time finding a spot since the cast and crew were already there, and maybe a whole bunch of extras, too, considering how crowded it was.

I found a spot on a side street where parking looked legitimate, then hurried back. A security guard stopped me before I got too close and I explained who I was. I'd worn a jacket over my regular outfit but peeled it back so the guy could see the HotRescues logo.

Mentioning Dante DeFrancisco opened yet another door.

I immediately sought out Niall Cransley. He'd met Dante after interviewing him for research a few years ago. They'd clicked, and Niall gave Dante the screenplay to read. He'd loved it, and Niall promised to keep Dante informed about his progress in getting the movie made.

When nothing happened after Niall shopped it around, Dante stepped in waving money — figuratively, of course, but that did the trick. The production of *Sheba's Story* was launched.

"Hi, Lauren," Niall called, seeing me as I approached the lot with no available spaces. Holding a cup of coffee from a shop in this center, he stood in the middle of a crowd of people holding similar cups.

Niall was taller than most of them, a beanpole of a man with narrow shoulders, a long neck, and a receding hairline. His smile was all large teeth surrounded by thin lips. He maneuvered his way out of the group and joined me. "What happened with Dante?

He didn't tell me much."

After Niall started walking away from his crowd, it had begun to disperse. I recognized a few people from when I'd visited the set before. Most were production staff, including some involved with costume, makeup, and animal handling. The human star, Lyanne, was with them, too.

I told Niall the little that Dante had related to me. "He'll be back soon but apparently wanted to make sure everything was handled appropriately," I finished. "He wants me to take pictures. I assume that's okay?" I made the last sound like a question.

"For Dante, sure. Let's go hear how it'll all be set up. I saw Hans heading toward that side street. He may be giving some direction by now."

On the way, we passed several poshly furnished crates along the sidewalk just outside the coffee shop and adjoining clothing store, dry cleaner, and deli. The crates contained a number of particularly young-looking Shebas. Maybe some of the white poodles were supposed to be her siblings. I'd understood that the scenes to be filmed here were to represent when the dog was still a fairly young puppy, just running away from an abusive situation.

Taking my camera from my purse, I shot a few photos, shoving back an urge to take the dogs out for a walk. Or at least a hug. Maybe I'd get that chance later.

"I saw the dog handlers walking this bunch just a few minutes ago, in case you were worried," Niall assured me.

I smiled up at him. "Guess you know me pretty well already, even though we were just introduced a few weeks ago."

"Dante's told me about you." He lifted a stringy hand as if to erase any complaints I might be ready to make. "All good things. He's pretty proud of how you run Hot-Rescues."

My smile grew even broader. That comment could make my day. Maybe my week. But not much longer than that. Especially now. I needed to spend more time at HotRescues than I was at the moment to make sure it continued to run so well.

"I'm glad we're in sync," was all I said.

We reached the end of the row of stores and stepped onto the sidewalk leading to the nearest street. There, I saw the people I most wanted to hang around with while I was here.

Carlie was there, which surprised me. I'd thought she was going to send one of her veterinary staff today. She was talking with

Winna Darrion, chief animal handler for the film. All underlings who exercised, walked, and fed the dogs reported to her.

With them was Grant, as well as the primary dog trainer, Cowan.

As Niall and I approached, I saw director Hans Marford coming from farther down the street.

"I need to ask Hans a few things before he gets started," Niall said. "I'll talk to you later." With his long legs he had no problem pulling way ahead of me toward his goal.

I edged up to Carlie as the group moved to circle Hans for instructions on how the scene would work. "What are you doing here?" I asked.

Today she was dressed more casually than yesterday, wearing slacks and a shirt with rolled-up sleeves. "The key vets I'd assigned to help here were otherwise engaged." She didn't sound pleased.

"Doing what?"

"One had a class already scheduled, and the others . . . well, you asked. Two older dogs were brought in last night with rather nasty cases of diarrhea. Been there, done that, so this time I directed the rest of my staff to administer tests, figure out the causes, and deal with it. That meant I'd be the one to come here to twiddle my thumbs and watch the filming. I assume it'll all go well, as usual, especially with your buddy Grant observing for American Humane."

I felt my face turning red and I looked away from her. "He is a good, dedicated animal protector," I said formally. "I wouldn't exactly call him a buddy, though."

"Of course." I tried not to react to the irony in Carlie's voice.

"Oh, and by the way, I brought my own filming crew." She gestured to a couple of guys with cameras who stood behind us, talking. "I figured that since I was going to be here anyway, this was more material for my *Pet Fitness* show."

She had gotten prior permission to film from the studio execs in charge of *Sheba's Story.* She'd had a crew there the first day we were on the set together but not after that. This filming on the streets could be more interesting for her show. Maybe she could even fill a whole episode with how this movie was being shot.

Hans began speaking, and we edged forward to listen. I took a few pictures, and Carlie's crew undoubtedly did, too. I noticed Carlie frowning. Good thing she wasn't on camera. I supposed she thought Hans's description might not go over well on her show, although it sounded okay to

41

me. At least at first.

Hans first explained what needed to happen. "In this scene, Sheba, her mother, and sister and brother poodles are all taken captive by a nasty man who treats them badly and wants to sell them and make a lot of money — no matter who wants to buy them. The narration to be dubbed in will indicate in Sheba's human voice that she sees through that and decides they'd run away. Unfortunately, their captor is out walking their mom at the time so Sheba can't save her, at least not yet. But the rest of them climb through an open window, run out of the yard, and onto the street to get away. The bad guy sees them and gives chase, but they all escape."

He went into more detail after that, pointing to where the cameras and dogs would be, and where the actor playing the nasty captor would start and end up.

"I get to just watch today." That was Lyanne talking to Niall, who no doubt already knew that she wouldn't be in any scenes to be shot that day. Both stood near me. I hadn't noticed when she'd joined us. I'd gotten the impression that she was quite a diva. Was she here to call attention to herself despite not being on camera?

"So you're just filming the dogs running

today?" Grant asked as Hans stopped talking. "As I understand it, the cars will be dubbed in later by computer animation." Grant had stood quietly at the front of the crowd, today wearing a navy T-shirt beneath his American Humane vest.

"Mostly, yes. But for the best effect, we have some vehicles ready to drive down the street here. Some of our best drivers will handle them."

"Then the dogs won't actually go into the street during the shots."

Hans stopped and stared at him. "Yes, they will, but only for part of the scene that will show up in the final film. Like I said, some of our best drivers will handle the cars."

"That wasn't how this was discussed before," Grant protested.

"It'll be safe. I guarantee it."

Which sounded like BS to me. Obviously it did to Grant, too.

And to Carlie, who maneuvered away from my side and to the front of the crowd, where Hans stood. "You need to listen to the American Humane representative," she said right into the director's face. "You know how important that 'No Animals Were Harmed' rating is. It's why we're here, and this whole film is about saving animals."

Carlie was always concerned about animal welfare, but even so, the intensity of her reaction surprised me a little. She usually tried to reason with people — on her show, at least — before verbally attacking them.

"You're here because that American Humane group wants a vet here, Doctor Stellan," Hans said coldly. There was something almost menacing in his gaze, as if he really disliked Carlie — not just her attitude. "And because you want to put this on your own show to boost your ratings. But this discussion is strictly between Grant and me."

"I don't think so." Niall had left Lyanne's side to join them. He probably wouldn't have had much clout if he'd just been the screenwriter, but what he said would have weight, thanks to his relationship with the financial backers. Me, too, in a way, but I'd stay out of it as long as others to whom Hans was more likely to pay attention were in the discussion.

"I don't think so either." Carlie motioned for her filming crew to get a little closer. "You're right about why I'm here: It's because I'm a veterinarian. And over the past few weeks, when I wasn't here I had to try at my clinic to save the lives of at least three dogs that were hit by cars. There was nothing I could do to prevent those ac-

44

cidents — although I was fortunate enough to save their lives. But I'll do all I can here to make sure you do this filming safely and appropriately."

That explained her overreacting — maybe.

"I swear it'll be done safely." Hans spoke through gritted teeth, which seemed to belie his words. But he looked away from Carlie. "You can always tell me if something looks too dangerous." He nodded toward Grant, then Niall, who both nodded back. "Now, let's get started."

The first few takes were done in a manner where the dogs seemed safe enough despite their excitement in running down the street and barking, with no cars following.

Matt arrived around lunchtime. L.A. Animal Services didn't generally show up on movie sets, but I still managed to get him okayed to join us as a friend of Dante's. They had met and seemed to get along fine, even if they weren't buddies.

Matt is six feet tall and nice looking, with brown eyes and short, dark hair. I liked seeing him in his official uniform — khaki shirt, green slacks, and jacket, with lots of patches and badges to show he was a captain in Animal Services.

And, yes, I'd seen him in a lot less.

I introduced him to Grant and saw them

45

size each other up but we were all on friendly terms as we observed the filming.

If I'd been asked, I would have said that Marford had just been goading Grant, Niall, and Carlie. The takes even after lunch all seemed pretty mellow. Apparently Marford was in agreement. He wasn't allowing any animals to be harmed. No cars were filmed with the dogs. As Grant had insisted, the scariest parts of the scenes for the canines would be added later by animation.

Take after take, cute poodles dashed everywhere, apparently running away from the bad guy. I could just picture how it would all look up on a movie screen when the film was done, hear in my head how the narrator, in Sheba's point of view, would describe what was happening. It would be exciting and poignant and great filmmaking, or at least it had that potential.

But then came the last take. It made my blood freeze. Cars were used. And those sweet little poodles seemed much too close to the rolling wheels of at least one of them.

Grant called a halt to the filming. To my surprise, Marford agreed. Or maybe he thought he'd gotten the scene the way he wanted it.

"We'll resume here tomorrow," he said. "There are a couple more scenes that'll be shot on the streets here under our permit."

"No more endangering the animals, you freak," Carlie demanded. "That last shot — it was scary. They could have been hurt, or worse. No more of this or even if you get the seal of approval from American Humane, I'll make sure you're depicted on my show as the monster you are."

"None of the animals was hurt," Marford insisted. "My drivers were careful. Everything is fine."

"It's not," Carlie said. "Don't even think about doing that again, or you'll be sorry."

Her crew, no doubt, got that on camera.

Which turned out not to be a good thing.

Somebody killed Hans Marford that night.

CHAPTER 4

Unsurprisingly, I didn't expect that.

I didn't like it either. In fact, I felt pretty awful about it. Hans was dead.

It wasn't clear at first whether he'd been murdered or the subject of a hit-and-run accident. I suspected the former, though, and so, apparently, did the cops.

Sure, he hadn't seemed as devoted to protecting animals as I'd have hoped for a director of the kind of film that *Sheba's Story* would be, but at least he hadn't allowed the dogs to be put in danger for most of the day.

Although I'd been concerned that his last take would be a harbinger of others to come . . .

Maybe someone else had felt the same way. But kill him for it? That seemed much too extreme.

Yet people sometimes murdered with even less motive.

The way I learned about Hans's demise was rather unexpected, too. Matt told me.

His affiliation with the film production was even more tenuous than mine. But he'd learned about it in his official capacity.

"One of the crime scene investigators from the LAPD called Animal Services around four A.M.," he told me as we spoke by phone early the next morning before I left for HotRescues. We'd postponed our dinner plans the previous night.

Talking on my smartphone at this hour was becoming a habit, one I'd be glad to break. Yesterday's call from Dante had changed the schedule of my entire day.

So would this one from Matt. I needed to find out what had happened.

Mostly to make sure . . . "Are all the dogs okay?" I asked Matt, realizing how taut my body had become at the thought they might not be.

Once again I was in my kitchen, Zoey at my feet. She regarded me curiously, and I patted her head reassuringly before planting myself at the table again for this conversation, willing myself to relax.

"That was why we were called in. Far as I know the dogs are fine, apparent homicide notwithstanding. A team of our officers is on the scene, which is why I heard about it.

I reported in that I'd been there yesterday observing, so I've been directed to go there, too."

"I'll see you there, then." I had to go, for Dante's sake as well as the animals'. "Any idea what happened to Hans?"

"Sounds as if he was struck by a car on the street where the filming occurred — and where those poodles were endangered."

It could have been a coincidence. An accident. Or so I tried to tell myself as I headed for the Northridge filming site.

The media had picked up on what had happened, at least part of it. As I drove I listened to the news report of a death at the site of a movie shoot in Northridge, with cops on the scene. But hardly any other details were given. For now, at least, they continued to report that it was an apparent hit-and-run. And maybe it was. Someone could have hit the director and panicked, driving off rather than calling for help. The coincidence of it happening on that street where the dogs had been somewhat in peril could have been just that — a coincidence.

I'd had to talk my way onto the set yesterday when all it had been was a filming location. Would it be harder today as a crime scene? Undoubtedly.

But Matt had gotten there first, in his official capacity. Today, he was the one to vouch for me.

"This is Lauren Vancouver," he told a uniformed officer at the edge of the cordoned-off area. "She's involved with animal rescue and is here to confirm that the animals are being handled safely."

The cop, probably a rookie considering how young he appeared, looked at Matt. "That's what Animal Services is here for, isn't it?"

"Partly. But —" Before he could finish, he was interrupted by a voice from behind us.

"The American Humane Association, too." I turned to see Grant Jefferly behind me, wearing his American Humane vest and a grim expression. "I heard on the news about trouble on this site, so I came right away."

I met his eyes. I hadn't paid much attention to their light blue color before, but their angry gleam now took me aback. I felt he was almost daring someone to accuse him of killing Hans — probably a silly reaction on my part.

Even so, I couldn't help recalling his last discussion with the director, at least the last that I had heard. They had not been at all cordial with one another.

51

I'd recently figured out the culprits in several murders. That didn't make me an expert. It didn't make me a cop or an investigator, or even someone who wanted to be in the position of figuring out a killer's identity either.

Besides, I liked Grant's attitude about the dogs. We'd gotten along well at this site before the filming started. I didn't want him to be Hans's killer.

"Is there some trouble here?" A man in a suit joined us, holding out a badge. "I'm Detective Maddinger. And you are . . . ?"

In the three other situations where I'd been involved with a murder investigation, the detective on two of them had been Detective Stefan Garciana, and Detective Joy Greshlam had worked on the third. I'd managed somehow to not tread too strongly on their toes, and both had been relatively civil to me — most of the time.

If I got involved in this one — not that I intended to be more than a curious by-stander — I'd have to check with Detective Antonio Bautrel to see what he thought of Detective Maddinger. Antonio was with the LAPD Gang and Narcotics Division and was also the boyfriend of HotRescues' head of security, Brooke Pernall.

I took a quick scan of Maddinger. He was

African American, a bit chubby, and had a thick head of gray hair over a skeptical expression that included a quizzical frown.

"I'm Captain Matt Kingston of Los Angeles Animal Services," Matt said before either Grant or I could introduce ourselves. "I was here yesterday observing the filming, and I was told that some other Animal Services officers are already here checking on the dogs' welfare. This is Lauren Vancouver, who represents one of the film's producers, and Grant Jefferly, the representative of the American Humane Association assigned to this production."

"We're sorry to hear about what happened to Mr. Marford," I said, "but we're all concerned with making sure that the animals are still being well treated."

"Er . . . right. Okay, follow me. You can't get near the area under investigation, but the dogs have all been moved into one of the vacant stores in that strip mall. First thing, though — were all of you here yesterday during the filming?"

"That's right," I acknowledged.

"I'll take you first to look in on the dogs. Then we'll need each of you to answer a few questions."

I'd been interrogated before in homicide

investigations. A young female detective was assigned to question me. Her name was Detective Wast, and she appeared to be all cop with no sense of humor. Nor did she seem to have any love for animals that I could detect. But I didn't have to like her to cooperate with her.

We stood outside the coffee shop in the busy parking lot, not far from the empty store where the dogs were crated. I'd seen the dogs but hadn't had time to get close to them. I encouraged the detective to hurry so I could start walking some of them as soon as possible. I hadn't seen any handlers or anyone else who might have been able to feed or exercise them that morning.

On the other hand, their crates looked clean, so they must have had some accident-preventing care.

"Okay, take me through yesterday, as you remember it, Ms. Vancouver. What time did you arrive here?"

Her voice was shrill, almost childlike, but there was nothing sweet about her attitude. She appeared to be in her mid-twenties, with short, black hair and small gold earrings in her earlobes. Her skin was pale, suggesting no makeup, which meant her thick eyelashes were her own.

I did as she asked but answered her ques-

54

tions succinctly, volunteering no additional information. I'd learned how to deal with this kind of situation the hard way.

"And were there any other people there besides Mr. Jefferly, Mr. Kingston, and you who were particularly interested in animals? I assume you'd be interacting mostly with them."

I pondered that for a moment. I didn't really want to involve Carlie in this. Though she and the director had exchanged a few harsh words, she wouldn't have killed him.

But even if I didn't mention her presence, someone else would. And they'd undoubtedly be less discreet about it.

"You mean besides the film crew types — the trainers and handlers and all?" I wanted to make it clear that there were others involved with the dogs in case they zeroed in on concern for the animals' welfare as a motive to kill the director.

"That's right."

"Well, the American Humane Association did urge that there be a veterinarian on the set at all times. A vet from The Fittest Pet Veterinary Hospital was here yesterday."

"And who would that be?" The detective poised her pen over her notebook.

"Dr. Carlie Stellan."

"You mean the star of that reality show

Pet Fitness?" Detective Wast smiled for the first time, and I smiled back. She might like animals after all if she knew about the show.

"That's right," I said.

Since she knew who Carlie was, surely she wouldn't suspect —

"If she thought some dogs were potentially in danger, I doubt there's anything she wouldn't do to save them. Some people I've talked to said there were concerns about how yesterday's filming was handled. I need Dr. Stellan's contact information, if you have it."

As soon as I could get away from the detective, I stood on the main street with a finger in one ear to ward off the sound of traffic. With my smartphone at my other ear, I called Carlie.

She didn't answer so I left a message. "It's about the filming of *Sheba's Story*. Hans Marford was killed near where the movie was filmed yesterday. Call me. We need to talk."

I wanted to give her a heads-up about what was going on and that she was as likely to be interrogated as I'd been. I hoped she'd return the call soon.

Meanwhile, I stayed near the crime scene. I wouldn't look for clues or interfere in the cops' gathering of evidence. But I wanted to make sure that Sheba, her miscellaneous poodle versions, and the other dogs were well cared for.

When I saw Detective Maddinger walking inside the yellow crime scene tape, I motioned for him to join me. To my surprise, he did.

"Yes, Ms. Vancouver? Did you think of something else to help our investigation?"

"Not yet," I said. "I'd really like your okay to take the dogs out of their crates and walk them. We humans may hate what happened here but at least we know what it was and its seriousness. All the dogs know is that something is going on, and they're being ignored."

"I've got a pit bull mix at home," said the detective, and his usually skeptical face went all gooey. "A really nice guy, never been used for fighting, of course. Ebby is really gentle."

Ah, another animal lover. I wasn't sure I'd be able to take advantage of that — and actually hoped I wouldn't need to. I had no intention of getting involved in this investigation.

But realistically? I already was involved.

I made a mental note about Ebby in case knowing about him came in handy someday.

At least the detective cared about animals enough to give me an okay to help take the dogs for walks. Apparently the initial interrogation of the animal handlers was also complete, since they, too, were in the building where the dogs were crated when I got there.

I threw the strap of my purse over my shoulder and borrowed an extra leash from Jerry. He, Elena, and I set off down the noisy main street with the dogs — not the quieter side street where Hans had been killed.

We passed the row of huge white trucks used to transport filming equipment. Evidently the show must go on — or at least no one had told the film crew to remove its stuff. Maybe filming would resume sometime soon. I'd heard mention of an assistant director to whom Hans was giving orders. Maybe whoever that was would take over.

"This is all so weird," Jerry said. I'd considered him an eager young kid before. Now, his sandy hair looked askew and his long face was pale and drawn. Everything about him, appearance and demeanor, was obviously strained.

In his charge was Sheba Number One, the poodle whose name really was Sheba. I had a younger white poodle — Blanca, who was

58

used in the puppy shots. Elena walked another adult poodle, Stellar, who was trained more for rolling over and acting scared than the other Sheba lookalikes.

"This is only the second film where I've been involved in production, though I've also worked on a few TV shows," Jerry continued as we passed the last truck and could finally see the street. "I can't believe what happened."

The traffic was backed up. Was it because the restaurants and clothing and gift shops to our right were busy, or because looky-loos were trying to see what they could about the nearby death? I wasn't sure.

"It's an omen," Jerry went on. "That's what some people would say. All of us who're working on *Sheba's Story* may be doomed. Not the dogs, though. I hope."

"Don't be silly," Elena said softly. "Relax, Jerry. It's okay." She patted his arm, and he visibly seemed to calm down.

I assumed Elena was a wannabe star like so many involved in the production — or at least she looked pretty enough to go in front of a camera. She was of moderate height, slim and busty with a smooth complexion and full, pink lips. "Whatever happened to Hans, no matter how he was killed, the only effect it'll have on the rest of us people —

59

and dogs — will be how our filming schedule gets changed. They'll have to name a new director, but this film has already gotten a lot of good media hype. It'll go forward, you'll see. And we'll all be fine. Especially you, Stellar." She knelt and hugged the poodle at the end of her leash.

Wannabe actor or not, Elena appeared good at her current assignment. Stellar thought so, too. She rose on her hind legs and gave Elena a doggy kiss right on the nose.

"Maybe." Jerry didn't sound convinced, but he didn't seem nearly as tense as he dropped back to walk beside me. "Do you have any poodles at your shelter, Ms. Vancouver?"

"I'm Lauren," I told him, appreciating his politeness but wanting to seem friendly to these kids. "There aren't any poodles at HotRescues right now, but we sometimes rescue them and have them available for adoption just like all our dogs and cats. Poodle mixes, too. And every type of poodle — miniature, toy, and standard sizes of all colors, not just white like this crew. Do you know anyone who's interested in adopting?"

That was a question I asked often in almost any circumstance. It was always fascinating to hear how many people said yes — and some even referred people to us who did eventually take a pet home. After I approved their situation, of course.

"I might myself," Jerry said. "Assuming Elena's right and I do survive this filming. I've worked with animals a lot lately since that's where there's been a need on some of the productions I've helped with. I've always liked dogs but haven't had one since I was a kid. My apartment building allows pets — and I may just want to take one of these guys home with me. Especially since they shouldn't be in any dangerous scenes now."

"I applaud you, then." I clapped my hands despite holding the end of the leash in one. "I understand that at least some of the dogs who're appearing in *Sheba's Story* were rescued expressly for the purpose of filming them but they won't be returned to the public shelters — not with all the bad publicity that would generate. They'll be needing homes when the production's done. I may be asked to help." In fact, that was something I knew Dante would insist on. "Maybe I can help you adopt one later."

"Really? Oh, thank you." The young guy stood still, grinning at me, and I wondered if I was about to get a hug. Not appropriate here, but if it helped to get a needy dog a new home I'd be glad to oblige.

Instead, he started walking again. So did Elena and I, and our three white poodles strutted in front of us. I saw smiles on faces of other pedestrians along the street and smiled back. No doubt we made a fun appearance.

"How about you, Elena?" I asked. "Do you have any pets?"

"Not right now." She was on my other side, and when I glanced toward her she didn't meet my gaze. I gathered that adoption wasn't currently something she planned.

"Well, if you ever —" I began, but my phone rang. I pulled it from my pocket. It was Carlie.

"Hi," I said. "Guess where I am right now."

"I don't give a damn, Lauren. How could you?"

I stopped walking, feeling my eyes burn as I held my young poodle, Blanca, back with one hand and clutched the phone with the other. "How could I what?" I hated that my voice rasped, but I felt almost as if Carlie had struck me.

It only got worse — when she hit me with, "You told the cops that I argued with Hans Marford. That I could have killed him. Why would you do that, Lauren? I thought you

62

help to clear your friends of allegations of murder, not accuse them yourself."

CHAPTER 5

I was flabbergasted. Should I apologize to Carlie?

I wasn't good at apologies. Besides, I hadn't done anything wrong. I certainly hadn't accused her.

I tried to tell her so. "I'm not sure who you talked to, Carlie, but if they said —"

I got no further. I realized the line was dead. She had hung up.

And I felt terrible.

I called Dante as soon as I got into my car a few minutes later, ignoring how bad I felt about Carlie and her unwarranted anger toward me.

I also ignored the crowd of people who milled around obviously hoping for insight into what had gone on here last night. Some were probably just curious. Others were clearly reporters for who-knew-which media — probably all of them, considering how many cameras were wielded. The news was never quiet about anything that could be sensationalized, and a killing on a movie set would undoubtedly keep the media jackals howling for a long time.

Dante had already heard the news. "I just got out of a meeting," he said as I looked out my windshield to find I was being stared at. I almost wanted to shout that I was nobody and I wasn't involved. Which in a way was only half true. "I was going to call you," he continued. "Glad you got to me first. What happened?"

"I don't know," I told him honestly, wishing I had some hot coffee. Better yet, something stronger.

It was mid-afternoon, so I could possibly justify a medicinal glass of wine to calm my sparking nerves. Not when I was about to drive my car, though. I just sat back in the driver's seat and closed my eyes.

"Things got a little tense here yesterday," I said, "when it looked like Hans was going to ease up on some of the protective measures that had been agreed on to make sure the dogs weren't hurt, but the actual filming was executed relatively safely — although I had concerns about the last take."

"Who did he argue with?" Dante was always perceptive. I hadn't mentioned an argument. There hadn't really been one. But there had clearly been some disagreement.

"No one, not exactly. But the American Humane representative and Hans faced off a little. I don't see that as being a motive for murder."

"Anyone else in the argument . . . er, disagreement?" I could almost see the ironic smile on Dante's nice-looking face — or at least it was nice looking when he wasn't frowning his irritation at someone who was causing him trouble or arguing with him. He liked being in charge and wasn't afraid to show it.

I hated to bring up Carlie again, especially after the way she had reacted earlier. But this was Dante, my boss. And, as I said, he was astute. He might be peeved if he later learned from another source about Carlie's presence during the disagreement. "Well . . . Carlie wasn't thrilled about the direction Hans appeared to be taking. But I wouldn't say she exactly argued with him." I wouldn't say that she didn't exactly, either.

"I was actually referring to you. You're not about to become a murder suspect again, are you, Lauren?"

My eyes popped wider. "Heavens, no!" At least I didn't think so. I hoped not. I had never wanted to be in that position the first

66

time, let alone a second . . . or third.

"Just checking. Okay, keep me informed if you learn anything. Especially . . ." His voice trailed off, but I knew that was a cue he expected me to react to.

I inhaled deeply as I said, "Especially what?"

"Especially if you decide to stick your nose into this situation and try to sniff out a murderer again. In fact, since I've got money tied up in this production, I wouldn't discourage it. Not with your success rate."

He hung up before I had an opportunity to shout out, "No way!"

I drove home to get Zoey. I'd left her there by herself that morning when I'd dashed off to the crime scene — after letting her outside and feeding her, of course. But she was used to a lot more attention than that.

After I changed into my blue HotRescues shirt, I took Zoey out for a very brief walk, and then she accompanied me to my shelter. We got there as fast as I could safely drive. No matter what had happened regarding the filming of *Sheba's Story,* and no matter what Dante's position was, I had responsibilities there — ones that might even help to take my mind off Hans's apparent murder.

Of course the word was out. When I walked into the welcome room, Nina was behind the desk. "What happened, Lauren?" She stood and looked at me with concern. Zoey dashed over to say hi and Nina knelt briefly to pat her, still watching me with sympathy from beneath her straight brown bangs.

"You can believe some of what's been on the news," I informed her. "Hans Marford is dead, and the police are saying it was a homicide."

"Murder?"

"That's the way they seem to be heading. He was the victim of a hit-and-run." Some of the newscasts had also said the car was one associated with the film, and that it had been abandoned on a nearby street.

"What happens to *Sheba's Story*?" She bit her lip as if waiting for the worst news possible about the production.

"Far as I know, the old saying 'The show must go on' will apply, but I don't know when or how, or who'll be the director."

"So whodunit this time?" The voice came from the doorway into the HotRescues shelter area. It was Dr. Mona Harvey, and the question was not one I'd expect from our part-time shrink who helped to screen potential adopters.

68

As usual, she was dressed professionally, not in our standard HotRescues garb for staff members but a doctor-appropriate beige dress. Her hair was short, light brown with even lighter highlights, and she wore glasses. Her outfit was accessorized today by the small black kitten she held in her arms.

"You're the psychologist." I took a few steps toward her as Zoey did the same to sniff at the kitty. "You tell me."

"Sure, if you give me an accurate profile of everyone on that movie set. And everyone else who might have had a grudge against Mr. Marford. And —"

"I get it." I hadn't thought I'd be in the mood to smile for a while, but I did anyway.

Our staff handyman, Pete Engersol, was the next to start questioning me, as soon as I got past Mona and Nina and into the HotRescues yard. Behind the thin yet strong senior citizen were a few of our volunteers, listening intently. Even the dogs in the kennels on either side of us seemed to watch with interest.

I wondered if I should call an all-hands meeting in the conference room on the second floor of our main building and impart everything I knew so far — to people only — which wasn't much.

"Honestly, I don't know what happened other than the fact that the director of *Sheba's Story* was killed last night," I said loud enough for everyone to hear. "If I learn anything I think you should all know, I'll tell you. Okay?" I didn't wait for a response. "Now, everyone, we've got animals to take care of. Please get back to it!"

"Okay, Lauren," Pete said.

No one disagreed, although Mamie Spelling, our most senior volunteer who was also once my mentor — and, later, a reformed animal hoarder — came over and patted my arm. "You seem upset, Lauren, dear. Would you like a hug?" She was short, with curly red hair and a sometimes distant smile.

"I sure would," I said and shared a hug with the small, frail woman.

She came with me as I started my afternoon walk-through of the shelter. All of the kennels near the entryway were filled, as always, since that was where potential adopters saw our inhabitants first. Those in the back, around the corner in the recently acquired and built-out property, had some vacancies. So did the cat house and the building for small dogs and puppies, which were also in the back.

It would soon be time for us to do a rescue at a public shelter. I'd have to let Matt know

70

and have him suggest which one to visit.

I enjoyed peering into the glass-fronted kennels and seeing some of our volunteers, new ones and old-timers, sitting on the ground with our dogs, socializing them for human bonding by playing with them. Talking to them. Letting them enjoy the company for as long as possible.

Some of our residents had only been here a short while. Others were long-timers, and some were in between.

I noticed that Hale, a Rottweiler mix, was alone, so I slipped into his kennel to hug him and play for a few minutes on his smooth, recently cleaned cement floor while sending Mamie to visit with another dog. Hale had been one of the pups Mamie had been hoarding. He'd been named by Carlie, and so had a terrier mix called Hearty who had been adopted last month.

I paid attention to Hale despite how my mind began to wander. Carlie. Did she hate me now? If so, it was her loss . . . well, hell, it would be mine, too. Especially since it would be based on a misunderstanding. A partial misunderstanding, at least. I'd have to call her again. Maybe even take some of our residents here to her veterinary clinic as an excuse to see her. Then I'd be able to talk to her and —

71

"Hi, Lauren."

My imagination had to be working over-time. And I didn't have much of an imagination. But that sounded like Carlie.

I looked over Hale's head through the glass gate to the kennel. I was right. It really was Carlie standing there, wearing jeans and a *Pet Fitness* T-shirt.

I gave Hale a final hug and a couple of small treats from my pocket. Then I left his kennel.

"What are you doing here?" I asked. At Carlie's blink, I said, "I'm glad you're here, of course, but I didn't expect to see you."

She appeared tense, with no warmth in her expression. That was unusual, but I kept myself from wincing.

"Got a few minutes?" she asked. "I'd like to speak with you."

"Sure."

We talked about the dogs in the kennels we passed on the way back inside the main HotRescues building. It was a good excuse not to talk about the explosive situation that had crept into our friendship and threatened to blast it apart.

"I'll be unavailable for a while," I called to Nina and showed Carlie into my office.

I didn't want to look or act official with so much already dangling between us. I motioned for Carlie to sit on the couch in the friendly conversation area of my office.

Her blond hair looked as if she hadn't combed it for a few hours, which was unlike her. I knew she had something she wanted to say or she wouldn't have come. Even so, I spoke first. "Carlie, I know you're mad at me. I only said that you were there because I knew the cops would hear about your discussion with Hans from other people. But that's all I —"

"I know, Lauren." She raised one of her work-worn hands. Her smile was sad. "I'm sorry. I was looking for someone to blame, and it shouldn't have been you. I came here to ask you for a favor."

"Of course," I said, not caring what it was. I would do anything to preserve our friendship.

But I nearly kicked myself for even having that thought when she told me what she wanted.

"I don't know how far all this might go," she said. "Whether the cops will really consider me a prime suspect in what happened to Hans. They have more reason to look at me than the little spat you saw. I'll tell you more — but before I do, I want to invoke friend-to-friend privilege. You know, like attorney-client privilege. I don't want you to tell anyone else."

I stared at her. "But that attorney-client privilege is a legal thing. I won't volunteer anything you tell me, but I can't promise someone won't twist my arm to give it up."

"I understand. But before I tell you anything, I want to ask . . . Lauren, if they really come down on me as a possible suspect in Hans's death, would you please do one of your wonderful, independent investigations to figure out who really killed him?"

Chapter 6

I started to argue. I'd been fortunate three times before in situations I should have kept my nose out of. Well, I should have stayed out of two of them, at least. I was a murder suspect the first time so I had no real choice.

But, yes, I'd been successful all three times. That didn't mean I would be again. Or that I even wanted to try.

Although I was a lot closer to Carlie than I'd been to the other two people I'd helped to exonerate.

Even so, I'd done enough. "I can help you find a private investigator to hire, Carlie." I leaned toward her on the sofa. Zoey saw me move and came from the side of my desk for a reassuring pat that all was well. "Brooke probably has a slew of people she could refer you to." But as I saw my good friend's face fall, I felt my own insides start to melt — and I'm not an emotional person.

"Could we talk about it a little more?" she

said softly. "Let's go out for coffee. There are things you need to know before you decide — including how very much your friendship means to me. And how much I admire and respect your intelligence. And —"

"Laying it on a bit thick, aren't you?" I asked dryly.

Her smile was sad. "I haven't even gotten to the good part — why I know I could be a suspect. There are things you're not aware of . . . yet."

She had me there. I might not be overly susceptible to emotions, but my curiosity had been known to rule my common sense at times.

"Okay. Let's go get some coffee."

I went through my usual routine first, hugging Zoey and making sure she was settled in with Nina behind the welcome desk. "I'll be back soon, I promise." At Nina's grin I said, "I was talking to you, too, not just my dog."

She laughed and patted Zoey, and Carlie and I headed for the door. "I'll make sure things run smoothly around here while you're gone," Nina assured me.

"I'll drive," I told Carlie.

In less than fifteen minutes, we sat at a

table on the crowded sidewalk outside a chain coffee shop not far from HotRescues. The spring weather was a bit cool but pleasant. I sipped a brewed coffee, and Carlie had ordered a mocha.

"Okay," I said. "Let's hear those deep, dark secrets you hinted at."

"I hadn't planned on sitting outside, but it's such a pretty day," she dissembled. "Too bad we didn't bring Zoey along." She looked up with her flashing violet eyes as if assessing how blue the sky was.

"Or Max." He was the cocker mix whom Carlie had adopted from HotRescues when we'd first opened around seven years ago — our very first adoption. That had led to our friendship. "Do you want to call him and tell him where you are — and why?"

She laughed. "You win," she said, smoothing her blond hair back with one hand. "I've been trying not to focus on why we're really here." She turned her gaze on me and her full lips pursed as she appeared to consider how to begin.

I just waited.

She took a sip of mocha and stared away again, this time toward the street where a few vehicles were parked nearby at the curb and occasional cars passed by. "Okay. Here it is — why I may become a suspect in Hans

Marford's apparent murder."

I expected her to say that she'd contacted him in the last few weeks to get some additional information about the filming of *Sheba's Story* that she could use in her *Pet Fitness* segment.

But I didn't anticipate . . . "I had an affair with Hans."

"What!" I nearly rose. The small movement I did make caused some of my coffee to slosh out of the top of the cup. Fortunately, I'd brought a few napkins to our table.

My shout caught the attention of people sitting around us. Some of them stared. I ignored them.

"It was a few years ago," Carlie continued softly, as if I hadn't just nearly made a fool out of myself — not my usual practice, of course. "*Pet Fitness* had only been airing for a few months. Hans was already a well-known movie director. Apparently he likes animals, although he certainly didn't make that obvious while filming *Sheba's Story* — at least not during that last outside street shoot."

She paused, and I stifled my urge to shake more out of her faster. I knew her well enough to realize she was once more gathering her thoughts.

"Anyway, he was on a break between films and approached the executives at the Longevity Vision Channel. He said how much he liked my show and requested an opportunity to get involved with filming an episode or two. I was new enough at it that I was thrilled. Impressed. And readily seducible. But he got his next major motion picture gig, and that was that."

"Was the end of the relationship amicable?" I asked. I was surprised. Although I'd seen Carlie in a relationship or two since we'd become friends, I hadn't imagined her in a brief affair with a well-known Hollywood director.

"I wasn't thrilled," she admitted. "But I was a big girl. I knew I'd get over it. And I did. Fast. That wasn't his real intention, though. He expected I'd be waiting by the phone for him to call and ask me to join him in bed the next time he was in town. I didn't. He showed up at my place anyway. That's when we had words."

"Nasty ones, I surmise."

She aimed her next wry smile toward the coffee cup in her hand. "Imagine really nasty and you'll have it." She sighed. "That was that. We hadn't spoken in between at all, and I knew I was asking for trouble by agreeing to have The Fittest Pet provide the vet services for *Sheba's Story.* But I was excited about the opportunity — both because of the subject matter of the film and because I was told I could do a *Pet Fitness* segment on it."

"Did Hans know you'd be involved?"

"Sure. When I was contacted because of my connection to you and HotRescues and therefore Dante, the studio executives proudly told me who the director was. I suggested that they check with him before confirming me as the vet. I didn't say why, but apparently he had no problem with it."

"I'd no idea that you knew each other when I was on the set those first days of filming," I said. "Did Hans ever acknowledge it when you were both around?"

"No, and neither did I."

My coffee was growing cold. "I'm going to go buy a refill. Want one?"

"Sure," she said. "I'll hold the table." She reached for her purse to pay me.

"Don't bother. I'd rather that you owe me."

She laughed, and I headed inside.

When I returned, she was staring again at her hands, which were clasped on the table. She looked startled when I put her cup down in front of her.

"I've been wondering," I said as I sat back

down. I kept my voice low because of what I was about to ask. "Why would you think you'd be considered a suspect in his death? You're someone to interrogate, sure, like the rest of us. But what you went through was a while ago, and I doubt anyone connected with the film was aware of it."

"A lot of people we both knew were aware of it then," she replied. "This was the first time we'd gotten together since, and I was attacking his treatment of the dogs the last time we spoke — right in front of people. Maybe it's a stretch, but the cops may find out and ask questions and —"

She caught my dubious expression and stopped. And looked down. And blushed.

"Okay." She still didn't meet my eyes. "He called me that first night after I came to the set. I was cordial, but I cordially told him where to shove his suggestion for a get-together. I also said I wouldn't stay away from the filming, since I was always concerned about animals. We got into a shouting match over the phone. I was in my office. One of my vet techs didn't realize I was busy and came in at just the wrong time with some paperwork for me to review. I don't know whether Hans was alone or where he was. But if the cops learn about that . . ."

"I get it," I said. "They'll be looking for any potential suspect with a grudge against Hans Marford for any reason."

"I won't reveal anything to them unless they ask me directly, and then I know better than to lie — although I might invoke my Fifth Amendment right and hire a lawyer, just in case. But if that happens . . ." The gaze she leveled on me then was pleading, and she reached over to grab my arm. "Please, Lauren. I know you can't make any guarantees, but with your score in investigating murders so far, I'd really appreciate it if you'd try to find out who really did it."

My sigh was long and deep. "Okay, Carlie," I said slowly. "Like you said, no guarantees. But if the cops zero in on you, I'll see what I can do."

She rose and gave me a hug. "Thank you, Lauren," she said hoarsely.

As she sat back down I took another swig of coffee and tried not to kick myself in the butt. After all, she might never be considered a major suspect.

We both had to get back to our responsibilities. Cups in hand, we walked slowly down the street to where I'd parked my Venza.

And stopped, half a block away.

There, on the sidewalk in front of a dry

cleaner's, was a scruffy-looking dog, chest-nut in color with long, curly fur. If I had to guess, I figured it was part cocker spaniel and part poodle.

It wasn't on a leash. No person stood near it. I looked around. There wasn't anyone else nearby. No one dashed down the street looking for this pup.

"Do you see that?" Carlie asked, looking around, too.

"A stray," I surmised. "Here, hold this." I handed Carlie my cup. "I'll go grab her." I'd checked as well as I could from a few feet away and believed the dog to be female.

She wore no collar. When I got closer, she shied away, running much too close to the street.

I drew in my breath in fear for her — then realized that I still wore my HotRescues work clothes. That meant —

I reached into my pocket and pulled out some treats. "Here, sweetheart." I held out my hand toward her.

She looked suspicious, but her nose must have told her that I really had some food for her. She slowly drew closer.

When she grabbed the treats from me, Carlie, who'd set our coffees down and sneaked toward us, picked her up from be-hind.

Fortunately, the dog seemed more shy than aggressive.

"See any kind of ID on her?" I asked.

Carlie shook her head. "Nothing."

We wandered around for quite a while, asking people, including those at the coffee shop, if they recognized the dog, but no one did.

"Let's go back to HotRescues," I finally said. "I'll check her for a microchip."

"And if she doesn't have one?"

"Let's strategize on the way. I'm sure I can get Matt to help me pick her up again from a public shelter if I have to turn her in."

That was the law here. Private shelters could take in owner relinquishments or could rescue animals from public shelters before they were put down for lack of space. But they couldn't take in strays.

There were ways to deal with that, though, that could still result in a living, adoptable dog.

"Let's call her Hope for now," I said as we settled the stinky pooch in the back of my Venza in one of the crates locked in there for just this kind of situation. I looked into the crate, seeing the scared eyes of the poor dog. "Hope, I have a feeling that your life is about to get a whole lot better."

CHAPTER 7

"She's adorable!" That was Nina, the moment we brought Hope into the Hot-Rescues welcome area. Her huge smile bisected her thin face.

I'd called ahead and Nina had closed Zoey in my office. My dog didn't need to meet Hope unless and until our new rescuee became an inhabitant at this facility. Less hassle that way, and there was always the remote possibility that Hope was ill — although Carlie had already given her a cursory examination.

Our plan was to go next to The Fittest Pet to ensure that Hope was checked out more thoroughly before we decided what to do with her.

For now, though, I went into my office and grabbed the microchip scanner. Hope cowered a bit as I knelt on the tile floor and ran the gadget over her while Carlie and Nina watched.

Yes! There was a microchip embedded in her back beneath her curly reddish coat. The small rice-sized gadget should help us find Hope's owner.

Who might be looking desperately for the poor, missing animal. Or not. I'd reserve judgment whether to feel sorry for the despondent owner who'd tried everything to find his or her pet, or to hate the careless, uncaring person who had let Hope get lost and wasn't even searching for her.

In my work with animals over the past few years, I'd seen and dealt with both.

At the moment, I looked at the information, grabbed my phone, and called the microchip registry company noted on the readout. The operator who answered quickly found a dog matching Hope's description with the same ID number and gave me the contact data. Since I'd dealt with this company before and they knew about HotRescues, getting them to provide me with the somewhat confidential information was no problem.

I jotted down the name and phone number. The name sounded familiar: Guy Randell. Same name as a Los Angeles city councilperson. Could it be him?

Carlie and Nina looked over my shoulder toward the pad of paper I held. "Really?"

Carlie said.

"It doesn't seem like that common a name, but it isn't necessarily who we think it is," I replied. I hugged Hope, then asked Nina to take her into the small kitchen and give her some dinner. "I'll bet the poor thing hasn't eaten for a while."

"Should I call Margo up here and ask her to give Hope a bath?" Nina asked.

"I'd rather have her health checked before she sees our groomer," I said.

Nina put a temporary collar on Hope and snapped on a leash. She seemed to know what they were for, since she didn't balk at accompanying Nina into the other room. I'd already used a leash with a slip-collar from my car to walk Hope briefly in the parking lot. She also appeared to be house-broken.

I wished, not for the first time when I met a new animal, that we had a better way to communicate. I'd love to know Hope's background from her own perspective.

For now, though, Carlie and I went into the rest room, sanitized our hands, and sprayed a light disinfectant mist over our clothes. Then we entered my office, where Zoey greeted us both effusively.

Sitting at my desk, I used the speaker-phone on my landline to call the number

I'd been given by the microchip company.

Sure enough, "Councilman Randell's office," said the friendly female voice that answered.

Keeping my tone professional, I said, "My name is Lauren Vancouver. I'm the administrator of HotRescues, a private pet rescue facility. I'd like to speak to the councilman about his dog. Is he available?"

"His dog?" the voice repeated as incredulously as if I'd asked to speak to the councilman's long-deceased great-grandfather. "Just a minute." Before I could say anything else, I was apparently put on hold since I didn't hear anything for at least a minute. Then, "Ms. Vancouver? Sorry to keep you waiting, but I checked. The councilman doesn't own a dog."

My turn for silence, but only for a moment. "May I speak with him, please? I got his information after checking out the microchip in a stray dog I found. I'd just like a clarification." And verification, in case whoever this was didn't know what she was talking about. I suspected, though, that I'd been put on hold so she could ask around to confirm whether the councilman did or didn't have a canine pet.

"Just a moment and I'll check."

Good thing I wasn't in a hurry to do

something else, since once again I was treated to a lengthy silence. I broke it by saying to Carlie, "This seems a bit strange, doesn't it? I mean, why would Hope's microchip give information for someone who didn't own her?"

Carlie shook her head slowly, her blond hair stroking the shoulder of her T-shirt. "I agree. I've never heard of anyone putting someone else's contact information into the database for a microchip. But —"

"Hello, Ms. Vancouver?" boomed a deep voice over the phone. "This is Councilman Randell. I understand there's some confusion — about a dog, is it?"

"That's right."

As I explained the situation about the dog we now called Hope, I heard the politico's ongoing "hmmmm," which grew louder as I told him how I'd gotten his name and this phone number.

"Interesting," he said. "But truly, Ms. Vancouver, I don't own a dog of any kind, let alone the one you've described." His tone grew a tiny bit curt, which made me wonder . . .

As we continued the conversation briefly, I did a Google search on the Internet — and learned that there was some controversy about Councilperson Guy Randell's position on a few issues regarding Los Angeles Animal Services. If the media got it right, the guy might actually be an animal hater. I'd known there was political opposition to some matters recently proposed to further regulate puppy mills and extend the time animals were held in public shelters but hadn't paid much attention to who was against them.

"You know," the councilman said eventually, "I think I'll have someone look into this odd situation. If they find anything, I'll have them call you at HotRescues. In any case, as far as I'm concerned the dog is yours to deal with as you wish."

"All right," I said. "Thank you."

I had a feeling that had I been in this man's council district, I would vote against reelecting him.

"What now?" Carlie looked concerned as I ended the phone connection.

"First, I'll contact Matt. Then we'll go to Fittest Pet so you can check Hope out."

I quickly called Matt and explained the situation. "Even though the councilman is purportedly looking into the situation, Hope seems to be a stray. I'll need to turn her in to Animal Services once her health has been checked. But I'll want to put a hold on her, assuming Councilman Randell's office doesn't contact me with anything helpful and her real owner doesn't claim her — which sounds as likely as the councilman inviting me to lunch."

I was glad for many reasons that I was now friends with Matt. For one thing, he helped to expedite this kind of situation. For another, he gave a damn about what would happen to the dog.

"You're sure you got the information right?" he asked.

I had him on speakerphone, and Carlie answered, leaning over my desk toward the receiver. "Why would a microchip service company lie? It's possible they got their records fouled up, but I've never heard of that before."

"Me neither," Matt said. "Well, check out the dog's health, Carlie. If you give me what you got from the microchip company, Lauren, I'll put that into our system and have someone follow our protocol to confirm the information you've got. Let me know if you hear anything new from the councilman's office, too. It sounds, though, as if you've just rescued another unclaimed stray dog, which could be a good thing since she'll probably wind up at HotRescues."

"That's great!" I said, meaning it. But my questions still remained. "I'd still like to know, though, if the councilman was lying."

"There are ways of checking out whether he had a pet," Matt reminded me.

"There are," I agreed. "I think I'll tell Brooke when she comes to do her security thing at HotRescues tonight to put on her private investigator hat for a little while and find out."

Carlie had her car here, and I could have just sent Hope with her back to The Fittest Pet Veterinary Hospital. But I'd arranged with Matt to meet him there. He would take Hope to one of the public shelters, then make sure all the requirements were fulfilled to allow me to come get her if the owner didn't show up — the most likely scenario.

Something was definitely screwy about Hope, at least about where she'd come from. But I'd do my darnedest to make sure that the rest of her life was happy — especially if I could find her a new, loving home soon.

Matt was waiting for us when we reached The Fittest Pet. Carlie and I had driven in a short caravan with Hope in the back of my Venza while I followed her.

The Fittest Pet Veterinary Hospital was in Northridge on Reseda Boulevard, not far from the streets where the filming of scenes for *Sheba's Story* had occurred yesterday. As I parked in Carlie's lot, my mind pounced once more onto the possible murder of director Hans Marford.

What had happened to him? Was Carlie really a suspect?

Would I have to help find who killed him to help her?

I hoped not.

"Hi, Lauren," said a muffled voice outside my car window. I realized then that I'd just been sitting there. Matt was right beside me.

"Hi." I smiled and got out, waving toward the back of my car. "That's Hope. I'll get her out of her crate and put a leash on her."

Carlie joined us and we all headed into the facility.

The Fittest Pet Veterinary Hospital is in a cute, single-story building of pink stucco. It's a circle, built around an outer patio where animals could be walked or otherwise given fresh air.

With Carlie along, we didn't have to wait till a doctor was ready to see our canine patient. Matt, Hope, and I were shown into an examination room.

"Cute pup." Matt stooped to pet Hope. "I can't imagine that someone who really owned her would disavow it."

"There are a lot of strange people in the world," I responded. "Although someone in the public eye like that . . . well, we'll just have to see."

Carlie, dressed in her official veterinary scrubs, soon joined us, followed by a vet tech who came in to draw blood. We lifted Hope onto the metal examination table in the middle of the room. Her exam took about half an hour. By then, preliminary results of the blood test had been received, too.

"She looks good," Carlie said. "I know that Matt has to take her to one of the public shelters now, so I'll have one of my technicians give her a quick bath first." She popped her head through the back door of the examination room and immediately a twentyish young woman came in and picked up Hope.

We stayed in that room talking for about fifteen minutes till Hope was returned to us — much cleaner and still a bit damp.

"Now, come out front with me and I'll tell our guys how to handle this on the computer."

We went out through the exam room's front door and down the hallway toward the reception area, Carlie leading the way.

I almost bumped into her when she

stopped abruptly and gasped.

Detective Lou Maddinger stood in the busy waiting room, surrounded by people maneuvering cat crates and dogs. The chubby, gray-haired detective saw us right away. "Dr. Stellan? I'd like for you to come with me to the Devonshire station. I have some more questions for you."

I wanted to ask him if they had made a final determination whether Hans had been murdered, but now wasn't the time. Besides, I felt certain that I already knew the answer.

I heard Carlie's soft moan — and knew that, like it or not, I was about to start conducting my fourth unofficial murder investigation.

CHAPTER 8

As I stood beside Matt in the crowded waiting area, Carlie slipped back inside the pet hospital with Detective Maddinger following. She needed to get her purse, call the lawyer I'd recommended, and direct someone to cover for her while she was gone.

I hoped that would be only for an hour or two. It was late enough in the day, though, that I suspected that the earliest she'd return would be tomorrow.

My fingers were crossed that she wouldn't actually be taken into custody.

"Are you okay, Lauren?" Matt's brow was furrowed with such concern that I wanted to hug him. He held Hope's leash, but the dog looked more frightened by the large population of animals in the reception area than ready to attack any of them. She sat on his foot.

"Sure." I pretended a lightheartedness I didn't feel. He knew me well enough to realize that, and those dark, straight eyebrows of his raised in challenge. "Really. Or at least I will be when you get Hope checked in and do what you need to so I can retrieve her and bring her back to HotRescues." I wiggled my own well-maintained brows in pseudo-flirtatious challenge right back.

He laughed. "You win. Let's go." He pulled gently on Hope's leash.

"I'll be a few minutes," I said. "I need to make a phone call about when filming of *Sheba's Story* might start again, and I also want to talk to at least one of the vets here who might be on the set."

"I gather that isn't just about wanting to make sure that 'No Animals Were Harmed.'" He did have one expressive face. Right now, it looked wry.

"Well, that — and I thought I'd try to be there next time so I can tell Dante how things go without Hans Marford."

"And to see if you can figure out who . . . disposed of him." Matt looked around. There were a lot of people nearby who might be eavesdropping. Maybe it was better to use euphemisms than to say outright that I wanted to solve the director's murder. "Is that what you're up to?" He didn't look thrilled with the idea.

I sighed. "I don't know. It's not that I want

to, but —"

"I get it. Especially since I understand how close you are to Carlie. But you also know how concerned I got the last time you got involved in . . . a situation like that. Not to mention the other times. I don't imagine it'll make any difference, but I'd rather you stay out of it." As I opened my mouth to explain why I needed to get involved, he raised one hand. "Okay. I get it. At least promise you'll be careful."

"I will. And I'll not do anything stupid, and I'll keep you informed — you and Brooke and Antonio. And —"

He laughed, then bent and planted a quick but enjoyable kiss on my lips, despite the crowd around us. I kissed him back. Why not? I really liked the guy.

But so as not to play favorites, I bent and gave Hope a hug, too. "See you soon, girl," I said, then rose again.

"See you soon, girl," Matt repeated, then he and Hope left.

I went up to the registry counter at the far end of the bustling room and asked the young female vet tech who was staffing it, "May I see Dr. Andelson now?" Cyd Andelson was the vet whom Carlie had assigned to mostly work with the film crew.

"She's with a patient," the tech, whose

nametag identified her as Sher, said with a smile that looked pasted on because she had been told to act friendly no matter how busy the place was. "Can someone else help you?"

"No. I promised Dr. Stellan that I'd check in with Dr. Andelson about the next filming being done for *Sheba's Story.*" I'd bent over as if imparting a secret. At this point, The Fittest Pet's involvement hadn't been revealed to the world.

Carlie had wanted to do that on her own show with a preview of what was happening on the various sets, and she'd been given the okay by her not-so-close former friend Hans Marford. I wasn't sure what the next director would say about it.

"Oh. Of course." The smile ramped into one that appeared genuine. "Will it take long?"

"I promise not to hold her up for more than a few minutes."

"I'll make sure she sees you next. Would you like to have a seat?"

I might have, had one been available. But I had a phone call to make anyway.

"That's okay," I said. "I'll wait outside."

I stood close enough to the door so Sher could see me through the glass. Then I called Grant Jefferly.

He answered right away. "Hi, Lauren. You'll never guess where I am."

"Fill me in," I said, smiling at his excited voice.

"I'm at Solario Studios. Niall called before and asked me to come to meet the new director on *Sheba's Story*. They appointed one of the assistant directors who already knew what was going on. The permit for shooting the street scenes is fairly short and they didn't want to go through an attempt to extend it."

"So who's the new director?" I asked, keeping my eye on Sher, who was speaking with the owner of a Great Dane that seemed very interested in a nearby Lab. Fortunately, the Lab's owner got the message and walked away.

"Mick Paramus."

I thought I remembered meeting the guy, but I'd met so many of the production staff I couldn't put a face to the name.

"Great," I said anyway. "When's the filming to start again?"

"Tomorrow. I just tried calling Dr. Stellan to let her know but she didn't answer her phone. Can you tell her?"

"I just happen to be at The Fittest Pet now," I said without going into detail. "I know Carlie's busy, but your timing couldn't be better. I'll make sure one of the other vets here comes to the set tomorrow. What time?"

Of course it would start early, which was a good thing. I'd be there, too, for at least part of the day.

And then I'd go back to HotRescues and start one of my now de rigueur computer files on murder suspects in the death of Hans Marford.

As I hung up with Grant, I saw the Great Dane's owner peel away from the reception desk. Sher was looking out the door toward me. I went back inside.

"Dr. Andelson can see you now," she said and had one of the other techs show me to an examination room.

Cyd Andelson popped in about a minute later holding a clipboard as if ready to take notes on a veterinary case. "Hi, Lauren," she said. I'd met her and probably all of the vets here at one time or another when I came in with animals from HotRescues for exams and shots. Cyd was in her fifties, a little overweight, with long, nondescript hair fastened at the nape of her neck. "What's up?" She looked around as if searching for a dog or cat I'd brought in.

"First thing — I meant to ask Carlie. Is the diarrhea epidemic here at Fittest Pet

101

taken care of?" Or would I have to tell Matt to have closer watch kept on Hope to make sure she didn't come down with anything?

"Of course." Cyd looked insulted that I would even ask. "All the dogs are doing just fine now. What's second?"

"Well . . . Carlie mentioned treating a number of dogs lately who were hit by cars." I'd wondered, though, if she had made it up to help explain the extent of her anger — without revealing what was actually behind it. "She'd said they were okay. Are they still doing all right?"

"Fortunately, yes. We were very lucky that none had been badly injured — and of course our veterinarians are the best."

I smiled at that, nodding my agreement — and encompassing her in it as well as Carlie. "There's one more thing," I said. "It's actually a heads-up. Filming's going to resume on *Sheba's Story* tomorrow morning at eight A.M. I don't know whether you're aware of it, but Carlie's . . . well, she probably won't be able to attend. She may not be easy to reach to check on her availability, so I figured I'd let you know. Can you be there, or can you get someone else?"

"Sure, I can come. I'm on standby for the production, and I can just let the staff know to get someone to cover for me here —

although we might be pretty shorthanded tomorrow." Her round face looked drawn all of a sudden, and tears appeared in her light brown eyes. "Word's gotten out that the police are questioning Carlie about the death of that jerk Hans Marford." Surprise must have shown on my face, and she gave a bark of a laugh. "We're a pretty close-knit group here at Fittest Pet. We saw Carlie leave with that guy in a suit. We also knew when Marford was hanging around her *Pet Fitness* set and when she finally had the sense to dump him."

I wasn't sure who dumped whom, but that didn't really matter. The problem was that it seemed clear that people knew about their aborted relationship. And that they'd been in contact again. And argued.

I suspected that the investigation I was about to conduct was even more imperative than I'd first thought.

It might be the only way to keep my dear friend Carlie out of jail.

CHAPTER 9

As soon as I got back in my car, but before I started driving away, I made a phone call — one I didn't really want to make but felt I should.

I called the local TV station, where Carlie's boyfriend worked. The relationship was only a few months old but I figured that Liam Deale should at least know what was going on — if he didn't already. The media had jumped on reporting Hans's death. Maybe they were following the situation closely enough to know when a "person of interest" was being interrogated, and I assumed that was what the authorities would call Carlie, at least for now.

Watching the parade of animals being led in and out of the busy veterinary clinic from the lot where I was parked, I used my smartphone to find the number, then called KVKV.

Liam responded almost immediately.

"Lauren? What's going on with Carlie? One of our reporters was at the Devonshire station and said she was brought in there a minute ago. He wasn't allowed to speak with her, and her phone is turned off so I can't talk to her either. I assume this is about the death of the director of that movie she's providing veterinary care for. Did she see something?"

Good. He knew about the film and Carlie's connection to it, and he apparently didn't suspect her of anything.

"Not that I'm aware of," I answered, "but even so, the detectives looking into the director's death want to talk to her some more about it."

"Is she a murder suspect?"

"Possibly," I said slowly.

"Ridiculous! Hell, I'll get my reporters on it right away and find out what's really going on. Meantime — are you looking into it?"

Liam had been dating Carlie during the last bit of investigating I'd done so he knew about my past involvement in investigations.

"I might be, but that's not for publication." I certainly didn't want him to get any of his crews to interview me.

"Whatever you say. But let me know if there's anything else I can do to help."

Another pause. "I know Carlie's protective of animals, not people so much . . . She couldn't really be involved, could she?"

I didn't like his changed tone — too much speculation and not enough denial.

"Of course not." That must have come out pretty loud, since a woman passing by with her corgi on a leash looked in at me with a startled expression. "Of course not," I repeated more quietly. "Keep me informed if you learn anything, and I'll do the same."

My irritation with Liam didn't spill over into my driving as I headed to HotRescues.

I thought about it, though — a lot. But my poor friend had enough to worry about without my suggesting that she upend her current love life. Once she was free and clear of suspicion, I might find a way to hint that a change might be in order. She shouldn't stay with a man who didn't fully trust her, and might even consider using her as the focus of a reputation-damaging story. Did Liam suspect, or even know about, Carlie's past relationship with Hans? Of course I didn't know that he would do something to harm her — but I had seen stories he had worked on for his station and some had seemed less news and more sensationalism.

I said hi to Nina, then took Zoey on a regular walk-through of my shelter. All the animals looked fine, for pets without their own homes. At least they had people who loved them, including me, my staff, and our volunteers.

Usually, just visiting them was enough to distract me from whatever problems were on my mind. But not today.

My disquiet must have been obvious. Volunteers with dogs on leashes drew close but just said hi and walked on rather than engaging me in conversation about their wards, which was the norm.

Fortunately, Dr. Mona wasn't there. I didn't want to have to explain my distress to her, and I had no doubt she'd read it on my face.

Eventually I returned to the welcome area and talked to Nina about some potential adopters who'd come in, fallen in love, and filled out forms. I'd have to meet them before deciding whether the animals they'd chosen were good matches.

My mood for now was such that I'd probably hate every human who came in, so I needed to wait.

Maybe I was wrong about Liam.

And maybe helping Carlie would be easier than I anticipated. I hoped.

It was late, time for Nina to go. "Are you okay, Lauren?" she asked first. "I'm going to the East Valley Animal Shelter to volunteer for a few hours tonight, but I could stay here with you."

"I'm fine." I tried to convince her as much as myself.

She still looked dubious but she left.

At least I didn't have to wait long before our overnight security guru, Brooke, arrived.

I realized that I'd subconsciously planned for Zoey and me to wait till she got here. I needed to talk to the former P.I.

Even more, I wanted to talk to her significant other, Detective Antonio Bautrel of the LAPD.

Brooke popped in right on time, at six o'clock. Zoey and I went to greet her in the welcome area.

Brooke looked bright and energetic and happy, the way she usually did these days despite her earlier health issues. The narrowness of her face was pretty, not gaunt, and her highlighted brown hair created an attractive frame for it. She wore a uniform consisting of a traditional black T-shirt that read SECURITY STAFF over matching black jeans.

She'd brought her golden retriever Cheyenne, and Zoey hurried over to trade sniffs.

One look at me, though, and Brooke's smile fell into a concerned frown. "What's wrong, Lauren?"

"Any possibility of Antonio coming to see you this evening?"

"He's on his way. Is there a police matter you want to discuss with him?"

I motioned for her to follow me to the small kitchen, where I handed her a bottle of water from the fridge and took one for myself. We returned to the small table in the welcome area where prospective adopters filled out applications. After closing the window blinds, I sat on one side and Brooke took the other. She remained patient, but her expression was full of concern.

"You know my friend Carlie," I said. Like most people here, she now used The Fittest Pet veterinary clinic for her own pet.

"Yes. Is she —" Her phone beeped. She pulled it out and read the text message. "It's Antonio. He's in the parking lot."

"Go let him in," I said. "It'll be better if I tell you both at the same time."

She unlocked the door from the welcome room to the parking lot, and Antonio strode in.

Antonio Bautrel was an LAPD detective in the Gang and Narcotics Division. He

109

must have just come from work since he was in a dressed-down suit, wearing nice trousers and a shirt but without jacket or tie. He wasn't a traditionally handsome man, since his nose was rather large and he had a jutting brow, but his demeanor was arresting — in more ways than one.

He gave Brooke a kiss in greeting. They broke away after several long, intense seconds, and he then looked at me.

"Hi, Lauren." Antonio's deep voice was breathless, edged in laughter.

"Hi, Antonio." I smiled back. "Hey, have a few minutes? I need to run something by you." The recollection popped the balloon of lightness around me, and I motioned for them to join me at the table.

They were both aware, of course, of my affiliation with the *Sheba's Story* filming. They'd also both heard about director Hans Marford's death. Antonio, like Brooke, knew Carlie socially, thanks to me, and professionally thanks to accompanying Brooke and Cheyenne to The Fittest Pet now and then.

I told them the latest about Carlie.

I also considered mentioning her earlier relationship with Hans to get Antonio's reaction but didn't want to make that revelation if Carlie was able, somehow, to downplay — or even hide — it. Besides, what she'd told me was probably some kind of legal hearsay, the way I understood it. I'd heard her say it, but it wasn't my own knowledge.

"Want me to find out what's going on with her?" Antonio asked.

"Yes," I said in relief. "Please."

"Then excuse me."

Brooke and I left Antonio alone in the welcome area while I joined her initial walk-through of HotRescues for the evening. Just knowing I had someone with clout on my side, someone who'd at least tell me what he could without breaching the official confidentiality shroud of the LAPD, made me feel better. I stopped in a few of the kennels and cleaned them as needed. I also spent some pleasant minutes hugging and playing with a few of our dogs while Brooke continued through to ensure that all looked secure.

That meant I was first to spot Antonio come through the door from the main building.

I quickly hugged the dog I was playing with, the Rottweiler mix Hale, and hurried to the pathway to meet Antonio.

"Did you learn anything?" I said eagerly. But my mood tensed and flattened just at the look on his face.

He nodded, his expression hard beneath his short, black hair, and I expected the worst.

And got it, or at least a close facsimile.

"I'm very sorry, Lauren." His tone was formal. "Here's the little I now know, and you'll need to keep it to yourself. Evidence is still being collected so Carlie is not under arrest, at least not yet. It sounds as if there weren't useful fingerprints in the vehicle that hit Marford — one connected with the filming — but it could have been wiped clean or the driver might have worn gloves. They are investigating this homicide as a probable murder. And there's a witness who's come forward about a relationship Carlie once had with the victim, one that apparently didn't end well. She's definitely at least a —"

"Person of interest," I finished harshly as Brooke joined us once again. "But she didn't do it."

"I hope you're right, but the investigation is ongoing."

Who was the witness? How much did he or she really know? Could it have been one of the people at The Fittest Pet who'd admitted knowing about the prior relationship — like Dr. Cyd Andelson?

Had things between Hans and Carlie been even worse than she'd said?

No. I had to trust her. I *did* trust her.

Didn't I?

"You don't know for sure that she's innocent, Lauren," Brooke said.

"Please stay out of it," Antonio said to me. "I know you've gotten involved in other cases lately and had good results, but —"

"But Carlie's my friend," I said. "And she's asked for my help. I promise to keep you informed about everything I learn, Antonio" — at least all in her favor — "and I'll be careful, but — well, thanks for the info. Hey, let's order a pizza, shall we?"

As far as I was concerned, the discussion was over.

But I had a film shoot to visit tomorrow.

CHAPTER 10

Filming that Thursday was to take place just down the road from where the scenes for *Sheba's Story* had been shot on Monday. It was in the same mostly commercial area, but less of the street was available for cars chasing dogs — whether real or set to be dubbed in later.

One block was still cordoned off with crime scene tape.

This scenario was actually pretty handy for me. In situations before when I'd tried to figure out the identity of a murderer, it was unusual to get a whole group of suspects together like this. Sometimes I got to assess several at once during the victim's funeral. On one occasion there had been a group meeting of suspects — when the victim was the head of an organization of affiliated pet shelters.

I shook my head in disbelief at the way my thoughts were roaming as I walked quickly down the sidewalk from where I'd parked my car. I could see the line of large white trucks at the curb, surrounded by bustling people.

In a minute, I'd reached the perimeter.

"Hi, Lauren." Dr. Cyd Andelson had approached from one side, and her smile looked relieved, as if she was glad to see a friendly face. The vet of the day hadn't penetrated the filming area yet. Her mousy brown hair was loose, though I was used to seeing it fastened at her nape at The Fittest Pet. I also usually saw her with a clipboard in hand, but she was carrying a script. Her button-down pink shirt wasn't tucked into her jeans.

I'd gotten used to dressing up a bit whenever possible when I'd come to a filming. Maybe it was because I represented Dante. It certainly wasn't because I tried to impress members of the film industry with how professional I could look. Today I wore a woven beige jacket over a blue short-sleeved sweater and navy slacks.

"Hi," I said to Cyd. "Have you seen Grant?" I figured on spending most of the day following him around — except when I got an opportunity to talk nonchalantly with people I thought could be murder suspects.

Of course, that included Grant.

"No," Cyd replied, "but a lot of people are already gathering inside the secured filming area. Maybe he's there."

"Then let's go."

We approached the hired security guys standing at the barrier leading to where the shoot would take place. There were three of them now, but that was the only change I noted. It didn't seem any harder to convince the guy we talked to that we were who we said we were, and that we were cleared to be present at the filming. The underlying process hadn't been changed despite the fact that the director had been murdered nearby. But even if he had been killed by someone not authorized to be present, tightening the screening process now wouldn't resurrect Hans. Was anyone else targeted for murder? Since we didn't know who'd done it or why, who could say?

It was something I'd consider as I asked my questions.

As soon as we'd gone through the makeshift gate, I saw Grant Jefferly standing nearby. Today he wore a teal blue T-shirt under his American Humane Association vest. He must have seen me at the same time, since his concerned frown as he surveyed the area turned into a huge smile that, as always, revealed his perfect white teeth. Maybe someone should cast him in a toothpaste commercial if he ever got a break from attending film sets. Even with that thought — or maybe because of it, I couldn't help smiling back. I liked the guy, or at least what he did.

"Hi, Lauren, Dr. Andelson," he said. "Glad you both could make it."

"Has any filming started?" I asked.

"No. The new director has called a quick meeting for" — he looked at his wristwatch — "ten minutes from now."

"Great. I'll be interested in hearing what he has to say."

We started walking along the sidewalk inside the area cordoned off for filming. There were a lot of people here, too. The first I recognized was Lyanne Shroeder. She sat on a folding chair on the sidewalk, and a couple of people were fussing over her makeup and hair.

Interesting. I didn't think she was included in any of the scenes that would be shot today. We'd probably learn more before filming started, but I'd heard that the scenes in today's takes were to occur prior to the time her character, Millie, even became aware of the dog who'd become Sheba.

Since she wasn't in a position where she was likely to run off quickly, she could become the subject of my first inquiry. I eased my way through the crowd toward her.

"Good morning," I said.

She brushed away the man working on making her lips pout even more and looked at me. "Hello, Lauren." She settled back in the chair, obviously assuming I was just being friendly.

"Are you in one of today's scenes?" I now stood beside her, and the woman fussing with her dark hair gave me a dirty look as she edged toward Lyanne's other side.

"I hope to be." Lyanne shrugged off her peeps and smiled at me. "I told Hans about my idea — showing Millie at a store near where the escaping dogs are running — without having them meet yet, since that's not in the script. But it could be such a poignant scene. The audience will expect that their paths will cross then, yet they don't for months."

"And Hans was going to film it?" I asked.

"Well, no. He didn't like the idea. But I'm planning on making an all-out effort to convince our new director, Mick Paramus, so I figured I'd be ready."

Interesting. A bit flimsy as a motive to kill Hans, but I made a mental note of it.

"Why didn't Hans like it?" I asked. Not

exactly subtle, but I was digging for information about any strife between Lyanne and him.

"He's — er, he *was* — such a by-the-script kind of director. A good guy, and his films were great. But he wasn't all that creative himself." Her frown evidenced her displeasure, but she wasn't admitting to any huge disagreement with the guy, creative or otherwise, that could have led to something worse.

She'd remain in the computer file I always made about suspects, but her page would be near its end . . . for now, at least.

"See you in a bit," I said noncommittally. Her assistants looked relieved when I walked away, as they could recommence their work.

Cyd hadn't waited for me, but when I looked around I saw both her and Grant at the far end of this block. That's where the dogs were, too — four on leashes held by the young dog handlers, Jerry and Elena; the trainer, Cowan; and the chief handler, Winna Darrion. I hurried in their direction.

The day was warmer than the last time we'd been here. I smelled a barbecue aroma in the air and realized that some enterprising local restaurant along this street must be attempting to make money by luring the cast and crew in to eat. Maybe they were using fans to make sure the delicious smell wafted around everyone.

The aroma seemed to inspire the dogs to do anything but obey commands. "Let them get it out of their system now," Winna was saying as all four dogs strained at their leashes, apparently trying to get beyond the cordoned-off filming area. She was short, and her dyed red hair clustered in a poodle haircut of her own. The T-shirt over her jeans looked well worn, a gray tweedlike knit. "Show me where you want to go, Blanca."

She loosened the dog's leash, and Blanca strained even more in the direction the others seemed to want to head.

I looked up and saw a place appropriately called the Hamburger Hangout just down the street.

"You don't let dogs 'get things out of their system,' " Cowan contradicted. He was a short man, very thin, and reminded me of a greyhound with his elongated face. A couple of extra leashes adorned his neck. "They're to obey us, not vice versa. We can distract them with treats. Let's show them, Sheba." The real Sheba sat on command and took the treat Cowan handed to her. But as soon as she was done eating, she again stood and tried to follow the other dogs.

Jerry and Elena laughed but dutifully followed Cowan's lead in trying to get their leashed dogs to ignore the smell of hamburger.

I approached them all. "This is so cute," I said. "But frustrating, I know. I'm always having to deal with trying to train the dogs at HotRescues not to go dashing off where I don't want them, or to stop barking — whatever they do that could make people less inclined to adopt them."

"It's not cute," Cowan growled. "This could cost time and money on the production if these people don't work with the dogs correctly."

I didn't point out his failings. "I'll bet poor Hans Marford wasn't happy when the dogs didn't do things on command the way they needed to for the filming."

"Absolutely not." Cowan's elongated face grew florid. "He wanted things to go perfectly."

"And when they didn't?" I prompted.

"He had a system of rewards and punishments. I always received bonuses for getting animals to do what he wanted them to."

Except, maybe, this time.

"I don't think so." Grant had been standing at the edge of this group. He'd shot me a worried-looking smile. "Isn't that part of

121

the reason he wanted to do that last scene with the dogs and cars running free — because the dogs weren't doing things the way he told you he wanted them?"

"Of course not." But the color of Cowan's face grew a brighter red.

He was rising to the top of my suspect file.

"If you all had worked with them the way I told you for that scene," Cowan continued, facing Winna, "everything would have worked out. Didn't Hans tell you that, too?"

The handler suddenly looked furious. "We did fine, didn't we?" She looked at her two young assistants. "Mr. Marford liked to come over and pat the dogs when filming wasn't going on, and he always seemed pleased with how they acted. Right?"

Both Elena and Jerry nodded, their eyes wide. Neither responded verbally.

This scenario appeared to give Winna and Cowan more motive to fight with each other than to harm the director.

And my approaching everyone here didn't seem to be as productive as I'd hoped. But I could continue to observe them.

Plus, getting them off on their own, without having a group around that they had to impress, might be a better way for me to conduct my inquiry.

But that wouldn't happen now. Niall darted over. I hadn't noticed him before but I wasn't surprised he was here.

"Hi, Lauren," he greeted me. "Cyd, hi. All of you — our new director, Mick, is about to talk to us. Please go over there" — he pointed to the far end of the roped-off street, where people were already starting to congregate — "right now."

I was definitely interested in what Mick Paramus had to say. "Can we bring the dogs?" I asked Niall.

"Why not? They're part of this production."

I therefore found myself surrounded by two poodles, as well as their young handlers, as I walked toward the new director's meeting.

"Good idea," Elena said. "I'd hate to have to leave all the dogs in crates while people here are just talking."

The white poodle whose leash she held was walking calmly at heel then. "Looks as if you really do have this pup trained."

"Somewhat. This is Velda."

"And this is Rossi," said Jerry, at my other side, introducing an older, golden poodle. "Elena and I are working with these two. They're not portraying Sheba so they don't get as much attention."

"They're both very cute," I said. "And on the road to being well-behaved, I think." I paused. "What was your opinion of how Mr. Marford treated the animals?"

"I think he liked them but didn't like that he couldn't make them obey his commands the way he did with people," Jerry said. His sandy hair was better combed than I'd seen it last time, and his expression didn't look as strained. In fact, he seemed to be enjoying himself.

Elena, on the other hand, looked a lot more harried than when I had last seen her. It had been soon after Hans had been killed, when we had both been walking some white poodles.

"How's Stellar?" I asked. That was the dog she'd worked with then.

"He's okay. So is Velda. I still think this film has so much potential, but . . ."

Her voice trailed off and I looked at her.

"But what?" I asked.

"But . . . well, despite what Grant is trying to do here, I'm not sure that no animals are being harmed."

CHAPTER 11

I wanted to hear more about Elena's opinion and where it came from, but she went loping ahead of me with Velda panting and pulling ahead of *her.* Jerry and Rossi joined them.

"Sorry," she called, turning her head to look back. "These two need their exercise. And — about what I said?"

"Yes?" I had speeded up to try to catch them.

"I didn't really mean it. Everyone's fine, especially now."

We had caught up with the throng of people who'd surrounded Hans Marford only a few days ago but were now circling Mick Paramus in the middle of the street blocked off for filming.

At least this noisy and energetic bunch appeared to be comprised of mostly the same people. I recognized those who worked with the dogs, or whose faces had appeared in the news, along with some others I knew I'd seen either here or on the Solario Studios set.

I hadn't paid much attention to Mick before, since he'd been an underling. Now, I glanced at the people closest to him. One was a young lady with long, straight blond hair who seemed to glance at him every few seconds, then at the electronic device she held and apparently used to take notes. Mick might have been an assistant before, but now it looked like he had an assistant of his own.

Mick was a lot more nondescript than Hans had been. He was of moderate height, and his facial features were not nearly as attention-grabbing. His hair was dark, somewhere between black and brown, and he didn't look as if he had shaved that morning.

One thing similar to Hans, though, was the way his voice carried. He didn't need a microphone as he greeted the people around him. "Good morning. Busy day planned — but first, a minute of silence in memory of our wonderful lost director, Hans Marford."

He lowered his head, and so did a lot of the others. I was among them, at least at first. But I kept an eye on Mick and noticed the way he moved his arm to observe the time on his wristwatch.

I didn't count the seconds but thought we were shy by about twenty or so when he called out, "Farewell, Hans. Now, here's our plan." He described that the filming would be divided into two parts. "We'll only need the dogs here for the morning." He looked in our direction. "We'll get some more takes now of them running down the street so we'll have extras to choose from. This afternoon, we'll only take shots of cars and trucks driving in the same area. Then we'll be able to use our excellent computer animators to blend them together digitally."

The others in charge of dogs on the set — Cowan and Grant — had joined us. So had Cyd Andelson. I saw Grant's face light up. Maybe this was a new beginning for "No Animals Were Harmed" in this movie. I felt happy for him, and even more so for the dogs.

"Excellent plan, Mick," Grant called. He proceeded to make notes on the pad attached to the clipboard he carried.

"Great," Mick said. "Now, I want to do things as well as my predecessor. Even better, if that's possible." Nice compliment to Hans, although I didn't believe he meant it. Didn't people in showbiz have to have enormous egos to succeed?

I hadn't talked with Mick yet. I had no feel so far for whether his success in getting the top director's spot here had been a product of his own ingenuity — like getting rid of the predecessor he'd just sort of lauded.

For now, I figured he wasn't at the top of my file of most likely suspects, but not at the bottom, either.

"Are you open to suggestions, Mick?" Lyanne had been standing at the front of the crowd to Mick's right and now strode up to him.

"I'll always listen," he responded loudly enough for everyone to hear.

I couldn't make out what Lyanne said, but my assumption was that she described the scene she'd hoped to get inserted into the film — where her character Millie was in a nearby store while the scary yet uplifting scenes of the poor, abused, dogs escaping played out at the same time.

"Hey, good idea," Mick boomed in his director's voice. He motioned for some of the crew to join him. "We'll shoot a few more scenes in the area, then decide whether to use them."

The crowd around him seemed to have heard him call "Action," although I hadn't. Maybe they were all just restless. But in moments they had dispersed.

I watched the initial filming of the dogs. Grant might have the final say-so about whether any animals were harmed, but I wanted to feel comfortable about it, too, especially since I'd need to report to Dante.

I'm happy to say that the scenes I watched were amazing and even heart-wrenching, with dogs running, and later with their stand-ins sitting and panting on command, or lying down and looking frightened, again on command, as cars — imaginary at the moment — zoomed by.

But not one of them looked even worn out, let alone hurt. It almost seemed as though they enjoyed it, with treats and pats afterward like applause after a great performance.

I imagined what this could wind up looking like in the final movie, with the audience fearful for the escaping dogs, cheering them on, loving them. This was the kind of rescue, fictional or not, that could help to call people's attention to the plight of abused or unwanted pets, and more than once my eyes teared up.

And I'm not an overly emotional kind of person.

I'm also not the kind of person who allows opportunities to get by me, so between the shots when we were all instructed to be quiet I edged up to other people who were also watching.

Most who weren't currently involved with the shoot were clumped in groups rather than engaging in the whole film-crew-united thing when Mick had taken charge.

Niall was among them, standing with some people I assumed were technically oriented since they carried computers plus other gadgetry I didn't recognize. I edged up beside Niall. When I told him how impressed I was so far with Mick, he agreed.

"Hard to tell how things will go with the whole film, though," he cautioned. "I'll keep in close touch with Dante and assume you'll do the same."

"Do you think Mick will be a better director than Hans would have been?" I asked, my tone utterly innocent. I genuinely didn't want Niall to be a suspect. I liked the guy. Plus, he was a close friend of Dante's.

But I was a close friend of Carlie's and wanted the truth to prevail.

Niall bent and spoke softly so only I could hear — though I doubted the crew members around us paid any attention. "Hard to tell this soon," he said, "but judging by this morning, I think so."

"Even though he seems amenable to adding that scene that Lyanne wants in?" Since Niall had been the screenwriter, he might not encourage such modifications.

"Is that what she talked to him about?" His voice rose. Uh-oh. Maybe this hadn't been a good time to mention it.

"I think so. It could have been something else. Even if Mick shoots a few scenes where Millie could be dubbed in later, that doesn't mean he'll do it."

"Yeah." Niall drew out the word. His expression looked thoughtful. Maybe he was considering how a scene like that would work into the script he'd written.

Or maybe he was considering how to do away with Lyanne, too.

I kept my sigh as muted as I could. Getting involved with murder investigations was definitely affecting how I looked at life, and other people.

Maybe, for now, that was a good thing. I had a whole bunch of others I could question here, and at least a few might be suitable additions to my suspect files.

At the lunch break, I called HotRescues and spoke with Nina. All sounded fine. Even so, I didn't want to stay away much longer.

I also wanted to continue to take advantage of having so many people involved with the movie together here.

Because filming of the dogs was over, most of those I'd been hanging out with were leaving for the day. I watched Elena, Jerry, and a couple of other dog handlers who'd shown up pack the dogs' crates, under Winna's direction, into the back of one of the white trucks to be transported back to the studio.

"They're all great pups," I said to Winna. "Your work with them, and Cowan's training, have definitely helped. I've heard that at least some have been spoken for and will have new homes when the filming is over, right?"

Her expression looked bleak beneath her bright red hair. "Yes, some, I think. But not all of them."

I gave her a reassuring look. The more people who knew of my intentions, the more likely it was that they would come true. "What you all do is shoot great films. What I do is to find new families for homeless pets. If I'm given the go-ahead when the shooting is done, I'll make sure they're all taken care of." Assuming that they'd all be considered owned by the production company, which could do an owner relinquishment to HotRescues. We'd work that out somehow.

"Really? Oh, Lauren, that's wonderful!" Her smile was enormous, and she gave me a hug, which I returned. There was a lilt to her step as she walked to the front of the truck and got in.

I decided to head for that burger joint that had smelled so good. But I wasn't only going to grab lunch there. I figured other people from the set wouldn't be able to resist any more than I could.

I'd join them — and engage them in conversation, I hoped, about Hans.

I left the area cordoned off for the shoot, waving to the guy wearing a security uniform. I wasn't sure if that was the same person I'd shown my ID to before, but I'd probably want to get back inside later. It wouldn't hurt to stand out a bit as someone who'd already passed muster.

The aroma of those grilled burgers met me again as I got closer to the hamburger joint. When I got inside, I looked around. It was one of those places where you ordered your food, got it on a tray and paid for it, then sat down. The decor was a bit cutesy for me — pictures on the wall were caricatures of smiling and dancing burgers — but the crowd suggested that the food was as good as it smelled.

I recognized a lot of the patrons occupying its tables. Fortunately, it seemed large enough to accommodate a substantial crowd. And that crowd included one of the people I especially wanted to speak with: Mick Paramus's assistant.

I stood in line and got my burger, keeping my eye on my target. She was busy chatting with others at her table. I was delighted to see a couple rise and depart, leaving empty seats. I headed there as soon as I could.

"Hi," I said brightly, looking at the three remaining people. "Mind if I join you? I'm Lauren Vancouver. I'm a pet rescuer, plus I'm kind of acting as Dante DeFrancisco's part-time representative for the filming of *Sheba's Story.*"

They all knew who Dante was and might even know who I was, since I'd been hanging around the filming now and then. I was welcomed, and I sat down beside the directorial assistant.

"I'm R. G. Quilby," she said. "That's R. G., not Argee." She spelled them out. "It's short for Rhonda Gwen." She spoke by rote, as if this was her standard explanation.

I got the others' names, too, but was more interested in their roles with the filming. The guy and girl were both set production assistants, and surprisingly they both reported to the very young-looking assistant

134

director R. G.

"Since I need to keep Dante up to speed about what's going on with the filming," I said to R.G., "can you tell me if it will take awhile for Mick Paramus to catch up to what Hans Marford was doing? I hate to sound crass about that poor man's death, of course." I watched R. G.'s face as I referred to Hans as a "poor man." Her lips tightened, and I got the impression that she would have called him something else. "But as I'm sure you've all been saying, 'The show must go on,' and 'Time is money,' and all those old platitudes."

"Mick's smart." R. G. took a sip of her drink as if it might contain something stronger than soda — even though the strongest they sold here was beer. "He'll catch up just fine." As she raised her head, her long hair flipped forward, and she used her hands to flick it back. Her nails were well-groomed, long, and polished in green.

"Great. Do you think — Okay, I know I sound like a jerk, but I'm protective of my boss." That was pretty much how I thought of Dante. Even though I was chief administrator of HotRescues, his input — and funds — were critical. "Is Mick in any danger? I mean, what's the scuttlebutt about who's rumored to have killed Hans?"

I figuratively gritted my teeth, hoping they weren't all assuming the police had the right suspect in custody.

"I don't really know," R. G. said slowly. "Either of you have any idea?"

The other two didn't.

"I'm aware that they think that nice lady veterinarian is a possibility," R. G. said, "since she argued with Hans that day before he died. But so did almost everyone around here."

"Any one more than the others?" I asked, hoping to deflect her interest in Carlie.

"Well, the American Humane guy, Grant, for one. And he was right, the way Hans was treating those animals. You know all about that, though, if you're in pet rescue."

I nodded. But I didn't want the killer to be Grant, either.

"But you know what I really think?" she said.

"What?"

She motioned me closer, obviously not wanting the others to hear. "Not for general knowledge," she whispered, "but I was one of Hans's assistants, too. I heard a rumor that he was in negotiations to direct another film after *Sheba,* and apparently the producers were also talking to someone else about the same film. He supposedly had a big fight — well, an argument — with the other director about it. But it might have turned into a physical fight, too. Or maybe the guy was mad enough to kill Hans over it."

"Is this something you or anyone else would have mentioned to the police?" I asked her.

She pulled back, looking shocked. "I'm not in any position to say anything about it. I wasn't involved, and, like I said, it was just a rumor. I have no idea whether anyone who really was involved said anything. Even assuming that the rumor was true."

Interesting possibility, I thought: two directors arguing over who'd direct a new film, resulting in the death of one of them.

Sounded like a perfect motive.

CHAPTER 12

To my surprise, Winna was still there when the filming resumed at around one thirty. The head animal trainer hadn't gone back to the studio with the dogs but was hanging out on the street.

I stood not far from where I'd been that morning. This time, though, Dr. Cyd wasn't with me, and Niall and Grant weren't around.

In fact, other than Winna, I saw no one who was particularly concerned about the dogs. Which made sense, since the canines weren't around, either.

Metal light stands were being rearranged to aim not directly at the street, but toward the end, where a bunch of cars and vans were being lined up. So were the stationary cameras.

These vehicles wouldn't chase real dogs, although I still assumed it would be made to look that way on screen. This seemed much better to me than the way Hans Marford had been setting things up in that last shot.

Maybe some catch-up was needed to get this production back on Hans's schedule, but it hadn't stopped. Not at all.

Right now, a lot of production staff milled around on the sidewalk. Some watched the setup. Others removed equipment I didn't recognize from rows of baskets in a tall cart. Another person thumbed through old-fashioned paper files in a container that sat on the ground.

I edged my way around most of them until I reached Winna, who stood with arms crossed, staring toward the cars. "This looks like a good way to do things, doesn't it?" I asked.

She looked up at me. Her bright red hair was askew but her expression appeared relaxed. I hadn't really noticed before, but Winna sort of resembled old pictures I'd seen of the comedienne Lucille Ball, with high cheekbones, full lips, and arched eyebrows.

Appropriate that she would be in the movie industry, I supposed. But she was a dog handler, not an actor. "I'll admit I'm a lot more relaxed than I was during the last filming in the Hans Marford regime." She smiled. But then her expression grew more serious. "Even so, I hate what happened. It may mean extra box-office time for the film, but *Sheba's Story* is supposed to be about saving animals and redemption. It's not a murder mystery — although Hans's death will turn it into one."

I mentally shuffled the computer pages with her as a suspect to somewhere near the bottom of my file. "You're right." And then we were all ordered to be quiet as the filming began.

Cars zoomed past us from the end of the street. Lights zoomed in on them, as did the cameras. I watched the open vehicles in which guys holding filming equipment both preceded and followed the cars. I saw Mick Paramus on an elevated stand on the opposite sidewalk watching and moving his arms and speaking into some kind of radio set, clearly directing who did what when.

I could visualize where the poodles would be at the front of the line, dashing ahead and between the automobiles that caught up with them — digitally and safely.

That was how Hans Marford's initial scenes had been, too, more or less. But that last one . . .

Well, I hadn't wished him dead and still didn't. But I thought his inability to direct this film now would keep its dogs safer.

The scene was going to be filmed again. The cars were apparently going around the block to be set up in the same lines as for this shot. Everyone here was engaged, even if I'd figured out who to talk to about the argument between Hans and the other director that R. G. had told me about — which I hadn't.

Presumably, there was one less car than there had been before, when Hans was in charge of the filming — the one that had been used to kill him.

After watching once more, I finally decided it was, at last, time for me to return to HotRescues.

I said good-bye to Winna first. "When's the next time the dogs will be involved in a shoot?" I asked.

"Not sure, but here's my card. Give me a call and I'll let you know."

I had other sources to check, but I took her card anyway. "Thanks," I said. "See you again soon."

Going to the film set had exhausted me even though all I had done was observe. After the short drive back, I dragged myself into HotRescues but perked up the moment I walked into the welcome room.

Two people, a man and woman, sat at the table under the window filling out an application.

"Hi," I greeted them. "You're interested in adopting?"

"That's right." The woman, in her twenties and wearing a form-fitting black T-shirt, smiled up at me. "We absolutely fell in love with Slinker."

Slinker was a gray cat with a beautiful face and fuzzy coat. He'd been an owner relinquishment several months ago. Another kitty who'd been given up at the same time had been adopted a while back, and I was thrilled at the possibility of Slinker finding a home.

I looked at the guy, about the same age as the woman and also casually dressed. I suspected he was a little less in love — with the kitty — but he glanced adoringly at his companion before smiling back at me. "Can we take her home with us today?"

I glanced toward Nina, who stood behind the desk smiling. "Dr. Mona was here before. And I helped to show them Slinker in the first place." She looked at the couple. "This is Lauren Vancouver, the director of HotRescues. She makes the final adoption decisions."

I suspected, with the vote of confidence

by both Mona and Nina, that my response would be positive. I'd need to see their completed form before I could say yes or no, though. "Why don't you finish the application and come into my office so we can go over it? Then we'll see." I hoped my return smile looked optimistic, although I couldn't assure them till I'd gone over what they said. Would the cat be kept indoors? That was a big thing. We didn't adopt to people who wanted their cats to roam their neighborhoods and just come home to eat — assuming they weren't made a meal of by a coyote or hit by a car.

I hurried into my office, where I was greeted effusively by Zoey. Nina would have put her in there while the welcome room was otherwise occupied by potential adopters.

My smartphone rang as I booted up my computer. I checked the number.

Matt.

"Hi," I said, figuring he could hear the grin in my tone.

"I've got a proposition for you," he said. "An update on Hope in exchange for making up tonight for our missed dinner. Oh, and I'm still waiting to hear about the background on *Sheba's Story.* I've only gotten pieces of it from you."

"I'll agree on one condition." I glanced down at Zoey, who sat on the floor beside my desk looking winsomely up at me.

"What's that?"

"We go someplace with a dog-friendly patio."

"Done. I'll bring Rex, too."

I looked forward to dinner for the rest of the afternoon — but that didn't stop me from being thrilled that Slinker was going home with a really nice couple — Bob and Faye.

I enjoyed speaking with them in my office. Zoey was pleased to have more people around, too.

Bob and Faye were married, had no kids yet, and wanted to dote on a household pet. Faye had had cats before but her husband hadn't. She promised to show Bob everything he needed to know — and he seemed delighted at the prospect.

"Slinker will sleep in our room, naturally," Faye answered almost indignantly when I asked. "Unless he wants to sleep somewhere else. But we won't let him out of the house."

Good answer, I thought. In fact, all of their answers were good ones.

Which meant they left that same afternoon with Slinker, a crate, some food, and toys

— from Dante's HotPets stores. Slinker had had all necessary shots and vet check-ups, and he was, of course, neutered, as all our animals were, as soon as they were old enough.

The adoption delayed my usual walk through HotRescues on my arrival. But it was worth it. And I finally got my opportunity to tour my shelter.

I smiled at everyone — staff, volunteers, and of course our resident animals, and they smiled back.

It had turned into a very good day. But would that continue?

I wasn't sure. For one thing, I had to call Dante. There were a couple of serious things we needed to discuss. Zoey and I soon returned to my office after our walk-through and visits to a bunch of kennels and the cat house. Then, sitting at my desk, I made the call.

"Hi, Lauren," he answered right away. "Good timing. I was planning on calling you in a while." Which with Dante could have meant anything from a minute to an hour or two. With his fingers in so many animal-related businesses and causes, he was a busy man.

"Great. How are things in the Midwest?" I pushed a key to wake my aging desktop computer from sleep mode. I'd had a deluge of e-mails but wasn't going to even look at who they were from till my conversation with Dante was over.

"They were resolved and I returned to L.A. late last night."

The break-in was resolved? Nothing Dante did ever surprised me, but I had to ask, "What happened, and how did you fix it?" I leaned back in my chair, waiting for an interesting recap.

He laughed. "Long story short? The kids the cops originally found around the warehouse after the break-in hadn't done it, but they had seen something suspicious. A homeless guy was responsible."

"Did he take anything?"

"Some food for his dog. And this wasn't his first break-in. I'd been worried about an inside job. Instead, it was a guy who really needed dog food."

"Oh." I pictured some poor, scruffy man and his poor, scruffy dog, just trying to eat. And then I pictured that poor, scruffy dog at a public shelter somewhere, about to be euthanized for lack of a good home or someone to care about him while his owner was in jail. Yes, I've said I don't have much of an imagination, but when it comes to worrying about animals my mind sometimes goes wild.

Unnecessarily, in this case. "So I didn't press charges," Dante continued. "Instead, I gave the guy a job helping with stock at the warehouse — under strict supervision of my manager, who will also let me know if the guy doesn't attend the Alcoholics Anonymous meetings I had him join. I also made sure he rented a room from one of the AA meeting leaders, a place where he could keep his dog. He's required to volunteer a few hours a week at a local pet shelter. I didn't stay long enough to make sure he was following through with everything, but I know my manager pretty well and he'll keep an eye on the guy and report any problems to me."

As with my imagination, I downplay any effusiveness in my personality. But I realized just then that, if Dante had been anywhere nearby, I'd have given him nearly as big a hug as I'd done with Zoey.

I looked down at my dog, who lay on the brown woven area rug I'd bought a while back so she wouldn't have to lie on the bare office floor. She seemed to sense my attention despite having her eyes closed and her muzzle on stretched-out paws. She wagged her fluffy tail and I smiled even more broadly.

After that, my conversation with Dante returned to L.A. and the film business. I reported where things stood, including a description of today's dog-free scenes.

"Sounds like things are progressing even without Hans," he said. "I still want to visit when they're filming a scene with the poodles. If you hear of any good time for that, let me know. I'll also check with Niall."

That provided a good opening for what I really wanted to talk about. "Great," I said. "And while you're talking to Niall, or anyone else involved with the production, could you check to see if they know about what Hans Marford's next film project was supposed to be — and who the director is now?"

A pause. Then Dante said, "You're still trying to figure out who killed Marford, aren't you, Lauren?"

"What makes you say that?" I made sure no defensiveness seeped into my tone.

"Why else would you ask about what other projects he was scheduled for? I'm not complaining, but what precipitated that question?"

Dante was always an ally, so I told him what R. G. had said about an argument between Hans and another director over a potential upcoming project.

148

Dante's resulting laugh sounded more ironic than amused. "So you're hoping it's this unknown director who decided to kill Marford to get him out of the picture — pun intended, by the way. Could be. And that would be a lot better than your friend Carlie remaining a suspect, or anyone else connected with *Sheba's Story*. I like it. Yes, I'll use my connections and see what I can find out. I'll call you either way, but I hope I can learn who that shady director is."

CHAPTER 13

A couple of hours later, Zoey and I joined Rex and Matt at a cozy restaurant that served mostly Greek food. The whole place was crowded, and our dogs weren't the only ones sitting on the concrete patio with noses in the air inhaling the delightfully spicy aromas.

I selected a Greek salad and beef kabob. Matt ordered hummus for us both as an appetizer, then chose falafel as a main course. We both decided on ouzo as our drinks, along with water.

Then it was time to talk.

"You know," I said, "Hope is still at The Fittest Pet. I talked to one of the vets and she seems fine. I'd like to bring her to HotRescues." I looked straight into Matt's face. That had been a question, though it wasn't phrased that way.

"I don't suppose Brooke has learned anything about Hope's origins — like whether our revered City Councilman Guy Randell was lying and actually owned a dog who looks like Hope." Matt was dressed casually that night in a bronze polo shirt over jeans. He looked good in it. He also looked good in his Animal Services uniform. And in much less, now and then, too.

"No, and no one from the councilman's office has called me, either, about whatever he claimed to be checking into."

I also was dressed casually, but I'd come right from HotRescues so I wore an open navy print cotton shirt over the regular shelter staff T-shirt.

"I'll talk to Brooke," I continued, "but I'd imagine she'd have let me know any juicy details she'd come across."

Matt smiled. I liked his smile. He looked handsome anyway, but there was a glint in his eyes that suggested he was fond of me, too, when he smiled like that.

"No doubt," he agreed. "Why not check with her now to see if she's made any progress?"

But I only got her voice mail. She was probably doing her rounds at HotRescues and was diligent enough to put her phone on mute.

I left a message, then said to Matt, "Assuming Brooke hasn't found out anything

151

useful, can I just take Hope to HotRescues? She can't stay at the vet's forever."

Which probably meant, legally, that as an apparent stray Hope needed to be turned over to Animal Services. And that meant that Hope, and I, would need Matt's help.

"I've given this some thought," Matt said. But I didn't hear the results for a few minutes, since our ouzo was served, followed quickly by hummus and pita.

"So what do you think?" I asked after we'd sampled our drink and appetizers.

"I think this stuff is pretty good." Matt's raised brows told me that he knew exactly what I was talking about but had chosen to tease me.

"I agree." I refused to play along. Instead, I dipped another pita into the hummus and took a bite.

He must have realized I wasn't going to push him. "Okay," he said. "Here's what I've come up with. The microchip company is a well-known and well-respected one. I'll need to confirm it with a higher-up at Animal Services — and I know who to approach — but I suspect we'll take the position that the information on the chip is true. At least the owner's name is. He didn't choose to pick up his lost dog or even send an underling. In a way, that's an owner

152

relinquishment."

"Yes, it is." My turn to really smile again. As long as whoever Matt checked with didn't stomp all over the idea, Hope could soon be taken in, loved and, hopefully, re-homed by HotRescues. "Any idea how long it'll take to get confirmation?"

"I've already got a message in to the most appropriate person," Matt said. "She was out of the office today but due back tomorrow. Could be we'll know then."

I was so happy about the possibility that I considered walking over to kiss Matt. But my standing would discombobulate Zoey and Rex. I could wait — at least until we headed out of here. And then a kiss might be more productive in leading to extra time together tonight.

Besides, there were other dogs I'd intended to quiz Matt about: Sheba, her many incarnations, and several of her closest friends.

Our entrees were served. Their aromas must have smelled enticing to doggy noses, since both Zoey and Rex stood at attention, muzzles in the air, when the server put our plates in front of us.

Both seemed to gravitate toward me. The charcoaled smell of kabob must be magnetic to dog senses. It smelled quite appetizing to me, too.

"Sit, both of you," I said. "If I have any leftovers, maybe — and only if you've been good dogs — I'll give you each a small piece."

"And are you willing to give a taste to a human if I promise to be good — and to give you a taste of my falafel?" Matt asked.

"Absolutely."

Once we'd exchanged pieces of our dinners and both canines had settled back down, it was time to delve into our next topic.

"I haven't told you a lot about *Sheba's Story* and the dogs that star in it, have I?" I looked at Matt. I was always surprised that a man could look as attractive as he did even when chewing.

He swallowed. "Only that the story is about a dog that ran away from an abusive situation and is eventually rescued, then adopted, by a caring person."

I nodded. "That's the gist. But there's more to it that should really help get people's attention even before they come to the movie." I started with the background, describing how Niall had written the screenplay first, shopped it around, and got Dante's attention. They'd both become co-producers, among others, when Solario

Studios bought it. "That's when things besides the script really became heart-rending. First, do you know how animals are usually filmed in movies?"

"In general. And in case you're wondering, you've captured my interest. I'm eager for you to get to the point."

I laughed. I usually don't dissemble, no matter what I'm talking about, but this time I wanted to explain so many facets of how the Sheba story would be filmed that I found myself jumping from idea to idea. "Okay. Sorry. Here it is: Animals in movies are often represented on-screen by several different counterparts that are trained for different aspects of the animal's character."

"Yes, I've heard that," Matt said. "So how many Shebas are there?"

"At least four," I said. "One is her as a puppy, and the others — the adults — have different skills they're trained for. Then there are her pack-mates, so there are quite a few dogs in the cast."

"Right." He watched my face as he took a sip of his ouzo. "And so . . ." he encouraged.

"And so, when filming was about to begin, Niall and some Solario Studios folks went looking for the right poodles . . . and found some who are perfect for the role. More

155

than perfect. They're all Shebas of sorts." I explained how Niall and the others had gone to poodle breeders at first but that hadn't seemed right.

Their next step was to visit animal shelters in the area, both public and private.

"Their timing couldn't have been more perfect when they got to the Pasadena Humane Society shelter."

Matt nodded. "Good group."

"I agree. In any event, when Niall arrived they'd just taken in a litter of poodle puppies about three months old, along with several older ones, including the pups' mother. It wasn't clear where they'd come from but they were all strays. No identification or anything. Someone at the shelter even mentioned that the person who'd brought them in claimed to have seen some of them running down a street — and that's just like an early scene in the movie. Perfect! Except for the poor dogs, of course. They were homeless and straggly and hungry."

"And taken to a city shelter by a Good Samaritan," Matt said, nodding his approval.

"That's right. By the time Niall first saw them, they were clean and well-groomed. Ideal for the Sheba production. He took them in after explaining to the people at

Pasadena Humane that they'd all be well cared for — and that they were about to become movie stars. Some of the staff checked early on during the filming to make sure what he'd said was true."

"Not surprising. And their story can only help with the *Sheba's Story* publicity."

"Absolutely!"

"So that leaves the question open about what happens to them all when the filming is over."

Matt was always insightful. He saw where I'd been heading even before I got there.

"Exactly," I said, and regarded him. "They're now in Los Angeles, not Pasadena. The Woodland Hills location of Solario Studios is in the city — and therefore in L.A. Animal Services' jurisdiction."

"Is Niall planning on adopting the dogs when the filming is over?"

"I don't think so, and even if he is it won't be more than one or two of them. Another couple might be adopted by Cowan if he thinks they have potential for other films, and one of the handlers sounded interested in taking one in."

"So the others . . ."

"Need good homes. And Niall, or Solario Studios, owns them now so they'd be owner relinquishments if they're given to me — to

HotRescues — to find them a new home. Right?"

I looked at him eagerly, waiting for confirmation.

"Yes, as far as I'm concerned. Will Niall, or someone from the studio, vouch for their current ownership under these conditions?"

"I'm sure they will," I said, hoping it was true.

I saw a hint of irony in Matt's expression, but, good guy that he was, he apparently wasn't going to question it further. "Then we're all set."

There were quite a few dogs involved, but I had a lot of room available at HotRescues. If I didn't have enough, I had a great resource — Southern California Rescuers, a loosely knit alliance of shelters that shared information on a Web site and helped each other find homes for animals in need. I'd recently become friends with Ilona Graye, who was not only affiliated with a great shelter that was a member of the organization, but she would understand what was happening here. She was a secretary at an entertainment law firm.

One way or another, these dogs would all be well taken care of.

"Yes," I said, swallowing my own purr of contentment. "We're all set."

I gave the dogs each a small piece of kabob meat when I finished eating. The serving had been generous enough that I even had a box to take home — not a doggy bag, but leftovers almost entirely for human consumption.

Matt insisted on paying, then Rex and he walked Zoey and me to my car. I'd had a fun time that evening and hated to see it end.

Fortunately, it didn't. Matt suggested that Rex and he follow us home.

"Great idea," I said. "I might even be able to scrounge up some wine and a bit of dessert." Hoping that my son, Kevin, might be around that weekend, I'd bought some cupcakes and gelato. His presence still remained iffy, so I could serve the treats to Matt for now, then replenish them if Kevin really did come home from college for a few days.

On my way home, Brooke returned my call. I answered on my hands-free phone device. She assured me that all was under control at HotRescues.

There were additional topics of interest between us. "I'm still digging into Councilman Randell's personal life," she told me, her voice echoing a bit in my car, "but haven't found anything helpful using online or other remote methods. I'm going to take Cheyenne for a walk in his neighborhood and see if we run into other pet-walkers who can tell me whether they've ever seen the councilman out and about with his own dog."

"Thanks," I told her. Maybe it didn't matter whether the councilman was lying or not since I was apparently going to be able to take Hope to HotRescues and find her a new home, no matter where she'd lived before. But I was curious. Plus, I didn't want the councilman or anyone else to object to any adoption I'd work out. And I also wanted to know if he really did have someone looking into the situation on his behalf — and, if so, what they'd learned.

Brooke finished our conversation by responding to the question I hadn't yet asked. "And no, Lauren, Antonio hasn't reported anything new to me in the investigation into Hans Marford's death."

Zoey and I reached our home, Matt's car close behind. He and I soon sat at my kitchen table enjoying the dogs' presence again at our feet — and each other's company — as we ate dessert and sipped the coffee I'd brewed.

We took the dogs for a walk soon afterward beneath the streetlights in my gated Porter Ranch community.

Then all four of us adjourned to my bedroom, the culmination of a really good day.

Too bad I hadn't booted up my computer, since I discovered a very interesting e-mail from Niall the next morning.

CHAPTER 14

Matt and I, and the dogs, had risen early and taken a short but productive walk. We'd eaten a quick breakfast of cereal and milk, embellished by slices of fresh banana and strawberries. Then Matt left to take Rex home and go to his office at Animal Services, while Zoey and I headed for Hot-Rescues.

I'd spoken with our champion handyman, Pete, as he got food from our storage building to prepare for our residents, and I'd even gotten in a quick chat with Brooke before she left. She promised to take her walk in Councilman Randell's neighborhood that afternoon, after her usual day's sleep.

And of course I'd done my morning walk-through of HotRescues, with Zoey accompanying me. I visited with a few of the dogs and cats and conversed with some of the early morning volunteers who came in to help Pete clean the kennels and cat house and to take dogs for walks.

Then, finally, after chatting with Nina in the welcome area for a few minutes, I headed for my office.

That's when I turned on my computer as Zoey circled for a few moments, then lay down between my feet and the legs of my desk.

I saw Niall's e-mail and opened it first thing. He had information for me about the director who'd argued with Hans Marford.

It was someone whose name was as well known. Maybe even better known than Hans's: Erskine Blainer.

Not that I really follow the film industry — at least I hadn't until now. But most people who watch movies would recognize Blainer since he's the type who appears on every talk show to pat himself on the back about his achievements.

And they were important achievements. He had directed film adaptations not only of some of today's bestselling thriller novels, but also some old classics like *The Devil and Daniel Webster* — which he made into a combined adventure/horror–legal thriller film.

The e-mail concluded with "Call me. I know which script they fought over."

Niall could have put it in the e-mail. The fact that he hadn't suggested he was concerned about security. My e-mail account was with a major provider, and I'd chosen a password that no one was likely to figure out.

On the other hand, I didn't blame Niall for being concerned, considering how insecure online stuff appeared to be these days.

I also wondered what that script could be, that its secrecy was so important.

It was nearly nine o'clock by then. Niall was a writer when he wasn't on movie sets. Did that mean he kept odd hours?

If he wasn't awake, I'd get his voice mail — and probably fret a whole lot till I heard from him.

Fortunately, he answered right away. "Hi, Lauren." He sounded so bright and cheerful that I couldn't have woken him. "I figured I'd hear from you pretty soon. You ready for this?"

His tone and words suggested he was about to reveal something particularly exciting. I inhaled in anticipation, even as the practical and most ironic part of me prepared me to be disappointed.

I wasn't.

"The script they were fighting over was actually written by a novelist who's also done screenplays before. But he's most famous for his series of young adult books. It's Carroll Cornahan."

"Really?" I kept the squeal that threatened out of my voice, but I'd actually read a couple of Cornahan's Val Avenger young adult books — while my kids were still living at home instead of at college. They were amazing even for adults. "They're finally making a movie of those stories?"

Zoey heard my excitement and stood up, looking at me quizzically. I stroked the fur under her chin absently as I waited for Niall's answer.

"The first one," he responded.

"A Matter of Death and Life?"

"That's it."

The story had gained amazing notoriety. It was about a normal-appearing family in middle America who happened to be descended from the Valkyries, so that all the women had power over life and death.

They might have precognitive powers as well. I certainly did — about this movie. I predicted that its box office take would be huge.

That was undoubtedly Hans's assumption, too, and probably Erskine Blainer's.

Was achieving the directorship worth fighting about? Maybe, but they were both such revered directors that neither one's careers would have been made by being chosen for this film.

Even so, if both had gone after it, their egos could have gotten out of control. Enough to argue wildly and publicly?

Probably.

Enough to kill over?

I'd never met Blainer. Even so, I'd have to add him to my suspect list. I only hoped I'd get a chance to talk to him to decide on his position in my file.

"In case you're interested," Niall said, "there's going to be another *Sheba* scene filmed tomorrow at Solario Studios. It'll involve the dogs. I'll be there, and so will Dante — I've already called him. Grant, too, of course. Want to come?"

"I'll try," I said hesitantly. But if Dante was going to be there keeping track of things from his perspective, I didn't really need to go.

I'd enjoyed watching the filming, but my obligations at HotRescues outweighed just having fun.

"From what I've heard, there's going to be a meeting at the studio of some of the people trying to get *A Matter of Death and Life* into production."

"Hans obviously isn't going to be the

director," I observed. "Does that mean —"

"Yes, from what I've heard, Erskine Blainer's been chosen, so he'll be there, too."

That meant so would I.

I thanked Niall and prepared to hang up. I didn't know him well, but he was apparently reading my mind.

"I've got a feeling I'll see you tomorrow at Solario," he said.

"I've got a feeling that you're right," I replied.

I had an internal meeting on a prospective adoption to attend a short while later. One of our volunteers, Ricki, had been the one to introduce Junior, a Doberman who was one of our longtime residents, to the couple who now wanted to adopt him.

Ricki was in school learning to be a veterinary technician, so she wasn't around HotRescues as much as she used to be. Even so, she was thrilled to be involved with Junior's finally getting a loving home. We'd picked a day for this meeting on which she didn't have morning classes.

Dr. Mona was there, too, as was our regular vet tech, Angie Shayde. We usually handled adoptions more informally, but the couple interested in Junior had admitted that they'd separated, then only recently gotten back together. They vowed they had mended the disagreements between them, and also promised that, although they never intended to split again, if they did they would keep Junior's interests primary and would work out custody in a way that would work best for him.

"Odd situation," I said at the beginning of the meeting as we all sat around the conference table upstairs in the main building.

Or maybe it wasn't so odd. People split up, and pet custody sometimes became an issue, but not always.

We'd had a dog when my beloved first husband, Kerry, died, and dear Bosley, our Boston terrier, had still been around when I'd married the jerk Charles Earles — and when I'd divorced him.

But in that situation, it was clear who had custody of the wonderful dog: the kids and I.

I'd previously met with the couple who wanted Junior, and they'd seemed very much in love to me. But I'd no idea how they had looked at one another previously before they'd split up.

"I thought they were almost disgusting in the way they were all over each other," Ricki said with a grin. "And Junior seemed to fit in perfectly. They both gave him a lot of attention."

"What do you think, Mona?" I asked our part-time shrink and adoption counselor.

She took off her glasses and regarded us earnestly, one at a time. She was dressed in a suit as usual but had taken off the jacket. Most of her formality was reserved for her own office in Studio City. "I think that, for Junior's sake, it's worth taking a chance. You always retain the right to visit a home where we've placed a pet. Plus, I talked to both of those people together and individually — with Junior present, of course. They each seemed to have Junior's interests at heart. Go for it."

I glanced at Angie. I'd always considered her classic oval face almost cherubic, and her short, curly hair seemed to underscore the effect. As usual, she wore a turquoise lab jacket.

She'd met the people, too, to go over Junior's health — which was excellent. But part of it was just to meet them as well. "Go for it," she repeated, nodding.

The decision was made. I'd call the couple and tell them to come in to adopt the new member of their household.

I smiled all the way downstairs to my office, with Zoey prancing near my feet.

I purposely hadn't brought my cell phone

since I didn't want to answer any calls, so I checked my messages before anything else. The first message informed me that I had to run. Well, drive fast, at least.

Hope was ready to be discharged from The Fittest Pet Veterinary Hospital.

I hadn't heard from Matt about her, though. I'd bring Hope to HotRescues, but would I be in violation of some regulations?

I decided to call to find out.

Matt answered right away. "Good timing," he said. "The supervisor here at Animal Services who I wanted to talk to just called me back. Your taking Hope is fine. As far as we're concerned, since her apparent owner — per her microchip — didn't want her back, she's an owner relinquishment."

"Yay!"

I kept smiling for most of my drive to the veterinary hospital and back again, with Hope protectively secured in the back of my Venza.

I'd had a chance to talk to Carlie at The Fittest Pet, but only briefly. She was in a good mood. No one had come to arrest her or even interrogate her further.

That made me happy. In fact, this day had been a good one.

But it wasn't over yet.

CHAPTER 15

I took Hope inside to meet Nina first. Zoey remained in the welcome area, too, and she got to greet the cute spaniel-poodle mix. They sniffed each other's noses, both wagging tails, and I knew they'd get along fine.

But Zoey would get to go home with me. I had to arrange for a kennel here at HotRescues for Hope. Our facility was clean and loving and an all-around great pet rescue shelter, but even with all the attention our animals got from staff and volunteers it still wasn't the same thing as going to a permanent family.

I'd try to make sure Hope was adopted as soon as possible.

Even so, I decided to hang out at Hot-Rescues late enough that day to chat with Brooke in case she'd taken the walk she'd promised. I wasn't sure where Councilman Randell lived, but Brooke, with her P.I.

ingenuity, would have no problem finding out.

"Come on, sweetheart," I finally said to Hope and snapped a leash on the Martingale training collar I'd given her at The Fittest Pet. She glanced up at me with sad, astute eyes that told me she knew her current fun and games had ended and she would wind up alone again.

Impulsively, I knelt and hugged her. "It's not what you think," I promised her. "You're here to stay until we find the right home for you. You'll get a lot of loving here. You'll see."

As if to bolster what I said, Zoey came up beside us and stuck her muzzle over my arm as I held Hope. That's when Nina joined our hugfest, too.

"She's right, Hope," Nina rasped, and I knew her emotions were as engaged as mine.

I sighed as I unwrapped myself and stood. "I'm going to put Hope in one of the kennels in the old shelter area rather than around the corner." Even though the new area was as delightful as the old, it was a little farther from the entrance — and I wanted Hope to be among the first dogs a prospective adopter saw.

Nina smiled as she, too, rose to her feet. "I thought you would. Thanks to our recent adoptions, there's one available near the storage shed in back that I think would work well."

"Sounds good." I left Zoey up front while walking Hope into the kennel area. She did well on a leash, which suggested she'd been trained. And that suggested she'd had a home.

With the councilman? If so, why had he denied it?

On the way back to Hope's new quarters — temporary, if all went well — I passed Mamie Spelling. She was sitting on a stool inside one of the front kennels, playing with Miracle, the part Basset hound and part Lab pup who'd been brought in to Hot-Rescues with parvo a few months ago. Miracle had done fine after veterinary care, and now we were showing her off for adoption as quickly as possible, too.

"How's she doing, Mamie?" I called through the glass and fencing at the front of the kennel.

"She's just great!" Mamie picked up a stuffed toy from the ground and threw it. Miracle leaped after it and worried it in her jaw, which made me laugh. "Who is that?" Mamie pointed toward Hope.

My onetime mentor looked especially happy today. Sitting there, she didn't seem as frail as usual, and there was no confusion on her face or in her words.

"This is Hope. She was —" I almost said she was a stray that I'd found not far from here, but I caught myself. "She's an owner relinquishment, and we're going to find her a new, much better owner."

"Amen to that," Mamie said emphatically.

I laughed and continued on. Pete Engersol came toward us with a large bag of food in his arms, handling it as easily as he always did notwithstanding his advancing age. "I heard you say that's Hope," he said. "Welcome, young lady."

I laughed. "Let's give Hope some extra love and attention," I said.

"Along with Miracle and Shazam and —"

"Point taken," I said. "Let's give her as much as we do all our animals."

"Will do." Pete continued on.

Dogs barked in the kennels on either side of us as Hope and I walked by, then only on one side as we passed the center building on the right. I always discouraged their noise, but dogs would be dogs, which meant they protected whatever turf they happened to have by barking at other canines.

We finally reached the empty kennel and I opened the glass front door and walked inside with Hope. The outer, outdoor area was clean. I went to the end and peeked into the enclosed portion of the kennel, which was inside a building so the dog could decide whether to be in or out. A fresh, clean doggy bed was already in place.

"Here you are, Hope," I told her. "Your new home. For now." I again knelt to hug her, and only looked into her sad eyes for a moment after I rose. "You'll like it here." I didn't promise, though. No matter how much love and attention we provided, who knew how happy she'd feel?

But what I could promise was that we would make her stay as warm and loving as possible.

It was already getting late, which was a good thing. My decision to stay at HotRescues until Brooke arrived meant that Nina and most of the rest of the staff and volunteers had left.

She arrived at nearly seven o'clock, dressed in yellow T-shirt and jeans instead of her usual black security outfit. Zoey and I had been listening for her and we exited my office immediately when we heard her enter the welcome area.

Cheyenne was with her, of course, and she went over to say hi to Zoey right away. Brooke carried a tote bag. "Hang on a minute," she said. "I need to change clothes." She hurried to the rest room at the end of the hall, leaving Cheyenne with Zoey and me.

She returned in a few minutes looking a little flushed, which worried me considering her earlier medical issues. But she sat down at the table beneath the window, took a deep breath, then smiled.

"Hi," she said.

"Hi back. Did you —"

"Yes, I found where Councilman Randell lives. Nice neighborhood, if you like large estates separated by attractive fences that make a definite statement about uncompromising privacy. Fortunately, there are wide sidewalks plus a lot of people who walk their dogs. Cheyenne and I weren't alone."

"Did you learn anything?" I hurried to sit across from her at the table. I looked at her eagerly while our dogs settled down on the floor. "Is Hope his dog?"

"Yes," she said. "At least I think so. Here's what I found out, both online and while taking a walk around there."

I'd already known that Councilman Guy Randell was a bachelor, although not necessarily an eligible one. From what Brooke had determined, he'd had a longtime girlfriend named Katrina Tirza.

"They recently broke up, though," Brooke said. "That may be how Hope got loose. The neighbors saw Katrina walking a dog who looked like Hope during afternoons for several weeks a while back. Katrina was known from parties and tabloids, so people recognized her. She stopped to ask other people about their dogs and sometimes mentioned that the dog she was walking — she called her Ginger — was the councilman's dog but he only exercised her by playing with her inside the house. Katrina thought the poor thing needed more attention, so that was why they were out walking. I've nothing but a gut feeling to say that Katrina may have let poor Ginger outside the grounds out of spite when they broke up, but it's certainly a possibility."

"Then why wouldn't the councilman have been thrilled to get her back?" I wondered aloud.

"Good question. Embarrassment?"

I shrugged. "Maybe. Does he have any staff who can confirm that Ginger was his?"

"Yes and no. Yes to the staff part, but no one who works for him will talk to the media or anyone else. The councilman himself may be a media personality but he likes to control what's said about and around himself. He'll fire anyone who

177

speaks out of turn and maybe even sue them. He only hires people under a contract with strict terms."

"Interesting perspective for someone in the public eye. How far away is the councilman's neighborhood?"

"That's another interesting thing. He lives in Beverly Hills."

Which was quite a distance from Granada Hills — where HotRescues was located, and where Carlie and I had found Hope running loose.

"Another one of those situations where I wish an animal who comes to stay with us could talk about what happened to her." I sighed. "Well, the good thing about what you learned is that we can genuinely continue to consider Hope an owner relinquishment." I told Brooke how Matt had finagled that a bit through Animal Services.

"Another good thing about it," Brooke said, "is that obviously the councilman didn't give a damn about Hope or Ginger or whoever. We do."

"Yes," I agreed, "we do."

I wished there was some way of making the councilman's horrible treatment of his dog public without getting HotRescues into a media hassle.

Maybe I'd talk to Dante about it and find

out his opinion.

I'd definitely think about it some more myself.

CHAPTER 16

The next day was Saturday. I supposed that the film industry, like animal shelters, never really had days off, since Niall had told me about the scenes that were to be shot that day at Solario Studios.

Dante had sent me a text message that he'd be there. His subtext meant I didn't have to go.

I, to the contrary, wanted to be there. I had a lot to talk to Dante about, both regarding *Sheba's Story* and the Councilman Randell situation.

Plus, maybe I could learn something about the proposed filming of *A Matter of Death and Life* and whether Erskine Blainer remained involved.

And whether he'd wanted to be involved enough to kill Hans to secure the opportunity.

I pondered whether to leave Zoey at home or at HotRescues, since I was heading there anyway for a shortened morning visit. I decided on the former. Zoey wouldn't be alone too long. I didn't intend to stay at the studio for more than an hour or two.

Plus, Kevin had confirmed that he'd be home for a short while over the weekend, starting that afternoon. He wouldn't be coming far, since he was a sophomore at Claremont McKenna College, and Claremont was only about fifty miles east of the San Fernando Valley.

Too bad Tracy couldn't come home as well. I'd called my daughter as soon as Kevin let me know, but Tracy, who attended Stanford, had plans — both social and academic. She sounded happy, which made me glad. But I missed her.

At least I got to see both my kids on holidays. My parents, and my brother and his family, lived in Phoenix, and although I talked to them at least weekly I hardly ever got to see them.

Today, after my quick trip to HotRescues, I headed to the studio. When I arrived at the entrance gate with its huge Solario Studios sign, I saw a familiar silver Mercedes in front of me. Dante showed his ID to the guard and was waved inside.

My entry didn't take much longer, and I

caught up with Dante's car in the parking lot.

He approached as I exited my car. "I thought that was you, Lauren." He was dressed casually in a white knit shirt with a HotPets logo on the pocket over black jeans. His wavy, dark hair was a bit askew, and his intense, deep brown eyes stared questioningly at me. "Why are you here? I told you I'd be here for this day's filming."

"There are a couple of things I wanted to run by you. Plus — well, I'm actually enjoying watching the filming of *Sheba's Story,* at least as long as the animals really aren't being endangered."

He smiled as he turned and began walking along the row of cars toward the path to the studio lot. Quite a few other people seemed to have arrived at the same time, and we headed toward the crowd.

"I'd better watch out or you'll leave HotRescues and take a job with American Humane," Dante said.

I snorted. "No worries about that. I'm perfectly happy with what I'm doing. But this is a nice diversion. And, by the way, I'm still spending plenty of time at the shelter. I did an adoption yesterday and there are others that'll come first thing next week. Then there's the dog named Hope, whom we just rescued. I need to talk to you about her. And how we should handle any of the poodles and other dogs from this film who aren't adopted by the cast and crew. And —"

Dante laughed, raising a hand into the air to silence me as we reached the wide, crowded pathway. "I get it. We'll talk. But not now." His hand turned to wave at a man who approached from the opposite direction from the flow of people. The crowd appeared to part like the Red Sea in Moses' story in the film version of *Exodus,* then converge again behind the guy.

He didn't look especially powerful. But he held out his hand to Dante as the two men met face-to-face.

"Hi, Morton," Dante said. Which made me both freeze and think, *Of course,* at the same time. This medium-height, medium-built man in a beige shirt and black vest over blue jeans didn't look like a studio mogul, but he had to be Morton Lesque, the renowned CEO of Solario Studios.

I could have crowed in delight about meeting him today, right here, in a situation where it wouldn't look like I was a nasty media person or stalker or anyone else he'd want to avoid . . . yet. But he was the ideal person to ask about the studio's intentions

183

regarding the potential filming of *A Matter of Death and Life.*

"Dante, welcome. Glad you decided to come. I know you've met Mick Paramus, but seeing him in action on set will reassure you that he's the right director to replace poor Hans on *Sheba's Story.*"

I thought about clearing my throat, or perhaps tripping Dante as the men started going with the flow of pedestrian traffic onto the lot. I wanted an introduction.

But I needn't have worried. As always, Dante did the appropriate thing. "Morton, have you met my usual representative for the shooting days? This is Lauren Vancouver, the excellent administrator at the private animal rescue facility I founded, HotRescues." I smiled across Dante's chest toward the other man.

"How do you do, Lauren?" Morton said politely.

"And Lauren, this is Morton Lesque, CEO of Solario Studios." As if I didn't already know.

"Delighted to meet you, Morton." We were a bit far apart for me to offer to shake hands, but that was all right. I didn't mind having Dante as our intermediary, at least for now.

The scene today was to be shot in an

inside studio location, and Morton led us to a vast structure that paralleled two other similar ones in the lot's center. The headquarters building was close to the parking lot, and other structures I couldn't identify were located in organized proximity to one another. I of course recognized those I'd visited before, including the one in which the luxurious dog kennels were located.

Not everyone in the crowd we'd walked in with converged on that building, but a lot of them did. We entered first. Obviously everyone here knew the hierarchy. Morton probably trumped all others present, with Dante coming in a close second.

And me? Well, good thing I was in such august company.

"I checked the set a little while ago," Morton said. "You might like it, or maybe not." He was looking at me as we walked along a wide corridor. "The scene to be shot today is when the Millie Roland character has been hunting for the stray dogs she saw on the streets and learns they were captured by the public shelter. All their lives are in imminent danger, and she finally finds them and promises to save them. It should be a real tearjerker."

"Sounds that way," I agreed. We stopped in front of a closed door. The sign over it read FILMING IN PROGRESS, but it wasn't lighted. I suspect that its being lit wouldn't have stopped Morton anyway, but he opened the door and motioned for us to enter.

Inside looked a bit chaotic. Lots of people and equipment filled the periphery of the room, not unlike other sets I'd visited recently.

But its center was exactly the way Morton had described. A row of shoddy and not very clean kennels was lined up and filled with dogs, which included three white poodles.

Our timing was perfect. As the door closed behind us, I saw Mick Paramus emerge from the side of the set and gesture toward the kennels. I couldn't quite hear what he said, but in a few minutes a scene was shot that was definitely heartrending. The character played by Lyanne dashed into the kennel area and stopped as she saw the enclosed dogs. The ones on either side of the poodles leaped at the wire doors, but the poodles just sat and looked mournful.

"I found you!" Lyanne's voice carried since the place was silent. "I'm so glad. I'll get you out of here soon, I promise. You'll become my family."

"Cut!" yelled Mick.

"Good one," said Morton. "Let's go talk to Mick to reassure you, Dante."

Just like that, the filming was interrupted, and no one seemed to care. In fact, Mick Paramus seemed delighted to stop and chat with Dante — and Morton, of course. Mick's assistant, R. G., was right behind him, electronic notepad in hand, and she, too, edged her way into the conversation.

I had little doubt but that the studio sorts would convince co-producer Dante that the show did indeed go on well despite the loss of Hans.

But suspicious person that I was, I wondered how Morton and Hans had gotten along. Was there a place for the studio executive on my suspect list?

While they chatted, I saw Grant Jefferly standing at the side of the pseudo-kennel area and wandered over. Or maybe not so pseudo. The dogs were, in fact, confined inside, at least for now.

"So are any animals being harmed in this scene?" I asked Grant in his usual American Humane vest.

He beamed at me. I smiled back, glad to see him.

But before he answered, a female voice from behind him said, "Not if we can help it." Elena emerged with a smile on her pretty and cheerful face. She wore a Solario Studios T-shirt over her jeans. "But I need to take some of those pups for a walk to make sure they keep their environments clean."

"I'll second that," Grant said. "Need any help?"

"No, I'll be fine. Winna and Jerry and some of the others are around, I'm sure."

"I'll help," I said impulsively. I'd talk to Dante later about his discussion with the director and the head of the studio, but doubted they'd be conversing about who might have killed Hans Marford. I hadn't approached the dog handlers on that subject yet, though, so I decided to take this opportunity.

Especially since I'd also be doing something I enjoyed — taking care of animals.

I was pleased to be given the leashes of the main Sheba plus a second poodle. Elena took a third white poodle as well as a terrier mix and one that was part pug. "Here." She handed me a couple of biodegradable poop bags.

"Thanks."

The crowd moved out of our way as we took the dogs outside the building and let them sniff and roam and evacuate. "This is fun," I said. "Do you enjoy working on

188

movie sets?"

I expected the pretty young lady to say yes, but that she really aspired to be on camera instead of way behind it. I wasn't disappointed. "I love it," she gushed, looking at me with big, shiny green eyes. "So much that I want to do it all the time. Different aspects, too. Maybe I could learn to do what Grant Jefferly does for American Humane. Better yet — well, I'm taking acting lessons."

"Sounds like fun. Did you think about trying for a role in *Sheba's Story*?"

She looked away as if one of her dog charges had yanked on his leash. I'd seen a sad expression in her eyes first, though. "Sure," she said, "but it didn't work out this time."

"What do you think of the change in directors?" This young lady's emotions weren't hard to see on her face, even if I couldn't rely on my own interpretations. But she looked more pensive than anything when she turned back to me.

"I really think Mick Paramus is a better director, especially for this kind of film. And I believe he cares more about the animals and their well-being. It's a shame, though, that the change had to be because of what happened to Mr. Marford."

Mick Paramus versus *Mr.* Marford? The difference in how she referred to them suggested a difference in how she thought of them, too.

"I agree that it's a shame," I said. "Hans Marford was a wonderful director. And despite how much I worried about his filming of that street scene, he didn't allow any animals to be harmed by it. I've nothing against Mick Paramus, but I'm wondering if Sheba's Story might have had a better chance of excelling if Hans Marford had remained in charge." I made that up as I went along, not really believing it — but wanting to see her reaction. She'd have discussed at least some of this with her fellow crew members, so I might get a sense of the general feel around here from her.

"No." She almost spit the word at me. Her glare made me want to take a few steps back — only the poodles I was walking had wrapped me up in their leashes. Where had this venom come from? But then she laughed. "Okay, you've caught me. I was so scared for the dogs during that street scene that I'd have kicked Mr. Marford off the film if I'd been in charge. Which I wasn't. But you're right. It came out well for the dogs. And I bet that scene will be really exciting on screen. I really am sorry that we won't get the opportunity to see what else Mr. Marford might have done with this film. But I'm really looking forward to it now, with Mick in charge."

I watched two more takes of that scene with Lyanne's character finding the dogs at the shelter. I stood beside Dante off to the side of the observing crew members, and way behind Morton Lesque who, unsurprisingly, had a prime front-row spot.

But when the crowd broke for a while, I was delighted to be invited to join Dante and Morton for coffee — in Morton's office, no less.

I probably wouldn't get an opportunity to chat with Morton alone, but that was okay. I didn't need to hide my nosiness from Dante. He'd probably find it amusing — as long as I did it in an inoffensive way that wouldn't insult Morton or Solario Studios.

Morton's office was a penthouse suite — well, at least it was on the top floor of the five-story office building on the studio lot. We walked through his secretary's domain and into a room that was large but sparsely furnished. Maybe that was to call attention to the glass-enclosed shelves along the wall behind the uncluttered mahogany desk.

It's probably not hard to imagine what

was on those shelves. Solario Studios was known for the awards it won for all kinds of movies. Some were emotional tearjerkers like *Sheba's Story* promised to be. Others were wild, blockbuster thrillers like director Erskine Blainer's interpretation of *The Devil and Daniel Webster.* In all, there were a lot of photos and plaques and replicas of the awards won by its producers and directors for a variety of films over the past fifteen years of its existence.

I noticed an empty area just to Morton's stage right after he sat down behind the desk. Was that where he anticipated keeping awards for *Sheba's Story?*

That was a premature assumption on my part, but unsurprisingly I loved the idea and script and hoped I'd adore the finished movie.

Was that empty space a reason why Hans Marford was dead? If so, who'd decided to change the production in such a drastic way?

I wasn't going to suggest that — not directly. But after Morton's efficient-looking secretary, who appeared even older than my mid-forties, served Dante and me coffee and chocolate chip cookies, I was ready to start my inquisition.

I couldn't right away, though. Morton and Dante were engaged in a friendly testosterone battle over who did better running their respective businesses. I couldn't compete — not since they were hinting at the huge amounts of money they brought in.

But at a lull in the conversation, I managed to pat myself on the back another way. "I've had a lot of success, too, guys. I save lives."

Dante laughed. "You sure do, Lauren." In case Morton didn't know who I was, Dante managed to impart to him a recap of my background, especially over the past several years as chief administrator of HotRescues.

"Then you're just the person I've been wanting to talk to," Morton said, surprising the heck out of me.

Not, apparently, Dante. "That's for certain, my friend. So how many lives can Lauren save around here?"

CHAPTER 17

They weren't, however, talking about how I might have been able to save Hans Marford. Not that I figured I'd had the possibility of doing that, either.

But it turned out that Solario Studios really did want to put a plan into effect before they had to implement it — one to ensure that the rescued dogs who played Sheba and her many film cohorts would find loving homes and happily-ever-afters once the shooting ended.

"A few of our trainers, staff, and even cast members have said they want to adopt one or another of the dogs." Morton looked at me earnestly from beneath his straight, ebony-dark brows, which went so well with the black vest he wore. His hair was sparse, but what was left of it was also black. So were the frames of his glasses. "But we've got a cast of thousands of dogs." He held up a well-lined hand. "Not literally, of course. But a dozen or more. All were rescued from shelters and trained specially to be in *Sheba's Story.* Obviously for the sake of making certain our film does well and is perceived in a positive light, we have to make sure they're not only unharmed but that they also have wonderful new homes."

"That's great!" I couldn't help exclaiming, particularly since this saved me one of the conversations I'd wanted to initiate. "I've already been considering how to do that — assuming that was what you wanted." If it hadn't been, I'd have found a way to shame the studio into it. And now I could try to ensure that the assistant handler Jerry got his choice of pets. "One question to start with: Who owns those dogs now?"

If he said no one did, that they were just stray dogs who happened to be prospective film stars, I'd have to tweak his manner of thinking. But perhaps Dante had already cued him on how to address this.

"Solario Studios does," Morton asserted without even an iota of hesitation.

"Excellent! Solario is here in Woodland Hills, which is a part of the City of Los Angeles. HotRescues is a private shelter that's licensed in L.A., and we're allowed to take in owner relinquishments. We can talk

195

about it further, but when the time comes, if you want to turn over any dogs remaining unadopted to me, HotRescues can take them in and find them new homes. Please give me whatever warning you can about the timing, though. We've expanded our facility recently" — I smiled at Dante, who grinned back — "but I'll still want to make sure we've plenty of room for whatever pups you ask us to rehome. And if we don't, I have contacts in other good shelters who can help."

"We sure will," Morton said. "It won't be far off. I don't think our filming of *Sheba's Story* is going to be delayed by our loss of Hans Marford as director. Mick Paramus has stepped right in as if he was always in charge."

"Looks like he's doing a good job," Dante inserted. "At least, I was impressed this morning."

"So far so good," Morton agreed. "I was curious about what you'd think. I'd heard about Hans's last day of filming, of course, and how a lot of people were worried about whether the dogs actually were being put in harm's way."

He was looking at Dante, but I was the one who'd been there that day. "As it turned out," I said, watching as both men's gazes

196

moved from each other's onto me, "no dogs actually were harmed. Hans Marford had promised that would be so, even while filming that last take. He claimed that all the drivers were skilled and the scene had been choreographed well." I paused for dramatic effect — not that I was any kind of actor, nor did I want to be. "But I'm with all those people you heard from, Morton, who were appalled by the dangerous possibilities." Now was the time to ask some of the questions that had been percolating inside me even before I had this opportunity to speak with the head of the studio. "I'd love to know who else agreed with me. Of course, I knew that Grant Jefferly of American Humane was as upset as I was. Maybe even more so."

"Aren't you friends with that vet Dr. Stellan who's got her own pet-oriented TV show?" Morton asked. "I heard she really argued with Hans about it. Maybe even killed him over it."

I groaned inside, wondering how he knew about my friendship with Carlie. In any event, that wasn't the direction I'd hoped to go.

"I'm aware that the police consider her a person of interest." I kept my voice level despite wanting to shout that, yes, I knew her, she was my friend, and regardless of whatever she'd felt about Hans she surely couldn't have killed him. But notwithstanding what Dante knew or believed, I had no intention of telling this studio executive that I had unfortunately taken on an investigation into this murder to help a friend.

I recognized that my life had turned into a potential screenplay, and I absolutely didn't want Morton Lesque to come up with any ideas in that direction.

Plus, I was the one who wanted information and he hadn't given me anything very helpful so far.

"I think it would be a really interesting thing for Solario Studios to turn this whole fiasco into a movie someday," I therefore continued, and I believed what I said — as long as I wasn't involved. "In mysteries I've read, the perpetrator is always the last person anyone would consider to be a suspect. I know both Grant and Carlie argued with Hans about that last scene, which makes them too obvious as killers. Who else criticized him to you, Morton? Is there anyone else you know of who despised Hans, whether because of that scene or any other reason?"

Unexpectedly, he laughed. "I don't suppose you're a closet screenwriter are you,

Lauren? You obviously have a good imagination."

That elicited a guffaw from Dante. We're close business associates more than friends, but he vetted me well before giving me the HotRescues position, and we've gotten to know each other even better over the years.

He knows that I have a limited imagination, especially when it comes to something other than pet rescue.

"No," I said firmly. "I'm sure that Solario Studios has dozens of screenwriters at its beck and call. That's never been an aspiration of mine."

"But finding the killer is, isn't it?" This came from Morton, who had a shrewd expression on his face. "Don't look so surprised. As you can imagine, I have a lot of people on the Solario payroll, and I get them to check out nearly everyone who visits the lot. Others, as well."

Not surprising, and it might be how he knew of my friendship with Carlie.

"I've seen online media references," he continued, "about how you solved murders in the past, Lauren. Are you working on this one?"

I wanted to turn into a molten puddle of goo and ooze out of the room. But I don't shrink from adversity or even embarrassment. Instead, I pasted a too-bright grin on my face. "What do you think? Of course I am. Yes, Carlie is my friend, and I know she didn't do it. That means I have to figure out who did. So, a couple more questions for you, Morton. The first one should be easy. Did you kill Hans Marford?"

The smugness on his face turned to shock, then anger . . . followed by a smile and a guffaw that echoed Dante's. I wondered if he had ever acted. He certainly had an expressive appearance.

"No, Ms. Vancouver, it wasn't me. Let's see. I'll guess what your next questions will be." He stuck the point of his index finger below his chin and looked up at the ceiling, while I glanced at Dante.

I couldn't read his expression, which wasn't a good thing. He was hiding what he thought, and that didn't bode well for me.

But surely he wouldn't fire someone as skilled and successful at rehoming pets as I was, just because I was being a bit outspoken here. He knew I was the outspoken type anyway.

"Got it," Morton said. He looked straight into my face. "You'll want to know if I'm aware of any other people who argued with Hans. The answer is yes. Next, you'll ask who they were. Well, Hans wasn't exactly the kind of man who got along with everyone. He was a good director, and that was what counted. The last person I know he actually argued with, though, was Erskine Blainer, because they both wanted to direct a particularly exciting upcoming film: *A Matter of Death and Life.* I was leaning toward Erskine anyway, and since Hans is gone, it's clear now that Erskine will be directing it. Did he kill Hans? I don't think so, but why don't you ask him? In fact, I'll figure out an excuse and set up a meeting for you."

That turned out to be surprisingly easy. Or maybe not, considering that head honcho Morton was the one to call Erskine as we sat there.

"Oh, you're headed toward the studio anyway?" Morton, still sitting behind his desk, grinned at Dante and me. "Yes, that's right. You and I have been wanting to talk some casting strategy about *A Matter of Death and Life* and one or the other of us has always had something to do instead. But I've got about a half hour to get us started. Oh, and there are a couple of people I want you to meet."

He hung up after a few platitudes and smiled even more broadly. "He undoubtedly thinks I'm going to introduce him to some people I want him to add to his cast. I'll bet he's already thinking up excuses why he won't select you for those roles. Unless, of course, you're exactly the actors he already has in mind for them."

I couldn't help laughing. "Thanks," I said. "I didn't mean for you to have to waste your time just so I can get an idea about his guilt or not, but —"

"We genuinely have been putting off this meeting," Morton said with a dismissive wave. "Besides, I want to see you in action with someone you undoubtedly really consider to be a suspect. At least, I hope you didn't really consider me to be one. And the sooner we get past all these accusations, the better." His stare again looked cutting and even cold.

Since I owed him now, for several reasons, I just said, "I'm not a cop, Morton, or anyone else in authority. And I certainly don't profess to know what I'm doing. What I tend to do is shuffle the names of suspects around in computer files. You were never near the top of those files, and now you're definitely near the bottom."

"Just near the bottom and not off the radar?" he demanded.

Dante broke in. "This lady never throws anyone's names out if they've got anything at all to do with whoever the murder victim is. Just in case she's wrong, or at least that's the way I understand it." He shot me a glance, and I nodded. "But I'm associated with the last production Hans Marford was on, so I'm undoubtedly in her files, too." He looked at me more intensely and I knew I was supposed to understand his unspoken message. "Where am I compared with Morton, here?"

"Oh, a page or two above him now. You had money involved, plus I know how much of an animal lover you are." I smiled sweetly and was gratified to see just a hint of a nod. I'd done what he wanted me to.

We gabbed a bit longer about *Sheba's Story,* plus I got a little more background information on Solario Studios' intentions regarding the production of *A Matter of Death and Life.* That was perfect timing, since there was soon a call on Morton's desk phone. "Yes, send him right in," he said, then turned to Dante and me. "Erskine's here."

A split second later, the office door opened and a large, beefy man in an unzipped green fleece jacket with a Solario Studios logo on the pocket strode in. His jeans were ragged — whether by a fashion statement or age, I couldn't tell. He had a round face with prominent lips that called attention away from the wispy yellow hair on his head.

My first thought was that he would have been more than a match in a fight with the skinny Hans Marford. But Hans had been killed by a hit-and-run driver.

"Hi, Morton," he said, ignoring Dante and me to clomp past us and offer his hand to the studio's CEO. I noticed then that he wore low-top boots that enhanced his overall strangely artsy appearance.

"Erskine," Morton said, standing and shaking hands. "Glad you could make it. I'd like you to meet a couple of people."

Only then did Erskine turn to look at us. His expression was assessing at first, then dismissive. He clearly didn't think we were actors Morton was about to ram down his throat, so he didn't care who we were.

Yet.

"This is Lauren Vancouver," Morton continued, chivalrously mentioning the woman first even though I was the least impressive of the two of us. He didn't explain who I was or why I was here.

"Hello," I said, without offering to shake hands.

"And that's Dante DeFrancisco."

Erskine's lack of expression changed into a huge smile. "Dante. How wonderful to

204

meet you." This time, a hand was proffered and Dante courteously shook it. I wondered if Erskine had any pets and knew Dante because of his HotPets stores, or because he knew Dante had money that he had just invested in his first Solario Studios film.

"Hi, Erskine," Dante said.

"Please join us." Morton pointed toward an empty wooden chair by itself under the window. Erskine obediently retrieved it and planted it in front of Morton's desk. The closest spot was beside me. I swallowed my cat-and-canary smile. Little did Erskine know what he was about to endure.

Well, okay, I wasn't going to do my worst interrogation here, not with Morton Lesque guiding the conversation. I was unsure how Dante would feel about my questioning Erskine, but I figured he'd mind it less than my butting heads with Morton.

I let the men start the conversation. For a while they talked about general movie topics, which soon began to focus on *A Matter of Death and Life.*

Then it really got interesting.

"Dante, I know you're one of the co-producers of that . . . er, wonderful upcoming production of *Sheba's Story,*" Erskine said, looking over me toward Dante. Had he really been about to denigrate the movie that he knew Dante was involved in? Or was his catching himself that way by intention, to indicate that what he did was even more wonderful? "I'd love to tell you more about my vision for *A Matter of Death and Life*. It'll have some of the emotion of that cute dog picture, but it's more likely to become a blockbuster. It's got sci-fi elements, and it's a thriller, and —"

"And it was just so convenient that Hans Marford died when the two of you were arguing over who could do the best job of directing it." That was me, cutting into the discussion.

All three men stared at me. I had to turn my head to ascertain that, but it was what I'd intended.

Then both Dante and Morton looked at Erskine, clearly waiting for his response. As if we'd scripted it earlier in our conversation.

His glare almost hid his brown eyes in his fleshy face. "Are you insinuating that I wouldn't have been selected if Hans . . ." His voice tapered off, and he glanced toward Morton in apparent embarrassment. He forced a laugh. "I won't put you on the spot, Morton, by asking who you'd have chosen if Hans was still around. But I'm going to put together a fantastic production. Just wait and see."

"I'm sure you will." Morton's tone sounded placating but abrupt, as if he waited to see what I'd say next.

I hoped I didn't disappoint him. Not that his approbation was critical, but he had gotten Erskine here to meet me.

"I'm a bit curious," I pressed, looking right at Erskine. "I assume the cops have asked where you were on the night of Hans's death. Can you tell your boss, Mr. Lesque, in case he's wondering? Loss of Hans on the current production of *Sheba's Story* could have resulted in a major delay, and therefore money lost to Solario Studios."

Erskine lifted his hefty form a bit from his chair. "Are you accusing me of killing him, Ms. . . ." He obviously had forgotten my name, which was fine with me. "Er, are you accusing me?"

"I'm just asking some questions," I said offhandedly. If I'd run into the guy in a dark alley I might have been nervous, considering his size and quick temper. But I doubted he'd attack me here with people around whom he wanted to continue to impress.

Those furious eyes closed for an instant, and I wondered if he had a method for getting his anger under control. It occurred to me that since he hadn't been told who I was, only my name, he might wonder if I was a cop. Or a lawyer. Either way, he apparently decided that coming clean was a good idea.

"Okay, it's like this," he finally said, lowering himself back into the seat. "Hans Marford and I argued, yes. He started it, since it was becoming clear that I was going to be chosen to direct *A Matter of Death and Life.*" I noticed that he didn't look toward Morton for confirmation. "We both walked away from the argument before we came to blows." Really? I'd have to, confirm that. "But he had more reason to kill me than I had to kill him. And I didn't kill him, if that's your next question." This time he did hazard a glance toward Morton, who nodded encouragingly. Did he believe Erskine? It didn't really matter.

"It was," I said. "Thanks for answering it."

"I would like to hear more of your thoughts about *Death and Life,*" Morton said to Erskine, obviously ready to change the subject. "Let me see these people out, and then we'll talk."

Dante and I rose. I was ready to leave, ready to put Erskine Blainer near the top of my suspect files notwithstanding his denial.

208

Maybe it was a gut feel, based on his attitude more than anything he'd said, but I didn't trust the guy.

Morton accompanied us to the outer office, where his secretary still sat at her desk.

"Thanks for coming," he told us both politely. "We'll talk again about *Sheba's Story* soon, and maybe about *Death and Life* and Erskine, too." He looked at me. "And I'm still not ruling out doing some kind of biopic, or even a fictionalized version of you, Lauren. It's been fun."

CHAPTER 18

"Hi, Mom."

I'd just gotten into my car to head back to HotRescues for the rest of that Saturday afternoon when my phone rang. It was Kevin.

"Hi. Where are you?"

"I'm here at HotRescues. Where are you?"

I didn't want to go into a lengthy explanation of my visit to Solario Studios, although the kids knew I was helping to keep an eye on the production for Dante. I just said, "I'm on my way there now. See you soon."

I wouldn't say I exactly speeded. Not since the most direct way was taking surface streets, and it was usually easier to speed on freeways — at the rare times there wasn't much traffic. But I did get there as fast as I was able.

I parked in the side lot and rushed to the welcome area door. But the only person in there was Nina, behind the leopard print desk as usual. Her deep brown eyes were usually huge and waiflike, but now they were narrowed thanks to her huge smile.

"I take it you know that Kevin's here," she said, standing and facing me.

"Yes," I said. "Where is he?"

"I let him go back into the kennel area. He's family to all of us. But —"

I felt my body stiffen. "But what?"

Those eyes of hers widened in a look I thought to be sympathetic, which immediately worried me. "He's not alone. Did you know he was bringing a friend?"

"No," I said, but he had brought friends here before. Why did that merit such an expression on Nina's face? And then I got it. "A girl friend?"

She nodded. "A very pretty girl friend. Maybe even a girlfriend."

She didn't have to explain what she meant by the duplication of words. Her attitude made that clear.

I chose not to ask why she thought that Kevin's friend could be, well, more than a friend. "I'll go say hi," I said. "Is Zoey in my office?"

Nina nodded, and I went to get my dog. She was always my companion around here.

She might also lend me moral support if I needed it.

Zoey leaped around in joy when she saw me, even more so when I snapped a leash on her collar. At the door leading to the kennel area, I stopped just long enough to gather my courage, then opened it.

I immediately saw that a couple of volunteers were showing potential adopters around, accompanying them through the first part of the kennel area and stopping to point out the inhabitants of some of our dog runs. One was Bev, a senior citizen in a yellow HotRescues knit shirt whose slight stoop indicated she could have osteoporosis, but if so she didn't let it slow her down. She used to just volunteer here once a week, but now she came more often. She was showing around two twentysomething guys who were looking into one of the kennels where a golden Lab mix named Flash peered out at them.

I hurried toward the group and said hello. The expression on Bev's lined face didn't look especially optimistic, so I assumed these young men might just be starting their quest for a new pet and weren't about to zero in on one to adopt that day. Or maybe they had nothing better to do on a Saturday than visit a pet shelter.

Things looked a little more encouraging when I reached our volunteer Sally, a short, vivacious brunette who only came in on weekends. With her were a couple in their thirties with a child who appeared around ten. They had stopped outside the kennel holding Bailey, a Jack Russell mix. Fortunately, Bailey was mellow enough that he might be a good fit with a family with a relatively young child. I hoped that they were interested enough to have Sally take the dog out and let him interact with them in our yard.

I waved at them as Zoey and I passed, which was when I saw Kevin standing outside Hope's kennel. With him was, as anticipated, a girl about his age. She was nearly the same height as my slim, tall son who looked so much like his dad, my beloved first husband, Kerry. Like Kevin, she wore snug blue jeans, but her T-shirt was gold and tight, unlike his loose black one.

And, yes, she had female curves. I was sure my son had noticed. I certainly did, but I couldn't hold that against her. She held Kevin's arm with one hand and pointed with the other inside the kennel where Hope stood on her hind legs. She was laughing. She was pretty. And Kevin had a huge smile on his face, too.

I sighed and stuck on my not-so-overly-protective mama demeanor as I approached them. "Hi," I said heartily. "Great to have you home, Kevin."

Would I embarrass him by giving him a hug and kiss? Well, so what if I did? I maneuvered around the girl a bit and kissed his cheek.

"Hi, Mom," he said, then stepped back. "Mom, this is Mindi Baranca. She goes to Claremont McKenna, too, and her family lives in Encino."

That address gave the immediate impression of a nice, middle-class family. Maybe upper-middle-class. Not Beverly Hills rich, although they could be, of course.

Or not.

And I quickly shut down that part of my brain. They were friends. Kevin had only recently turned nineteen. They weren't engaged or anything like that.

I hoped.

"Hi, Mindi," I said. "I'm Lauren. Welcome to HotRescues." I tried to make my greeting warm but not too warm.

"Hi, Mrs. . . . er, Lauren. Nice to meet you. This is such a wonderful shelter. Kevin has told me all about it."

The ice inside me started to thaw, whether or not I wanted it to. The girl had taste. First, she obviously liked my son. Second, she liked HotRescues. Third, she had started to address me politely and formally. Although if she'd only referred to me as Mrs. Vancouver, I'd have felt like she was telling me I was old — and I'm only edging up to middle age.

Mindi looked about Kevin's age. She had straight, ebony hair that framed her face then touched her shoulders. Her facial features were attractive, and she didn't wear a lot of makeup.

"Thanks." I saw Mindi's gaze go back to the kennel where Hope had sat down. The auburn cocker-poodle mix had a poodlelike long tail and was wagging it hopefully. "Would you like to play with Hope?"

"I'd love to!" Mindi exclaimed right away. Then she looked at Kevin. "We have time, don't we?"

He looked at me. "We're here to go to a birthday party for a friend from college whose family lives in Burbank," he said. "There's a dinner first, and we need to get ready. But, sure." He turned back to Mindi. "We've got time. Can I let Mindi into the kennel for now?" At my nod, he manipulated the gate covered in shatter-free glass and carefully swung it open. Mindi slipped inside while Kevin waited with me.

"Thanks, Mom," he said and gave me a hug.

Kevin's red-brown hair was, interestingly, a similar color to Hope's. He had intense brown eyes beneath straight brows and a ready smile.

We both watched as Mindi sat down on the tile flooring and Hope slid beside her and turned over for a tummy-rub. "Mindi loves dogs, and hers just passed away. Her parents were keeping him, of course, but he was old and got sick, and she's so sad. She really likes Hope, though. She'll need to bring her parents back here, but is Hope available for adoption?"

"Yes," I said firmly. "Although . . ." I gave him a very abbreviated description of how Hope had come here as a quasi-owner relinquishment and that I was still having a check run on whether the councilman had really abandoned her in the first place.

"Then he may reclaim her?" Kevin looked as crestfallen as if I'd told him that I had to turn our Zoey over to someone else.

"Not likely. But I'll step up our inquiry. I'd love to see Hope get a good home. Have you met Mindi's parents?" This, at least, gave me a good reason to inquire rather than just being a nosy, and concerned, mother.

"No, but I'm going to drop her off at their place now so I'll scope them out as potential adopters, and their home, too."

I laughed and hugged Kevin again. "You know what's on my mind, don't you?"

"Yep." He looked straight into my eyes with his laughing brown ones, drew me aside, and spoke quietly. "And I know what else you're wondering. Yes, she's kinda my girlfriend. But it's not too serious yet, so don't worry."

I didn't worry. Not even when Kevin didn't return home after their party that night till two in the morning. After all, I'd no idea of the hours he kept at school. Or what Mindi and he did, or didn't do, there.

Well . . . okay, I did worry. I'm a micromanager of things I can control and hate being in the situation of having no say over something important.

Being a mother is great. I love it. I love my kids.

But, yes, I do worry.

Maybe not so much about my daughter, Tracy. She's had a long succession of boyfriends and seems to know how to handle them. She wasn't ever particularly serious about any, but they were handy accessories going to parties and school events. Far as I knew, that hadn't changed.

Kevin, though? Well, he'd dated some in

high school, but not a lot. And the few girls he had taken out had seemed able to manipulate him. I'd tried to stay cool about it but, hey, I'm his mother.

I did like this Mindi, though — at least, the little I had seen of her. Maybe it was the way she loved dogs.

Plus, I rather enjoyed meeting her parents the next afternoon when the kids brought them in to HotRescues to visit Hope.

The Barancas were a little older than me, a nicely dressed couple who both used baby talk when socializing with Hope in our special outdoor visitors' area just beyond the rear storage shed. I sat at the picnic table watching the four of them tease and play with Hope, who seemed to lap up the attention and beg for more.

Eventually they all had to leave. Kevin and Mindi were heading back to school, and the older Barancas back to their Encino home.

The students took off first, having already packed Kevin's car. I took him into my office briefly, Zoey at our feet. "So glad you came this weekend," I said, giving him a hug. "Mindi seems very nice. Drive safely on the way back and give me a call when you get there. I love you." The last two sentences were a reiteration of what I told him every time he came home.

"Yes, Mom," he said resignedly but then a huge smile lit his face. "Love you!" And then he raced out the door. I smiled back in that direction, then sighed and followed.

Their departure gave me a chance to talk briefly with the older Barancas in our welcome area.

Judy was short, her trimmed hair graying and her face prematurely lined, with a large smile that turned wistful as we discussed their possible interest in adopting Hope. "We all felt so terrible when we lost our last dog to old age," she said. "Mindi took it the worst, but of course she's not around home now, and it's hard on us to have a house that's emptied of both her and our pet." She looked at her husband, Joseph, who was kind-looking and hefty in a work shirt and jeans.

He nodded. "Will we be able to take Hope home?" He sounded as if he'd take her right away if he could.

"Not yet," I said. "There are a couple of kinks in her background I want to get clarified. But I'm nearly positive she'll be available within the next week or two."

I became even more determined to make sure she was.

When they were gone, I called Brooke, who had no more specific information for

me on Councilman Randell's dog ownership — or not. But she did have something
else that intrigued me.

As I hung up I realized that, despite my
noninterest in showbiz, it was consuming
me these days. I now had to show up before
a local talk show was filmed tomorrow.

Not only that — but I got a call from Carlie. She really wanted to have dinner with
Matt and me tonight.

To discuss the Hans Marford situation?
She dissembled, but I had a feeling that
murder, and perhaps her status as a suspect,
would be topics of discussion.

I could hardly wait.

Chapter 19

Fortunately, Matt was available to join us for dinner, along with Rex. They both came to HotRescues to pick Zoey and me up.

It had been a good weekend. We'd adopted out three dogs and two cats into great-looking families, plus had another four applications submitted. I was in the cat house on the new part of the HotRescues property when Matt called to say that Rex and he had just pulled into our parking lot.

I'd left Zoey in my office since some of the cats got nervous around dogs, even one as sweet and mellow as she is. I'd been playing with a few of the kitties, teasing them with feathers dangling from narrow plastic rods. I loved watching them study the feathers then swipe at them with their curled paws.

They grumbled when my cell phone rang. I pulled it from my pocket and looked at the caller ID.

"Hi, Matt," I said as I answered. "You here?"

"We sure are. The office is empty, though, so we can't get in."

It was late on Sunday and I'd let all of the staff leave. Brooke would be sending one of her security people to remain here overnight, but whoever it was wouldn't arrive for another hour.

"Be right there," I said.

I said my farewells to the cats, most of whom seemed quite blasé about the situation. I made sure that the carpet-covered cat trees were all lined up for them to play on, grinned at them, then left, hurrying toward the main welcoming building.

It was March, so despite the time being near six o'clock the grounds were naturally lit, not from our security lights. I got to say quick greetings to the medium- to large-sized dogs in our kennels. Most of the smallest were in one of the buildings near the cat house. I'd visited them before, and now I felt bad that I couldn't take time to acknowledge each little dog as I went by. Which was silly, in a way. We'd had a lot of volunteers here this weekend, and most had spent time sitting and playing with and socializing our dogs. The pups might feel neglected at the moment, but they'd been

222

spoiled. As they should be.

I let Zoey out of my office before I opened the door for Matt and Rex. They both strode in, and the two dogs sniffed noses as Matt and I kissed.

"Where are we going?" he said in a minute, and I was glad to hear his breathlessness. Guess he'd enjoyed our kiss, too.

"We're going to meet Carlie and, I think, Liam, at Ira's Deli." Ira's was a delicatessen on Ventura Boulevard that had been around forever, a popular place that served good food.

And, it had an outdoor patio in the back and welcomed dogs. Otherwise, it would have been far off my radar.

Matt drove us all there in his Animal Services–issued vehicle. He'd already had a chance to change out of his official uniform, and he now wore nice gray slacks and a button-down blue shirt. I'd also changed quickly before my final rounds at Hot-Rescues, when neither staff nor volunteers would be able to see how I'd bent the rules a little for myself. My shirt was white, and I wore a light blue vest over it to go with my navy slacks.

Carlie and Liam were waiting for us in the patio area. Carlie hadn't brought Max, though. They both rose as we approached the table.

Carlie's face looked drawn, her expression sad, despite her effusive greeting to all of us — especially the dogs. She was wearing a nice rust-colored pantsuit, one I thought I recognized from an episode of *Pet Fitness.* "So glad you could make it, Lauren." Her tone, too, had an edge of too much gaiety, so I knew her mood wasn't a good one.

Liam held her chair out for her again, and she sat. Unlike Carlie, he was dressed casually, in a KVKV-TV T-shirt and jeans. He was a cutie, with a wide smile and curly brown hair all mussy on top of his broad-browed head.

Although he worked for the local TV station, I was never quite sure of his function there. I knew he appeared on-camera now and then, on certain pseudo-newsy shows, probably more paparazzi-related than genuine topical information. But he was apparently more of a station executive, helping to plan its schedule and make sure that all went well.

For someone as opinionated as me, I wasn't especially comfortable around Liam since I hadn't decided whether I liked him or not. But he apparently made Carlie happy, so my view didn't really matter. Maybe I wouldn't hint for her to reconsider seeing him after all.

We all ordered beer and sandwiches as the dogs sat tableside, their noses in the air. The patio wasn't too crowded, but the other nearby customers all had food in front of them, which kept the dogs' olfactory nerves in play.

"So," I finally said after we finished pleasantries and our beer was served. "How are things?"

I looked at Carlie, knowing that things for her couldn't be going all that well — the reason for this hastily-called get-together.

"I've been asked — no, told — to go to the Devonshire police station tomorrow for some additional questioning," she said bluntly. "I'll have that nice lawyer you referred me to, Esther Ickes, along. But . . . Lauren, how's your investigation into Hans's death going?"

I glanced toward Matt and met his gaze. He'd sucked his lips into a grimace, but his eyes looked a bit sympathetic. Good. He wasn't going to scold me for getting involved. Not now, at least.

"I've been asking a lot of questions," I said. "It's helped that I've been on the studio lot and otherwise at filmings."

"Thanks to your buddy Dante DeFrancisco, I presume," Liam said.

I didn't like his snide tone, but I nodded. "It helps to have a wealthy producer in my corner. Anyway, here's what I learned yesterday."

I described my conversations with studio exec Morton Lesque and competing director Erskine Blainer. "So far, Erskine has reached the top of my suspect list and I'm keeping him there for now. He wanted to be the director of *A Matter of Death and Life,* and with Hans gone he was a shoo-in. But that just seems too easy."

"Just because the other murders you solved turned out a bit more complicated doesn't mean the easy answer here isn't the right one," Matt reminded me.

"Could be. But . . . Look, Carlie. What I'd suggest when you're at the station tomorrow is — first, do you know what detective will be questioning you?"

She nodded solemnly. My good friend was usually so vivacious and outgoing that I hated to see her like this . . . scared.

But could it be because she had reason to be scared?

Had she killed Hans Marford?

I wished I'd found something concrete to exonerate her. Or proof that someone else had committed the crime.

But I had neither.

"It's Detective Lou Maddinger," she said.

"He seemed intelligent and willing to listen to other possibilities," I said. "At least tell Esther about Hans's argument with Blainer, and his sometimes difficult relationship with his boss, Lesque. It would be better if she threw out other possibilities than if you did. Meantime, I heard on the lot yesterday that there will be more filming involving the dogs later this week — a good reason for me to go there. I've done some Internet searches and didn't find any ex-wives listed for Hans, but from what you've said, Carlie, I suspect he's got other past relationships that went south. I'll ask more questions of some of the crew as subtly as I can. I'll also try to follow up with less visible crew personnel since they might hear things without being noticed. We'll get to the bottom of this soon."

"I hope so," Carlie said with a sigh.

She did manage to eat half of her sandwich. My corned beef was quite good, and the guys scarfed theirs down a lot faster than we did.

Our conversation turned in other directions, which was a good thing. Even Carlie seemed to cheer up.

We talked some about Hope and her suspect origins. I wondered if I should have kept quiet with media-guy Liam present. After all, I was potentially slandering a city councilman.

"I'm hoping to get a chance to ask his former girlfriend a few questions tomorrow, on the sly," I said. "Assuming I get to see her. She's going to be interviewed for some political show that'll be aired on cable TV and the Internet." Brooke had given me the information earlier when she called. She'd offered to go there and see what she could learn, but I had decided to do it myself.

"I'm invited to go there, too," Liam said. "KVKV might buy the rights to air it on local television. Would you like to come as my assistant?"

I grinned at him. "Heck, yes!"

Liam Deale suddenly rose a lot higher on my evaluation scale.

Matt and Rex stayed at my Porter Ranch home with Zoey and me that night.

Yes, he managed to get some scolding in, both on the way there and before we went to bed, about my nosing around yet another murder investigation.

"But you're going about it in a good, thorough way," he told me late that night. "And you know I'm only saying something because I worry about your safety."

I smiled at the good-looking guy who'd already showered and now only wore his underwear.

"I appreciate it," I said just before I kissed him.

We didn't say much more before heading to bed. And not even the dogs bothered us that night.

CHAPTER 20

The next morning, I drove over Coldwater Canyon to Sunset Boulevard. Even this early, there was a lot of traffic. Or maybe because it was early on a Monday morning and a lot of people used canyon streets rather than the San Diego Freeway to get to their jobs.

The interview of Katrina Tirza, Councilman Guy Randell's ex — or whatever she was — was scheduled first thing, unfortunately too early for me to pay a visit to HotRescues.

I'd been intrigued by the idea of the interview when Brooke had let me know about it. She had already learned how private the councilman attempted to keep his private life — and how he fired people for daring to talk to the media without his okay.

But if Katrina was an ex-girlfriend, she'd already been fired. Was she about to blab his secrets to the world?

Would she talk about Hope — or Ginger, which apparently had been the poor dog's prior name?

If she didn't do so during the official interview, I might still be able to get her to answer questions off the record — but ones that would give me sufficient answers to know how best to deal with Hope's potential adoption.

And if it was as sleazy as I believed the situation to be, I might find a way to make it public. After all, there were a lot of animal lovers in the councilman's district. They might not want to reelect someone who abused his own pet that way.

The studio was on Sunset, in an area where I hadn't realized there were any film studios. But in L.A., studios mushroomed everywhere, so I wasn't surprised.

I had to park on the nearby street, but fortunately the meter accepted credit cards. I had a bit of a walk, especially since I'd worn shoes with two-inch heels to go with my official-looking black suit. But fortunately, when I got into the lobby and saw the security desk, Liam was already there.

"Ah, here she is," he said, gesturing toward me. "My assistant. Come on, Lauren. It's nearly time for the interview to begin."

I smiled at him, showed my driver's license to the guard, and was hustled through the entry gate and toward the nearest bank of elevators.

"Thanks," I said softly to Liam as we waited. He was dressed in a suit today, too, and carried an impressive-looking video camera. "I doubt I'd have come up with a story good enough to get me upstairs. And if I waited for . . . our subject myself, I'm not sure I'd even recognize her."

Aardvark Filming Studios occupied the whole fourth floor. "They do a lot of independent shoots here," Liam explained.

We walked into the lobby and Liam again called me his assistant to the woman behind the desk. We were told to go down a hallway and enter the third door on the right.

We entered a mini-auditorium, with tiers of seats arched around a small center stage. An usher pointed to two seats about midway down the stairs. One was on an aisle, and I figured that Liam would be able to do his filming from there. His takes wouldn't be as good, though, as the ones that would come from the larger cameras at the periphery of the stage.

Two people were already seated right in

the center, with the cameras pointing toward them.

One was a woman I recognized from news shows. Her name was Marissa Karigan, and she'd always seemed like a shameless gossip to me — maybe even worse than most other paparazzi. I'd guessed her to be in her fifties, probably considered herself over-the-hill, so she enjoyed embarrassing those who were younger than her, especially if they'd achieved notoriety for something other than talking too much.

And the other? She looked familiar, too. The long-haired, model-thin twentysomething female looked a whole lot like a new volunteer at HotRescues: Cathy Thomas, I believed her name was.

What was she doing on the stage?

She saw me at the same time, and her eyes opened wide. But I didn't have time to talk to her. We were all told by the apparent stage manager to be quiet. The filming was about to begin.

I could be wrong — but I seldom was. The two women could just look alike. Katrina was dressed a lot more stylishly than Cathy, who had to wear our HotRescues shirt while volunteering. She also appeared to wear a lot more makeup. But their names had some similarity, as well as their appearances.

What if Cathy Thomas was actually Katrina Tirza? Not that it mattered a lot that a volunteer used a pseudonym, since they were well supervised while handling our residents, but I didn't like any kind of fraud being perpetrated on HotRescues. We did some background checks on our volunteers, primarily to make sure they didn't have any claims of animal abuse against them, but we might start doing even more now, depending on what I learned.

With Liam leaning into the aisle, obviously filming it all, I listened closely to the interview. Mostly, as I'd expected, it was a tell-all about the councilman and how he treated his staff. And Katrina. She kept saying that she really shouldn't answer anything, that Councilman Guy Randell was a really nice guy and devoted to the city, and all the standard verbal pats on the back. She actually didn't criticize the politico. But the questions Marissa asked were nasty and incisive, and Katrina didn't deny any specifics on the councilman's behalf either.

Sly, intelligent woman, I thought.

Then what had she intended to achieve by volunteering at HotRescues?

Of course, Hope had been found a long way from the councilman's Beverly Hills home. Katrina could have dropped her off near HotRescues. But as Cathy the volunteer, she'd have been told in our orientation that we couldn't take in strays.

But Hope — or Ginger, her name according to her chip ID — might not have been an ordinary stray.

My mind kept churning on all the things I now needed to know instead of focusing on the content-free interview — until I subconsciously heard what I'd been waiting for. I hadn't been certain the topic would be addressed, despite the controversial nature of the councilman's position on animal issues.

On the other hand, if Katrina and Cathy were the same person, it made sense for the interview to latch onto that subject.

"Well, yes, Councilman Randell is an animal lover. He champions legislation that will help protect our poor homeless pets. Mandatory spay-neuter, no puppy mills, that kind of thing." That was Katrina talking. Lying, actually, or at least stretching the truth. I'd already looked up the councilman's position on some pet-related issues.

"But does the councilman have a dog of his own?"

I waited for the answer, staring at Katrina. She'd been watching the interviewer the whole time, so she wouldn't have caught my eye then anyway. But I had an illogical sense, for a moment, that she was avoiding looking at me. Assuming, of course, that she really was Cathy.

"Well, he sort of did. For a while." She looked away from the interviewer, although not toward me, clearly uncomfortable.

Or was that just part of her act?

"For a while?" Marissa pressed.

"He's so busy that he really didn't have enough time to spend with a dog," Katrina said.

"Then what happened to the dog he had?"

"I think he gave it to a friend to adopt."

She *thought* he did? How long ago? Did she know that the councilman had denied ever owning a dog when we'd called about the information on Ginger/Hope's chip?

"But did you ever follow up on that?" Marissa wasn't giving up, which was fine with me.

"No," Katrina said softly. "But I've wondered. And worried. Poor Ginger . . . well, I really loved her. But Guy — the councilman — he decided it was best if no one ever knew he'd even tried owning a dog. And that was fine. He was acting in everyone's best interests."

Really? It didn't sound that way to me.

And Katrina/Cathy had seen Ginger recently at HotRescues. But she might not have realized it was the same dog, even despite their resemblance.

I hadn't told our volunteers how we'd come to take Hope in other than to say she was an owner relinquishment.

"Then you don't really know whether the councilman ever found Ginger a good home." Marissa was really pushing this point. Hard. Which made me wonder.

Had interviewer and interviewee gone over topics before they began?

If so, did Katrina have an agenda that included a discussion of the councilman's adopting then giving up a dog? And a further discussion about her not really knowing what had happened to the poor thing?

Was this real, or was it an attempt to make the councilman look bad in the public's eye?

One way or another, I wanted more information.

And I vowed to myself that, no matter what the answers, I wouldn't allow poor Hope to suffer as a result. As we left about a half hour later, after the interview had ended, I didn't tell Liam what was going through my mind.

He clearly sensed that something was, though. He looked down at me quizzically as we rode in the elevator with a bunch of other people from the audience. I'd tried to rush onto the stage to confront Katrina, but there'd been too many people going the other direction and I hadn't reached her.

Guards had told me that neither of the people who'd been onstage were available for further interviews or discussion, so I'd had to leave.

Out on the sidewalk in front of the building housing the studio, Liam finally asked, "What's wrong, Lauren?"

I decided to dissemble. I didn't know Liam well, but I did owe him since he'd gotten me in to the interview in the first place. "I'm not sure," I said. "I was just interested in that discussion about how the councilman might or might not have had a dog before, and might or might not have found it a good new home."

"Could that be your Hope?" he asked. He'd heard enough at our dinner conversation, and maybe through Carlie, too, to know my concerns.

I shrugged one shoulder. "Possibly. I've got more research to do, though. That's for sure." I even considered attempting to call the councilman again to let him know about this interview, but I felt certain he either knew about it or would learn soon — possibly from that nasty interviewer Marissa, who might seek his public response. She would doubtless hope for something antagonistic, which would draw in even more of an audience.

"Well, I'll keep an eye on things from my perspective. And I'll send you any links to discussions or whatever about the councilman's possible ill treatment of an animal. It might be interesting."

Speculation gleamed in his light brown eyes, and I couldn't help recalling that this man was, before anything, a media representative. I didn't know for sure that KVKV liked to focus on scandal — but, then, these days, what news organization didn't? And I had even seen him occasionally on-camera discussing gossip.

He was a good possible resource, but I needed to do my own snooping before involving him again.

I went home to pick up Zoey before heading to HotRescues. By then it was past noon, so I went through a drive-thru line to pick up a hamburger for lunch.

And yes, I did give Zoey a taste. I felt bad for leaving her alone all that time, and she deserved at least a small treat to try to make up for it.

As soon as I arrived and parked, Zoey and

I walked into the welcome area. Nina wasn't there, but our longtime volunteer Bev was behind the desk. A delightful senior citizen, she had a history at HotRescues and we trusted her to greet people and answer the phones.

"Hi, Zoey," she said as my dog sneaked behind the desk for a pat. "Hi, Lauren." Bev looked up at me. Her lined face beamed as if she expected me to react to her greeting Zoey before me, but I understood.

"Hi, Bev," I said simply, then inspiration hit me. I leaned over the counter. "Bev, do you happen to know a new volunteer named Cathy Thomas?"

Her brow puckered even more than usual as she thought. "I have met someone here lately named Cathy. Why do you ask?"

"I just . . . ran into someone who reminded me of her. Have you seen her socializing any of the dogs or cats?"

"I think so . . . Yes, I think I saw her in with Hope the other day."

This just got more interesting all the time.

Nina came in just then, and I asked her to join me in my office. With Zoey lying at my feet, I asked Nina to pull the volunteer application, attendance record, and any other info we had on Cathy Thomas.

"What's wrong?" she asked right away.

She knows me well enough to recognize when I'm concerned.

"Just some discrepancies," I waffled. "I'll tell you about them later, once I figure a few things out."

"You'd better," she said, then left.

I couldn't spend all day worrying about how Hope happened to have gotten here. She *was* here. And I'd make sure that nothing bad happened to her ever again.

Better yet, she might even find a new home with the Barancas, but I'd have to wait on that, for now.

I was itching to take my first walk of the day through HotRescues. First, though, I needed some information to be able to plan the rest of my week.

I called Grant Jefferly. I reached him immediately, so I figured there was no *Sheba's Story* filming going on at the moment.

But there would be again, tomorrow afternoon.

"I'll be there." After I hung up, I called Carlie, intending to leave a message to let her know I was taking some positive steps to try to help her.

To my surprise, she answered the phone. Her voice sounded hoarse, though.

"Where are you?" I asked. Had her latest interrogation by the police been short, sweet, and absolving her of suspicion?

"I'm in the bathroom at the Devonshire station," she hissed softly. "Taking a potty break. I just needed to get away. They're asking the same kinds of questions as if they expect me to fold and tell them what they want to hear — like that I did kill Hans. Which I didn't." She paused. "Have you found out anything to help me, Lauren? Is that why you're calling?"

"I wish," I said. "But I'll definitely try harder tomorrow. I'm going to the next filming."

CHAPTER 21

It was late on Wednesday morning. I'd just completed an adoption at HotRescues. The match seemed like a good one — a cat going home with a really nice retired schoolteacher. Trite, maybe, but they'd already bonded. I was happy for them both.

I'd just placed Zoey into Nina's able care and left my real shelter to head for the fictional one put together at Solario Studios.

I reached Woodland Hills fairly quickly, then turned onto the street where the film studio was located. As before, I hesitated an instant, staring at the large SOLARIO STUDIOS sign over the entrance gate before driving up to the security guard.

I'd talked briefly to Dante on my way over here. He wasn't coming over today, but he vested me with whatever authority I needed to ensure that the filming progressed as well as possible.

Including the perfect treatment of the dog

stars and extras.

I didn't mention my other plans to him, and he didn't ask — although I was sure he wouldn't be surprised by them.

After parking and glancing around at the large number of people heading for the soundstage where the day's filming was to occur, I headed toward the building where the temporary kennels were housed.

Jerry and Elena were walking poodles — what else? — on the small patch of lawn around the building's front door. They had stopped while the dogs sniffed the ground, and seemed to be engrossed in a conversation when I arrived — the people, not the dogs. Shaking his head, Jerry reached out toward Elena with his free hand and she caught it, gripping it tightly. Obviously these two did have a relationship outside their studio work.

I hated to interrupt them, but Elena noticed me and smiled. "Hi," I said, then stooped to pat the dogs. Pretty young Elena, who again wore a Solario Studios T-shirt and jeans, held the leash of the real Sheba today. Jerry, less officially dressed in a shirt that featured some musician I'd never heard of, had Sheba's counterpart Stellar, who did so well in looking scared.

How did I tell the two white poodles

apart? Well, I am a pet expert and could distinguish their features.

But besides that, the collars they wore now, while off the set, had each of their names attached in bas-relief metal.

When I stood again, I asked, "Are both of these girls scheduled to be filmed today?"

"Sheba is," Elena replied enthusiastically, nodding so her soft brown hair bobbed. "There's a scene where Millie argues with one of the people at that miserable shelter where Sheba's been jailed. I can't wait to see her get mad and tell the shelter person off, even if it is just Lyanne in the role. Poor Sheba actually went through something like that in real life before she was brought to the shelter where she was chosen for this film. And the dogs? They'll just be watching, probably from inside their kennels, but I'm sure the cameras will shoot their reactions. It'll all be so cool!"

I loved her enthusiasm over the filming. Would she ever be able to participate on camera? As I'd noted before, I had no doubt that was her ultimate plan.

"And they may need some extras on the set," she continued, "playing people visiting the shelter looking for a new pet. I'm hoping I'll be able to help out."

Of course she was.

Jerry, on the other hand, seemed more laid back despite his obvious interest. "It should be a fun day," he said. "I don't care if I get to be an extra, but these dogs will need special attention if they're going to be locked up most of the time."

By then, Sheba had squatted to relieve herself, but she was still sniffing the grass and didn't seem in any hurry to go inside.

"When do you need to take these two to the soundstage?" I asked.

Elena shrugged, and Jerry said, "Don't know for sure. I think one of Mr. Paramus's assistants will come for us and go inside to talk to Winna about the other dogs who'll be needed."

We continued to stand there. I figured I should go inside and talk to Winna myself, or maybe to Grant, who'd undoubtedly be there watching over the dogs. Except —

"You know, I'm looking for some information," I said impulsively, looking at both young assistants. "This experience with *Sheba's Story* has inspired me, and I'm working on a screenplay that's a fictionalized version of Director Marford's death. What I'd really love, though, is to expose the real murderer. Of course, the police will hopefully figure that out before I do, but I'm still doing my research. Who do you think ran him over, Elena?"

She frowned pensively. "Well, honestly? I don't know. But that veterinarian Dr. Stellan and he were arguing. And the American Humane representative, Grant, too."

"They're too obvious. How about . . . well, for the sake of my research, if you were the killer, Elena, why would you have done it?"

Her shining green eyes opened wide in what looked like shock. "Me?" she squeaked. "I would never — I don't like your research, Lauren. Use your own imagination. I know a film script is supposed to be all made up, but don't turn perfectly innocent people like me into killers."

"I'm just asking questions to get ideas," I said. "Okay, Jerry. Your turn. Tell me who you think did it — and if it could have been you, why would you have killed him?"

"Let's make this fun," he said with a grin. "Mmm — I think you did it, Lauren. Because he threatened the animals. But if I'd done it, it would have been because . . . I thought the film needed more publicity while it was being shot, so killing the director was a good way to get some."

Clearly it was a joke to him. That was fine. Except for the part where he accused me.

"Thanks," I said. "I think. Anyway, I'm going inside. See you later." I left the two of them talking. Actually, it appeared that Elena was doing most of the talking and Jerry just stood there shaking his head.

I was soon in the area that I'd come to consider a doggy hotel, a poshly furnished locale in the middle of the building. Lots more poodles were in their kennels, with soft bedding on the wood laminate floor. Other dogs, too, who had smaller roles in the film.

As I passed by their enclosures, most barked. The few who didn't looked at me so hopefully that it was all I could do to keep walking.

But there were humans at the end of the long row — Grant and Winna, as well as some other young handlers whom I didn't yet know.

"Hi, all," I said. "Everything under control here?"

"It sure is," Winna said with a huge grin. The chief animal handler was dressed entirely in white that day, which under-scored the redness of her curly hair. I wondered how she expected to keep her outfit clean around all the dogs — or maybe she considered a bit of dirt a sign of her competence. "We need to take most of this gang over to the set in a few minutes since there's going to be a scene in the fictional shelter."

In contrast, Cowan, the trainer-in-chief, was dressed all in black, which only served to accentuate the compactness of his stature and girth.

"Yes, I know," I said to Winna. "Where Millie confronts one of the shelter staff who's mistreating Sheba."

"Exactly." Winna looked impressed.

"But of course none of the animals will really be mistreated," Grant said, making sure that the American Humane presence was remembered. I was sure that he was saying that to caution Winna and Cowan as well as to make a statement.

A few minutes later, I helped this gang, including assistants, put a bunch of the dogs on leashes and walk them out of this building and to the nearby one where the scene would be shot. I wished the camera staff Carlie always brought with her for filming were around. I thought we all created a delightful picture, crossing the studio lot. Too bad I hadn't brought my own camera. I hadn't been taking photos for a while. My phone? Maybe, but I hadn't become skilled in using it that way.

Since I had a few minutes where everyone

would be somewhat distracted, as they should be, by the dogs, I managed to blurt out the same questions that I'd asked of Jerry and Elena. They'd been strictly an impulse then. Now, I thought they could actually help me to help Carlie.

Or just seem stupid. And I hated that idea. In fact, I wasn't happy at all with the game I'd begun playing, but I hadn't yet come up with a better way to try to clear my good friend Carlie. As a result, I did it again.

"You know," I said, "I've decided to work on a screenplay about Hans's death. Can anyone tell me who you think killed him and why?"

I got a dirty look from Grant, who was right beside me. I felt bad for an instant since I liked the guy. But only for an instant. "Me, of course. I'm a suspect since I argued with Hans. But guess what? Even if I had a bit of a motive, I didn't do it."

"Right," I said. I looked beyond him toward Winna. "Did you do it? And if so, why?"

She guffawed as she maneuvered the two leashes in her hand. She had two dogs, a Yorkie mix and a poodle, under her control. "I'd have been on Grant's side, against the scary scene with those dogs on the street. Did I kill him?" She paused to spread out

250

her arms, notwithstanding dogs and leashes. "Do I look like a killer?"

Cowan was less exuberant in his response. Walking at my left, he shot me a glare even angrier than Grant's. "What the hell are you doing, Lauren? I liked the guy, actually, even if I didn't like that particular scene set-up. You want a suspect to throw into your damned screenplay? Use your buddy the vet."

That wasn't what I wanted to hear.

Inside the soundstage, the crew was busy moving lights and taking final steps to make the place look like a shoddy kennel where animals might be abused.

Dr. Cyd Andelson was there since Carlie wasn't. To start things off, I approached and asked if she'd despised Hans Marford enough to kill him, making sure that others like Niall were around. Of course Cyd denied it. So did Niall when I played my little screenwriter game with him. He seemed outraged — because I questioned him, or because he'd already started working on a similar screenplay himself?

Would that have given him a motive to kill Hans?

The scene at the pretend shelter was filmed at least a half-dozen times before I left. Grant was in the middle of it all, ensuring that every one of the dogs was well cared for, given sufficient water to drink, and so forth.

Mick Paramus was hard to take aside for my silly confrontation, but I managed to do so. He seemed distracted, but he laughed and agreed he had one of the best motives of all to do away with Hans. He was having an absolutely wonderful time as director of this film. Killing someone to get such a fantastic appointment? Well, sure.

That attitude made me slip him figuratively toward the bottom of my suspect files, although I didn't eliminate him. He could just be playing along.

The problem with all the questions I'd asked so close together was that, even in reflection, I couldn't say for sure if I now could zero in on any of these people as top suspects.

After I eventually returned to HotRescues and took a quick visit around the place, I sat down at my computer for a while and listed my recollections of everyone's feedback when I'd all but accused each of them.

Niall, maybe?

Winna. Of course.

I shuffled who was where in my files, then gave up, and Zoey and I headed for home.

I'd done all I could that day on Carlie's behalf but I still had no real answers, just more questions.

Had I stirred the real killer up by making him, or her, think I knew who it was but was just playing a silly game to put that person off guard?

Unlikely. But I could hope, couldn't I?

I'm not stupid, by the way. I realized that by asking so many questions, I might have annoyed the real killer. I intended to be careful and not put myself into a situation where anyone could get revenge by harming me. I'd stay where there were other people around, like at HotRescues. When I went home, I had a security system. All was well.

Or so I thought — until I got a phone call at three o'clock in the morning, from Brooke.

"Lauren," she said in a muted tone. "There's someone here at HotRescues. I've called the cops, including Antonio. They're on their way. But I thought you'd want to know."

CHAPTER 22

Rousing Zoey, I shooed her outside into our fenced yard for a quick middle-of-the-night outing, then decided to let her come along. After I finished hurriedly dressing in jeans and a Stanford sweatshirt Tracy had given me, I loaded Zoey into the car and we zoomed off toward HotRescues.

This wasn't the first time there had been a problem in the middle of the night at my shelter.

But that first time, months ago, was what had led to our hiring someone to sleep there overnight every night.

We still had security cameras mounted within the shelter area — more of them now, and better quality.

I used my hands-free system to call Brooke again once I was on the way. "Has Antonio arrived yet?" I asked immediately. "And is Cheyenne there with you?"

Our security director's dog was an adorable, well-trained golden retriever who, I felt certain, would do everything she could to protect her mistress. Even so, without knowing who the intruder was — and whether he or she was armed — I didn't feel at all comfortable relying on the dog to save either of them.

"He just called," Brooke responded. "He's about five minutes away."

I was still ten minutes away. Not that I'd be much protection. Besides, Brooke knew better than I did how to take care of herself.

"Are you in your apartment? Do you hear anything?" Dumb questions on my part, at least the last one. I heard a lot of dogs barking in the background but they didn't sound near her. The first answer was probably yes.

It was. "I'll stay here till I've got backup," she said.

"Good call." I felt somewhat relieved. I really liked Brooke.

Besides, HotRescues was my responsibility.

But I remained frightened, not my usual reaction. Not only was I responsible, but I cared. What if whoever was there had come to hurt our residents?

Maybe it was only an animal wandering through the yard — a raccoon or skunk, maybe. Not the best situation, but not

255

especially dangerous, either.

Yet I knew better. Brooke was fully aware of what was happening around her. She would most likely have viewed some of the security camera footage already.

It had to be a person.

I could only pray that Brooke, and all the animals, remained safe.

I heard no sirens as I approached the HotRescues parking lot. Were the police already there? Had they decided to remain silent so they could catch whoever was trespassing in the act?

Pulling into the lot, I recognized Antonio's dark sedan sandwiched between two police cars. I saw no people around, so they must all be inside the fence.

I took a deep breath as I got out of my car, unhooked Zoey from her safety restraint in the backseat, and snapped on her leash. I watched her for a few seconds. She sniffed the air, then the ground — nothing atypical. She didn't seem alarmed, and she could be very protective if necessary.

I relaxed a little but remained on guard.

I tried the door into the welcome area. It was locked, a good thing — maybe. Had the cops entered this way? Had Antonio? If so, who'd locked it behind them?

I reached into my pocket, eased out the key, and carefully unlocked the door.

It was dark inside. I flipped on the lights. That wouldn't hurt anything, would it?

"Hands where I can see them," said a stern voice. A uniformed cop emerged from the hall where my office was.

Zoey growled, then barked. "It's okay," I told her, raising one hand all the way into the air and the other high enough for the cop to see it. I didn't want to choke my dog while still holding her leash. I identified myself. "My security director called and told me about a break-in," I said. "Have you found the culprit?"

"Still looking. I'll need to see your ID."

"She's fine, Officer." That was Antonio's voice, and he, too, came out of the hallway. "She's who she said she is."

"Okay, sir." The cop nodded, then disappeared again in the direction from which he'd come.

"What's going on?" I asked. I was used to seeing Brooke's guy dressed up in a suit, like the detective he was. Now, though, he wore an LAPD T-shirt over torn jeans, and his short, dark hair was unkempt. "Where's Brooke?"

"She's showing a couple of cops through the kennel areas. They're trying to assess

257

how bad the damage is."

"Damage?"

I'm sure I sounded as panicked as I felt. Antonio smiled reassuringly as he gave me a quick hug. "It's okay. Nothing much. But some of the kennel gates were opened and dogs got onto the paths. No fights or anything. They were just loose — although . . ."

"Although what?"

"Well, there were some packages of meat here and there. We've been picking them up rather than leaving them where they are as evidence. We're not sure whether they're poisoned, and not all the dogs have been put back into their kennels."

"Oh, no!" I felt myself sway but pulled myself together immediately. I wasn't the swooning type, not ever. And if I was really going to fall apart, I'd do it when I was alone — after making sure all our animals were fine. Or if they weren't . . . well, Carlie was a damned good vet, and others on her staff would also do anything to ensure that any injured pet was cared for fast and right. "I need to get back there."

"I'll come with you."

We hurried into the kennel area. The brightest security lights were on. Usually, they were on a dimmer setting at night. All the dogs seemed to be in their kennels along the main path. Not wanting to rely on my memory while I was upset, I checked each kennel card posted on the outer part of the gate to make sure that the one or two dogs inside matched the photos.

We went around the corner toward the storage building. "Any idea where the intruder got in? Could he still be here?" I was breathless as I asked Antonio my questions.

"We've looked around. Best we could tell, he got in right there." He pointed toward the gate at the rear of the shelter, where we brought in large containers of supplies like food.

"Wasn't it locked?" I suddenly was ready to chew out Pete, though I knew our handyman was always careful. Could he have messed up this one time? But Brooke usually checked all entry doors when she did her rounds.

"The lock appeared to have been picked from the outside. There are deep gouges visible."

Not only would I have that lock replaced, but I'd also have a brand-new gate installed. One with a lock that could never be picked.

"And the intruder?"

"No sign of him yet."

"You're sure it's a he?"

Antonio looked down at me grimly. "Unsurprisingly, with all your equipment here, there are pictures. Brooke glanced at them before, but we wanted to secure the facility before really focusing on them."

"Right."

We turned the next corner. I saw Brooke with two uniformed cops, including the one who'd first confronted me. "Oh, Lauren." Her shrill voice told me how upset she was. She was awfully pale. It could have been the bright lights back here, but I didn't think so. As I often did, I thought of her apparently conquered illness, which had brought her here in the first place to relinquish Cheyenne.

"It'll be okay," I reassured her loudly enough to be heard over the nearest barking dogs, hoping it was so.

"But —"

Antonio must have been worried about her, too. He approached and put an arm around her. "She's right," he told her. "You did good, calling us as quickly as you did."

I wanted to hear all the details about how she first became aware of the intruder and what she'd done, but not until the cops had cleared the place and were confident that all was well.

I'd stay here for the rest of the night

anyway, and hoped that Antonio would as well.

The group of us continued to look around, checking on the dogs outside, then the cats and smaller dogs in their respective buildings.

All looked fine, and it appeared that, with Brooke's help, every one of the animals was back where it belonged.

Eventually we headed back inside the center building. That was not only where the upstairs apartment was for whoever stayed here all night, but most security viewing equipment was downstairs there, too.

"Want us to hang around, Detective?" the cop who'd first seen me asked Antonio.

"Not necessary. I'll look at the tapes from the cameras, then bring them to the Devonshire station."

Only after we got copies made, but I wasn't going to interrupt him. I wanted to keep the pictures.

But I needed to see them first.

My mind had been churning over the timing for this break-in. Yes, someone could have decided to invade HotRescues anytime.

But this was the night after the day when I'd been really pushy at the *Sheba's Story* filming.

What if Hans Marford's killer was exacting a form of revenge, or at least warning me to back off if I didn't want to see my dear animal charges hurt?

I became more certain of that when we reviewed the film in a downstairs room in the center building that had been kept as a tiny security headquarters.

The person had, not unexpectedly, worn a disguise — a ski mask. The outfit was dark and loose, so the wearer's sex was indistinguishable.

There were shots of him or her in several different areas, wearing gloves and opening gates so dogs poured out of their kennels and onto the path.

The intruder wore a backpack, and extracted the packages of food to place on the ground here and there. Of course some of the dogs dug into it.

I prayed the meat was safe for them. So far none appeared sick, but I'd called Carlie just in case. Her backup vet, Cyd, was on the way to give everyone a cursory check. We'd have to wait until morning, or even later, to get an analysis of what they'd eaten. So far, I was optimistic that it had been part of the warning and not designed to harm any animals . . . this time.

At one point, when the intruder reached the spot in the newest area of HotRescues where they could have either continued along the path through the outdoor kennel areas or gone into the nearby cat house, the person looked a little confused. At least the gesture he or she made gave that appearance. The left hand reached over the head and scratched behind where an ear must have been under the mask.

The person continued on, out of this camera's range. Other cameras picked up some movement, but no other shot was as clear as that one.

And it told us nothing.

CHAPTER 23

The police kept a presence at HotRescues for the rest of the night. So did I.

Dr. Cyd Andelson left soon after she'd arrived, but not before doing a cursory check of each of the animals. All the dogs seemed to crave attention even in the middle of the night. Some cats, too. None appeared to be ill, so I had no problem with her departure — though I promised to call for an immediate revisit if anything changed. Before she drove off, we called Carlie together from my office to give a report.

"Glad all the animals are okay." Carlie sounded as wide awake as I was. "I'll talk to you tomorrow, Lauren." I was sure she'd want to discuss the reason for the break-in. Without giving details, I'd hinted that it had to do with *Sheba's Story*. When I returned to the kennel area, Antonio was trying to convince Brooke to go home. That would have been fine with me under the circumstances, but our security director refused. She did, however, take Cheyenne back to the upstairs apartment where they should have been sleeping that night.

I chose not to confirm whether Antonio stayed there with them but assumed he did.

I returned again to my office. Zoey promptly jumped up onto the sofa in my little conversation area and fell asleep.

Me? Well first, sitting at my desk, I sent an e-mail to Dante to let him know about the break-in. I thought about calling, or even texting him, but though he needed to know what had happened, there was no reason to wake him. Everything was under control . . . for the moment.

I did call Matt, though. Our relationship was growing, or at least I liked to think it was. If I didn't let him know what had happened, I'd hurt his feelings, and I didn't want to do that.

His voice was groggy but he answered right away. "Lauren? What's wrong?"

"Does something have to be wrong for me to call you in the middle of the night? What if I just wanted to hear your voice?"

"Yeah, right," he said. "You'd never admit to something that romantic. So, tell me. What's wrong?"

He had come to know me well enough to

get that right. I'd always have an excuse ready, even if I really did just want to talk to him.

I told him what had happened. "But all the animals seem fine," I reassured him hastily. That's one of the things I like about Matt. He really cares about animals. "We still don't know what the intruder was trying to feed them, but the police are having it analyzed." I paused. "I'm afraid the break-in might have something to do with *Sheba's Story.* I was digging for information today. Or —"

"Or?"

Another possibility had crossed my mind. "Well, it could relate to that abandoned dog I took in. If the councilman really did own Hope and wanted to hide it, maybe he sent someone to do something to her, or to steal her."

"But is she still there? If so, is she okay?"

"Yes," I acknowledged. "I'm probably just looking for reasons that maybe aren't there." And blaming myself. "Maybe this was just a random act of trespass and threat against my animals, just for someone's perverted sense of fun, to show it could be done."

But I couldn't help thinking it had been some kind of warning.

■ ■ ■ ■

Zoey and I took another slow walk around HotRescues under the glowing lights we'd kept on full power, observing everything. Cops were stationed on the grounds, and a crime scene team had also taken over the back gate where the intruder had apparently gained entrance.

When I returned to the main building, Matt was inside with Rex; Antonio had let them in.

"You didn't need to come," I told him, although I didn't even attempt to hide my big smile. I felt glad to see him. Even relieved.

Not that I'm some wimp of a woman who needs a man to protect her. But his moral support meant a lot.

"No, I didn't," he said. "And I can't stay long. I've got some training exercises scheduled for my animal rescue teams later today. But I wanted to see for myself that you're all right."

I glanced around the office. Antonio had headed back to be with Brooke again. We were alone, except for our dogs.

That was a good enough reason to kiss Matt, and I did.

"I'm fine," I told him.

"You might be interested to hear that the break-in here made the news," he said as I ushered him into my office so we could spend the little bit of time we had with each other sitting and talking. And maybe even making out.

I'd been about to sit down but remained standing instead. "What! Who told the damned media?"

"They have their ways," Matt reminded me. "Probably listen in on all police scanners, or have informants at all police stations, or even hire people to hang out there themselves."

I sighed. "I'm glad I sent Dante an e-mail. With his corporate public relations staff, he'll be able to turn this into good publicity for HotRescues somehow. Our security was violated, but the animals all came out of it fine."

"Could be," Matt said.

We snuggled on the couch for a while. I'd already told him my suppositions on why the break-in had occurred and had half expected him to scold me for being too nosy and not careful enough. I'd already decided how to argue against any criticism he had. But he didn't get into it.

I think I fell asleep. But eventually, I heard

a noise outside in the welcome area. I moved my head off Matt's shoulder to look at my watch.

The dogs both stood at the closed office door, wagging their tails. It was about seven o'clock — time for staff to begin arriving to help feed animals and clean their runs.

Time, too, for me to start my day.

I did, however, agree that Zoey and I could go with Rex and Matt to the nearest fast-food place for a quick breakfast on its outdoor patio.

We were the only ones there, although crowds kept arriving. Some got takeout, and others ate inside. I enjoyed my egg sandwich with cheese and bacon. Not the healthiest food, but I'd need whatever energy I could muster to get this day started. Matt had a scrambled eggs breakfast.

And the dogs? They managed to scrounge table scraps from us. Not the healthiest thing for them, either, but the aromas and our eating undoubtedly sparked their appetites. They'd get their healthy dog food breakfasts later.

Matt drove us back to HotRescues. Before Zoey and I exited the car near the entry building, Matt said, "You'll be okay?" He made it a question rather than a statement.

"Of course. But thanks for worrying about us." I included Zoey and all the animals inside my shelter in my comment and figured that Matt recognized it as such. I leaned over from the passenger seat and gave him a quick kiss. "If you'd like to get together later for dinner to confirm it, I'm available."

"Unfortunately, I'm not," he said, which made my upbeat mood threaten to cave in a bit. "We've got an emergency preparedness meeting this evening." And since in his role as a captain of L.A. Animal Services he was the head of that team, I knew he'd have to attend. In fact, I wanted him to. He was always good at what he did, and being prepared for emergencies was a worthwhile goal.

I felt a little sorry for myself as Zoey and I got out of the car and entered the welcome area but immediately pasted a smile on my face. Nina was there, and she looked worried.

"You heard about what happened here last night?" I could have made that a statement rather than a question, too. She had risen from behind the desk and approached to give me a hug.

"I got here early and talked to Brooke and Antonio. Plus — well, it was on the KVKV news this morning."

She listened to that station — the one where Carlie's Liam worked? Well, why not? He'd been helpful to me, and he was obviously a pet-lover. Although most of the broadcasts on that channel were typical snoop-into-the-life-of-uncooperative-celebrity types, so were nearly all news shows these days.

"We're still waiting to hear what the contents were of the food bags the intruder brought," I said, "but all the animals seemed fine when I left, and, more important, when Dr. Cyd came to check them out."

"They all seem fine now, too," Nina said. "But I'm glad they had a vet checkup."

Zoey and I went down the hall to my office, where I put my purse into a drawer and changed into my blue HotRescues knit shirt, an extra one I kept there for emergencies. Then we went out for our first stroll of the day through the kennel areas. Or the official day, anyway. We'd done plenty visiting of our inhabitants in the wee hours this morning.

It was late enough that the kennel area was fairly busy with staff and volunteers. I didn't see any potential adopters being shown around yet, but I had hopes for this Thursday.

271

If nothing else, the mention of Hot-Rescues on the news might remind people to come here if they'd otherwise been considering a visit to check out pets they might like to adopt.

A number would come out of sheer curiosity. But even some of them could make potentially suitable adopters.

My normal greetings from Pete and Bev and other volunteers were fairly poignant instead of the usual wave and cheerful good morning.

"Are you okay, Lauren?" asked Mamie. She had just exited one of the kennels, where she'd let one of the bigger dogs, Rottweiler mix Hale, slobber all over her. Even this sometimes confused senior citizen had heard about what had gone on here.

"I wasn't here when all the excitement happened," I told her. "I'm fine. More important, all our residents are fine, too."

"I'm glad." She gave me a huge smile beneath her red, curly hair, then turned to enter the next kennel, where Shazam, the Doberman, had sat down to wait for her. He was one well-behaved dog, and I was always surprised he was still with us.

Zoey and I continued on, although I stopped to say something encouraging to each of the dogs we passed, even those who kept barking at us.

Then I stopped. I had just noticed some-one at the end of this row of kennels, near the large storage shed. A volunteer. Or was she?

It looked like Cathy Thomas, which meant it was Katrina Tirza, Councilman Randell's ex-girlfriend who had accused him of aban-doning his dog, Hope. And, yes, that was where she now stood, right outside Hope's kennel.

She'd apparently spotted me, too; she started to turn as if to run out the driveway to the side of the storage building.

"Wait," I called to her.

Her back still toward me, she lifted her shoulders as if waiting for a blow.

I wouldn't hit her any more than I'd strike a dog. But if the blow she expected was an interrogation, then she was right to worry.

"Hello, Katrina," I said.

She turned toward me. She was appar-ently in her Cathy persona, since she wore a yellow HotRescues volunteer shirt. It was snug on her and showed off her cleavage. I'd noticed before, when she was here as a new volunteer, that she was quite pretty, with pouty lips and long, dark hair and huge brown eyes embellished with long lashes.

I hadn't realized that could be a reason

she attracted politicos, like Councilman Randell.

"Hi, Lauren," she said. "I — I saw you the other day in the audience when I was being interviewed by Marissa Karigan."

"I saw you, too. So . . . who are you, really?"

Instead of responding, she turned and looked inside the kennel, where poor, sweet Hope gazed out at us, sitting at attention with her tail wagging tentatively. The adorable cocker-poodle mix would have a new home soon, but I still felt obligated to make sure that there'd be no repercussions from the councilman who denied ownership — or anyone else.

"I'm Katrina," she said with a sigh. "I just . . . well, things are complicated. I don't want to say anything else to get Councilman Randell in trouble with his constituents or otherwise, but I fell in love with his dog. And then when Hope — I mean Ginger — wasn't there anymore, I wanted to make sure she was okay. I'd been able to track her down — and I can't say exactly how, but I knew she was at HotRescues. That's why I became a volunteer, so I could confirm that she was all right." She seemed to hesitate, and looked down at the ground. "If I were in a position to, I'd adopt her. But I'm not.

I just want to make sure she gets a good home — no matter what Guy . . . er, never mind."

"She's one of ours now," I said, trying to keep anger out of my voice. What had really gone on with poor Hope? Was she being used in some kind of tug-of-war between these two people?

"I heard on the news about what happened here last night." Katrina had taken a step forward, holding out one hand as if trying to soothe me. "I needed to come and check on Hope." She hesitated. "Could the trespasser have been sent here to steal her? Or to do something to make sure no one would ever find out where she came from?"

I felt startled. I wasn't the only one to have those suspicions cross my mind. But Hope hadn't been singled out.

It could still have been a warning to keep quiet about things relating to the filming and Hans's murder. Or something else altogether.

"Has anyone from the media asked you for an interview about the break-in?" she persisted. "If you do talk to anyone publicly, you might at least hint about the connection to a politician, just to make Guy back off in case he was involved."

I had no intention of talking to anyone in

the media or otherwise about what had happened, especially with our residents potentially in danger again.

But if Councilman Randell had had the break-in staged to somehow keep me quiet because he really had owned, then abandoned, poor Hope — or Ginger — he'd done everything all wrong.

If I got any evidence that the break-in was his doing, I'd be the first to step in front of a camera and make sure that all his constituents knew it before they considered reelecting him again.

CHAPTER 24

Katrina left after our discussion. And my direction to her that Cathy Thomas was no longer welcome at HotRescues.

She looked sad but didn't argue.

Though she'd gone through our orientation to become a volunteer, that had apparently been a ruse so she could come into the kennel area and check on Hope. Which continued to puzzle me. If Hope had been the councilman's dog and his abandoning her had triggered Katrina's worry, why hadn't Katrina simply taken in the poor stray — even just to find her a new, appropriate home?

Something didn't sound right. I continued to muse about it as Zoey and I finished our rounds and headed back to my office.

I got another surprise — sort of — when we reached the main building. Dante was there. Not that his visit was anything but welcome, and it certainly made sense after the break-in. But he wasn't alone. He had his German shepherd Wagner with him, not to mention his lady friend, Kendra Ballantyne, and her tricolor Cavalier King Charles spaniel, Lexie. They stood in the welcome area chatting with Nina when Zoey and I entered.

"Hi, Lauren." Kendra was the first to greet me as the two dogs came over to sniff noses with Zoey. Kendra was thirtysomething, pretty, with shoulder-length brown hair, and well dressed for a pet-sitter in a button-down pink shirt and black slacks. Or maybe not dressed well enough for a lawyer. She was both. She was also smart, and the combination had been enough to attract rich, good-looking Dante. "Good to see you, but what happened here last night?" She was also direct, probably an offshoot of the lawyer part of her.

I could see from the proud yet irritated look in Dante's eyes that he'd intended to ask that question himself. Oh, well. Didn't matter who asked, or at least I didn't think so. I'd answer as best I could.

"Let's go into my office and I'll tell you about it," I suggested.

In about a minute all three people sat on the sofa and chairs in my conversation area. The dogs were friendly enough to just lie down at our feet.

I started the discussion. "Dante, do you happen to know Councilman Guy Randell?" Dante knew everyone — everyone important, that is. Maybe he could help sort out what was really going on with Hope.

"Sure. I've contributed to his campaign. Why do you ask?" He didn't look pleased about what he obviously considered a nonsequitur to what he was here to talk about.

I briefly explained the situation with Hope, or Ginger, and what Katrina Tirza/ Cathy Thomas had told me. "She seemed to think that the break-in had something to do with the councilman wanting to tamp down any negative publicity about the dog he allegedly abandoned."

I glanced toward Kendra, who was seated right beside Dante on the sofa, as I used the word "allegedly." I wasn't a lawyer, but I knew enough not to directly malign someone unless I was certain of his guilt.

I caught the brief smile in her sparkling blue eyes. "What do you think?" she asked. Wasn't that more like something a shrink would say than a lawyer?

Nevertheless, I answered. "I don't think so, although I'll reserve judgment. Especially because — well, I've been wondering if the person who broke in here is someone involved with the *Sheba's Story* filming."

"Why do you think that?" Dante asked in a skeptical tone that iced its way up my back. I didn't want to look stupid to the man who was, in essence, my boss, even though I ran things around HotRescues — and did a damned good job of it.

And I wasn't stupid. Not about this or anything else.

I kept my voice level as I explained how I'd been asking questions around the set.

"So you think someone's trying to warn you off?" Kendra asked. Her tone sounded more interested than skeptical. Good. Dante might listen to her.

"I don't know," I said. "I also realize that I might be attempting to read meaning into the break-in that's not there. I suspect the cops won't spend a lot of time on investigating. It's probably not high on their agenda, since no one was hurt, not even any animals, for which I'm really grateful. We don't know yet what that supposed food was composed of, but it apparently wasn't poison."

"You could be right, Lauren," Dante said slowly. His skepticism seemed to have evaporated. Or maybe he had just wanted to see my reaction to it. "I'd thought it could have been a message for you. I heard from Niall about your foray into accusing everyone in the production of killing Hans — or asking them all to reveal their own suspicions. And Niall wasn't the only one. We decided to stop here this morning to make sure everything's okay, but Kendra and I are on our way to a meeting."

Dante had never struck me as the dramatic type, but he stopped as if challenging me to ask something about that meeting.

No need to disappoint him. He'd stoked my curiosity.

"What kind of meeting?" I asked.

"We're getting together with Niall, Morton Lesque, and maybe others at Solario Studios. I thought I might need legal advice, but rather than hiring someone official I'm bringing Kendra along for her take on what happens." They shared fond looks again, then Dante turned back to me. "None of the people working on the movie seems thrilled right now with your being my agent at the filming sessions. I may need to convince them to let you back on the lot on my behalf. Do you think I should do that?"

The stare in his dark, intense eyes was challenging.

I glared back. Without reservation, I said, "Hell yes, if you want to make sure your investment in *Sheba's Story* is being protected. I'm your extra set of eyes. And if solving Hans Marford's murder also helps to protect the production, well — there's no one better than me to figure that out, Dante."

I caught the look shared between Dante and Kendra but was unable to fully interpret it. Doubt? Irony? Pity? A combo?

I started to rise. The dogs sensed my movement and all three sets of eyes opened and focused on me.

"Kendra has a good reputation in that arena." Dante smiled at her.

"Oh, but Lauren has been doing such a good job on her own that I don't want to interfere," she said.

I ignored her irony and sat back down. "Tell you what." I looked straight at Dante. "Give me a call after your meeting with Morton and the others. I really think I'm contributing a lot as your representative. It won't hurt the production if I also keep the killer on his toes and prevent him from harming anyone else because his guilt would be too obvious."

"Okay," Dante agreed. "I'll call you."

"If they convince you not to let me back, please give me one more shot at persuading you otherwise. I really think it's in your best interests to have me there. Niall's your friend but he has his own agenda. My agenda is twofold: to be there for you, and to be there for the animals, too. Nothing there about benefiting me. And if you make it clear that you're backing my presence, you shouldn't have to waste time on meetings like this one unless you choose to. You can just watch filming when you feel like it."

I waited to see if he agreed. I guessed that he did, because he rose, and Kendra and the dogs followed his lead.

"I'll talk to you later, Lauren," he said, and they all left HotRescues.

I did get a call early that afternoon — not from Dante, but from the Barancas, asking how their adoption of Hope was progressing. I told Judy that we were still confirming Hope's availability, but that so far everything looked good.

After all, even if the story had occurred as Katrina described it, no one had placed dibs on the poor canine who'd been affected, one way or another, by becoming a stray.

I was just being extremely cautious. Maybe too cautious.

Or was I just using Hope as bait to get the truth?

Probably both.

But at the moment I didn't see any reason

283

these people shouldn't be able to become family to the dog.

"One more thing I have to do," I said, thinking about how Dante said he'd make some inquiries. "If it turns out the way I think it will, I'll give you a call and you can come get her."

If it didn't, it would subtract some brownie points from their daughter's boyfriend, my son — but nothing I could do about that except try.

My second call came while Angie Shayde and I were in the cat house playing with some adorable, young kittens. I heard my name called on the intercom and ran back to my office to answer. I sat back down at my desk and picked up the receiver for the shelter's landline.

It was Carlie. "What did you do, Lauren?" she asked.

Confused, I said, "I visited all the animals here with Cyd when she was checking on them last night after the break-in. Is something wrong?"

"I mean about Hans's murder. I've been hearing all sorts of angry stuff from people who said you'd accused them in order to try and help me. Did you do that?"

The answer was yes, but considering her accusatory tone I wanted to soften it a bit.

"I was playing a game of sorts to see how all the players reacted. I was hoping to get a good clue about who might have done it. Unfortunately, that wasn't the result. Not yet, at least. But the break-in could be related." Or not.

"Well, thanks. I guess." Her tone had softened, although this conversation was bothering me enough to motivate me to start doodling on a pad of paper on my desk, and I never doodle. I realized I was drawing a lot of question marks of many sizes and thicknesses, and made myself stop. "But be careful, Lauren. Even though you mean the best, I'd hate to see someone like that intruder harm you or any of your HotRescues people or animals, especially if it has something to do with helping me."

"Me, too," I assured her. "And, yes, I'll be careful."

My next phone call was one I'd been waiting for. This time, I was just about to leave my office to go visit the building that housed small dogs to go check on some puppies we had recently rescued from a high-kill shelter. I grabbed my smartphone when it rang, though.

It was Dante. I sank back onto my desk chair, with Zoey watching me with concern. I waited for the worst.

"Well, Lauren," he said. "We've had our meeting."

At his pause, I asked, as I was sure I was meant to, "How did it go?"

"Were your ears burning? You were definitely a subject of conversation."

"Yes, they've been tingling all day," I said, rolling my eyes but glad he couldn't see that.

"There's going to be a filming of a major scene at the studio tomorrow," he continued. I waited for the other shoe to drop: he either had to be there himself or send someone else. I wasn't allowed to be there. "I'm going to attend."

Was he angry with me for his having to interrupt his regular work schedule that way? Hell, attending on his behalf disrupted my usual routine at HotRescues. It would be good if I could get out of it — sort of.

"Okay," I said, waiting for him to tell me to butt out.

"You're going to attend with me," he finished.

I grinned in relief.

CHAPTER 25

I spent a fair amount of time at HotRescues the next morning. For one thing, I wanted to assure myself that none of our residents was suffering a delayed reaction to whatever food had been dropped on the grounds two nights before, when they'd also been let loose.

Of course, if they'd been poisoned, they'd be showing signs long before now. Plus, Antonio had checked with the crime lab and sent a joint e-mail to Brooke and me to let us know that the stuff appeared to be a combo of several cheap dog foods available at grocery stores — although the analysis had not yet been completed.

Mostly, I wanted to make sure I fulfilled my responsibilities here. Going to the *Sheba's Story* set wasn't my job, no matter how much I wanted to stay in Dante's good graces.

And no matter how much I wanted to

ensure that Hans Marford's real killer was caught so Carlie would no longer be a suspect. Still assuming she was innocent — and that was definitely what I wanted to assume.

I also spoke with one of the managers at EverySecurity Alliance, the security company we'd once relied on at HotRescues. We still utilized their services, but on a more limited basis now that we had Brooke full-time, and she had other security personnel who contracted to stay overnight here. We'd had EverySecurity patrol a lot more often last night, though, to ensure no further break-ins and scheduled them for additional patrols in the future. They had become more adept at keeping an eye on things ever since some intrusions a number of months ago, before Brooke was in charge, when a person had been killed right on our grounds. They'd had to improve, or get fired by Dante.

Eventually, after all the regular greetings of animals, staff, and volunteers, I left Zoey again in Nina's able care and headed for Solario Studios.

I went through the same old thing at the guard gate, showing my ID and mentioning Dante. It looked like the same old guard asking questions, so I was perturbed that he didn't just let me onto the studio lot. But I supposed he had his protocol to follow. And, eventually, he did wave me through that impressive entry gate.

I had to hunt for a space in the large parking lot. Apparently, the studio was busy that Friday. Was everyone here for the *Sheba's Story* filming, or were there other movies being shot here today?

I decided to visit the dogs first. I felt sure they'd be friendlier to me than the people I was likely to run into. I hadn't accused any of them of murder last time I was here, unlike the cast, crew, and even the executives. I'd go say a cheerful hello to all the people, too, but decided to work into it gradually.

As I walked down the street between the tall, mostly windowless gray studio buildings toward the one I'd started thinking of as the doggy hotel, I spotted some dog handlers in the distance, including Winna. She held leashes of two poodles, and along with her were four of her staff, also walking dogs.

I approached, skirting around people who had to be actors, considering the amount of makeup they wore and their gala outfits. Were they there as extras for the scenes at the end of the movie depicting the party at the animal shelter that the character Millie

Roland was opening? That was what I'd heard was being shot today.

Eventually I reached the dogs and their handlers. "Hi," I said cheerfully. "Can I help?" I held out my hand to Winna for a leash. One of the dogs she walked was the real Sheba, but I wasn't sure which rendition of poodle the other one was.

"Only if you promise not to start accusing me of murder today." She glared from beneath her curly red mop of hair. It should have felt comedic, but her look chilled me. Could she have been the intruder at HotRescues, trying to warn me away from questioning her?

I didn't think so. She was too short, for one thing.

But could I really know the intruder's height from the pictures? And since the person had worn a ski mask, there was no way of telling his or her hair color or style.

"Okay," I said mildly. "I won't accuse you. Not any of you." Her young staff had circled behind her as if to have her back in case of trouble. Their dogs sniffed each other's muzzles and rears in a friendly canine way. The dog handlers formed a charming pack — excluding me.

That was their prerogative. Would they also protect each other, or someone else connected with the film, if they knew who'd actually killed Hans?

"All dogs needed inside," commanded a female voice from off to the right. I looked in that direction and saw R. G. Quilby. Director Mick Paramus's assistant was dressed in an attractive red suit and held an efficient-looking clipboard.

Winna stuck her nose in the air as she looked away from me and started following R. G., still holding the leashes of both white poodles.

Of the animal handling assistants, Elena, also in control of a poodle, looked at me with an embarrassed expression on her youthful, pretty face. Once again, I figured she was hoping to be discovered as an actress on the set, since she wore a bit too much makeup like the people I'd spotted, and was dressed in a lovely, flowing knee-length dress. I hoped she wouldn't have to perform any gymnastics to keep her poodle doing what was necessary for the scene. She quickly followed Winna.

So did the other two handlers, whom I didn't know. Jerry Amalon hung back. He held the leash of the poodle I felt certain was Stellar — the dog trained to roll over and look scared. He was dressed better than usual today, too, in a button-down yellow shirt and beige slacks instead of his usual T-shirt and jeans.

"Hi, Lauren," he said in a soft voice. We both started walking after the dog-handling crowd. "I don't know if I should say anything, but you're probably persona non grata around here. Everyone was talking about you a lot yesterday."

"I don't suppose anyone happened to confess to the murder while they were acting angry that I was pushy, did they?"

The kid laughed. "No, not that I heard. But don't be surprised if no one else talks to you."

We'd reached the building housing the soundstage used the last time I'd been here for filming a scene from *Sheba's Story*. The others, dogs and people, had already gone inside.

"Why are you talking to me?" I asked.

"Because no one's looking now, for one thing," he said. "And because I'm not a real suspect. Ask me anything. I won't have any answers for you."

I laughed. "I'll bet the others recruited you to talk to me to waste my time."

"I'll never tell." Jerry grinned and followed Stellar inside.

The film set was bustling as things were still

being organized. I looked around, seeing where the handlers took the dogs. Not much speculation involved. The scene had been designed to resemble an animal shelter — one almost as nice as HotRescues, with a lot of kennel runs with glass gates opening onto a concrete path past them.

There was only one row of kennels, and they all appeared located within one large room, like the way Save Them All Sanctuary was designed. That was the shelter for special-needs animals, which I found particularly appealing, since they took in pets that were hard to adopt out like seniors and the disabled.

I'd helped to solve a murder there recently.

This set was a fictional shelter, of course. Though some of the people working on *Sheba's Story* had visited HotRescues, this clearly hadn't been patterned after it.

Dr. Cyd Andelson arrived and I greeted her. She took Winna aside to discuss any medical issues that had arisen with the dogs. I'd check with her later to see if there were any problems.

After taking in the vastness of this room, I began to zero in on groups of people until I found the ones I was looking for. Off to the side of the kennel set, Dante stood with Niall, Grant, and Mick Paramus. They all

293

were deep in conversation — one in which I wanted to become engaged. Edging through the noisy crew and others manipulating lighting, cameras, and more equipment, I headed in their direction.

Dante moved back from the circle to let me join. "Hi, Lauren. We've been discussing how this scene will be shot. No likelihood of danger to the animals. They'll mostly remain in the kennels, being oohed and aahed over by the people who've come to the opening of the shelter to eat, drink, be merry, and contribute a lot of money."

I met his eyes and smiled briefly, silently acknowledging that he was describing himself — at least the part about making large contributions. "Sounds good. You're okay with it, Grant?"

Grant wore his American Humane Association vest, but he, too, had dressed up a bit this day in a nice shirt and slacks.

This wasn't a wrap-party day. There were many other scenes to be shot. But it looked like everyone had decided to act as if they were invited to the pseudo-celebration being filmed today.

"That's the way it was planned." Grant smiled warmly, which made me flush just a little. I nodded.

No one else said anything for a long moment. None met my eyes, either.

I gathered I was persona non grata in this crowd as with everyone else, as Jerry Amalon had warned. Oh, well. I could don a pretty thick skin if I had to.

In fact, I could even turn this into a joke.

"So — anyone going to confess on camera today to getting rid of the old director so Mick could take charge?" I asked with a grin while raising my eyebrows.

"Not on camera, I expect," Dante responded as if I'd been serious. In some ways, I was. "But we're not being filmed right now. Anyone ready to talk?" He turned to scan the faces around us. No one met his eyes, either. He laughed. "Okay. Lauren and I have talked about her inquiries the other day. I expect that all of us would be relieved to know the truth. Well, all except whoever really is guilty. Maybe the timing's not right. Let's hope the killer decides to confess around the time *Sheba's Story* is being released. We'll get an even bigger audience that way."

As Dante joked — sort of — I looked at each man in this group, in turn. I saw nothing on anyone's face that shouted a confession of guilt. Oh, well. Clearly my little game the other day had accomplished nothing but making people uncomfortable in my presence.

But they'd have to get used to it. That's what Dante's funding told them, as long as he wanted me around.

Things were finally ready. One of those nimble double-jointed cameras on a boom lifted high above the set, and a bunch of guys with cameras resting on their shoulders came close to the kennel area, too. The dogs were already in position.

Mick Paramus moved away from this group and took a position near the set. "Action," he finally called, and the shoot began.

It was definitely a party scene. Lots of extras flowed in and made a fuss over the kenneled dogs, then went off to sip carbonated water from champagne glasses and look festive as Lyanne Shroeder, playing a beaming Millie Roland, thanked them all for coming and invited everyone to contribute to her new Sheba's Shelter.

The repetition went on for four shoots.

"Time to take the dogs out for a walk and drinks," R. G. finally yelled, after a consultation with Mick.

Good call, I thought. Grant Jefferly, who'd been off screen near the kennel area, smiled and nodded.

I'd been sitting in a folding chair beside

ones occupied by Dante and Niall. Niall had whispered his cheers and criticisms to Dante after each take.

I kept Niall fairly high on my suspect list, even though he was Dante's friend. He had a lot at stake with this production, since he'd written it and was one of the producers. He apparently hadn't gotten along well with Hans. Plus, he seemed to really like the job Mick was doing.

Was that enough reason to have killed the former director?

Then again, there was still Mick Paramus himself. Not to mention that other director Erskine Blainer, who had nothing to do with this film but everything to do with *A Matter of Death and Life,* the other movie Hans had hoped to direct.

How was I ever going to resolve this?

Or maybe, this time, I wouldn't be able to. If not, what would happen to Carlie?

I followed the dog handlers while they took the canine stars for a walk. "They're real troopers," I told Winna. "So are all of you. I think you're taking great care of them."

"Thanks." Her word was brief but not too curt, so I wondered if she was thawing a bit toward me.

Dante left after three more takes but

dubbed me his agent in front of this crowd again. I was sort of glad, but I really wanted to get back to HotRescues.

I nevertheless enjoyed watching the party scene, celebrating the opening of this fictitious shelter. When the scene wrapped, Winna let me take not a minor canine's leash, but the real Sheba's to walk her, then take her back to the dog hotel. Too bad I hadn't brought my camera again today. But, then, I'd mostly wanted to take pictures for Dante when he wasn't here.

The four young assistant handlers followed us. One moved around to open the gates of the posh kennel areas, which were carpeted and furnished with comfy-looking dog beds.

All of us handlers walked our dogs up to the doors of their living quarters and unleashed them, ready to close them inside — when a loud noise reverberated throughout the room.

I gasped and jumped — and lost hold of Sheba's collar. I noticed that most of the others no longer controlled their dog charges either. Dogs, seven of them, started running around.

I realized quickly that the noise had been caused by Elena, who apparently hadn't been watching where she was going and had somehow tripped in such a way that a folding chair near the kennel area had been slammed into the glass front, shattering it.

Clearly, these weren't built with materials as substantial as we used at HotRescues. Were the dogs' paws in danger? Elena was, at least, shooing the pups away, using her feet to shuffle the glass into a pile.

Even so, we had a canine riot on our hands.

"Sheba, sit," I commanded, but the poor dog was clearly too frazzled to listen. Same went for the rest, or so it appeared.

Winna dashed after one poodle waving a leash and commanding, "Sit!" The assistant handlers followed her lead.

That's when I noticed it. As Jerry followed Stellar, who also ignored his commands, he was obviously as agitated as the rest of us.

So agitated that he reached his right hand over his head to scratch his sandy hair above his left ear in an awfully familiar gesture.

CHAPTER 26

I stood still for a long moment, keeping my eye on Jerry. He bent to pick up Stellar to keep her paws away from the glass. Noble, and correct. I did the same with Sheba. Good thing they weren't large dogs.

"I'm so sorry," Elena cried. She, too, hugged the dog in her charge. Winna was a little farther away so her poodle wasn't in any danger.

Good thing all the humans, including me, wore rubber-soled flat shoes, since they were what had been recommended for the running around to be done during the filming. Athletic shoes are what I often wear at HotRescues, too. They were substantial enough not to allow glass to get through to any feet.

Jerry didn't meet my gaze, though I didn't have the sense he was avoiding me. He seemed oblivious as he carefully picked his way around the glass, helping the other handlers with their dogs.

So why did this apparently nice kid break into HotRescues, let our dogs loose, and show that he could, if he'd wanted, poison our inhabitants?

And did all of this mean he had killed Hans? If so, I had to assume it was because he hadn't liked how the dogs had been put into danger that last day of Hans's being in charge. Or was there more to it than that?

How could I find out — and if he was guilty, prove it? Which I had to do, to help Carlie.

Too bad Dante had already left. I wasn't sure enough that Niall was guilt-free to talk this over with him, nor did it make sense to tell Grant Jefferly or Dr. Cyd.

But I had friends I could discuss this with, even though they weren't here.

I considered my next move. The filming, at least that involving the dogs, was apparently over for the day.

With smiles at all the others who protected the dogs, I helped to put the canines into enclosures far away from the broken glass. Then I stood off to the side with the other handlers. All of them. Including Jerry.

"I'm glad the glass in the front kennels at HotRescues is more solid than what's here," I said to no one in particular, although I

301

kept watch on Jerry from the corner of my eye.

"Really? You have glass on your kennel doors, too?" asked Elena. "I figured that real shelters looked more like the ones I've seen other places, with wire fencing and gates."

"A lot do," I said. "Even nice ones, although some pretty ratty shelters use fencing that's dented and rusting. Ours were always nicely maintained, but we recently remodeled at HotRescues. We decided on glass for some of our runs to make it even easier for potential adopters to see our dogs and fall for them."

Jerry looked at me. "Really? I've never seen that, though I don't get to many shelters. Does glass help?"

"We hope so," I said noncommittally. I wanted to shout at him about his last shelter visit, but confronting him here wouldn't be productive.

How could I get him to admit what he had done at HotRescues?

"I'd like to visit HotRescues one of these days," Elena said. "I heard you'll be taking in the dogs who were rescued for *Sheba's Story* when the filming's over if they aren't otherwise adopted."

I smiled at the young handler, who'd put her dog into one of the kennels and now stood outside its gate. "That's my hope," I said. "And you know you all have a standing invitation to see what a real shelter looks like — mine — and to meet my volunteers and staff, in case that helps with the care of the pups here."

And if they happened to take me up on it now, I would love to see Jerry pretend that he'd never been there before . . .

I turned to Winna. "When's the next filming involving these sweethearts?"

She shrugged. "Most likely tomorrow, but I'm not sure. We're always around to take care of them anyway, at least as long as shooting continues, so it doesn't matter."

Not to them, maybe. But I still wanted answers.

"There'll still be some filming tomorrow even though it's Saturday?" I asked, recalling that weekends didn't matter to people busily shooting a film.

"I think we're off on Sunday this week, aren't we?" Elena asked.

"Could be," Winna responded.

"Guess it would sort of be a busman's holiday," I said, "but maybe you could all come visit HotRescues then."

No one accepted my invitation. But I'd come back tomorrow — and in the meantime, I might get some backup to put the

303

plan that had started germinating in my mind into motion.

For now, it was time for me to go back to HotRescues.

"You're sure it's him?" Brooke asked.

Zoey and I had waited until late that evening. One of Brooke's contract staff members was hanging out overnight, but Brooke came when I asked her to so we could discuss what had happened that day.

So had Antonio. And Matt. We all were out at a large family restaurant a few miles from HotRescues, after leaving Zoey and Cheyenne with their own dinner at the shelter. Matt's Rex was alone at their house, so he definitely would go home that night.

We had all ordered beers, just what I needed to try to relax. I was extremely keyed up over what I'd seen and what I thought I now needed to do. But these folks were more than friends. I'd listen to their input and advice.

Then do what I decided.

"All I know," I said in response to Brooke's question, "is that the gesture that young dog handler Jerry made isn't something you see often. But it's the same thing the intruder did on the security video. Could it be someone else? Sure, since the intruder was disguised and we couldn't tell much about him. That's why I want to try to check Jerry out to see his reaction at HotRescues."

"Makes sense." Antonio took a long swig of his beer, a darker one than I'd ordered. When he put his glass back on the table, he looked at me with his incisive dark cop's eyes from beneath his jutting brow. His uneven features would have unnerved me if I hadn't known what a good guy he was. Had he been in one of his detective suits, I'd have felt like I was about to undergo one heck of an interrogation, even without his asking anything. "But there's something you need to agree to, Lauren."

I almost called out, "Anything." Instead, I smiled and caught Matt's gaze. Darned if he didn't look as piercing as Antonio. I didn't look away from him, though. I had a feeling that Brooke would look as serious.

"What's that?" I managed somehow to keep my tone light.

"We'll have plenty of backup in the area of HotRescues," Antonio said. "Even so, you're not to let yourself get off alone with this Jerry, no matter what happens. Even if a dog is in trouble. Got that?"

I nodded. "Okay."

"Will you be able to get everyone there at

HotRescues on Sunday?" Brooke asked.

"I'm pretty sure of it," I said, "as long as Dante backs me up."

We enjoyed our dinners, then went back to HotRescues. From there, we all headed home.

But Zoey and I perked up awhile after we got to our place and the doorbell rang. I knew who it was.

Matt had gone home to get Rex. Now, they were going to stay the night.

I was getting tired of this. Not just trying to prove who killed Hans Marford, but also spending so much time at Solario Studios and other filming locations.

It wasn't as if I hadn't plenty to do at HotRescues, which was where I was at the moment. Temporarily.

At least today promised to be interesting, since Dante was also going to be at the studio again.

Yes, he'd returned my call early that morning just after Matt and Rex had dashed out of my place. I'd told Dante about that strange gesture the kid Jerry Amalon had made — again. "I'd like to get him to come to HotRescues tomorrow to see his reaction to being back there once more. Maybe he'll repeat that move out of nervousness, or just for fun, to taunt us in case we hadn't seen it the first time."

"Maybe," Dante had agreed. "Tell you what. I'll meet you at the studio today and make sure you get your wish. All the dog handlers from the production will come to HotRescues tomorrow so you can observe Jerry's reaction."

"Really?" I exclaimed so enthusiastically that Zoey, who'd been lying at my feet at my office desk, sat up and woofed. I laughed.

I stopped laughing, though, when Dante laid out the conditions under which he would decree that everyone — including Jerry — show up at HotRescues. One: I had to promise to stay around other people the entire time the handlers were present — staff, volunteers, whoever. Two, I had to call EverySecurity before anyone showed up and have them make certain that all the security cameras were working and that they would watch those cameras in real time. And, three, Brooke's Antonio had to be present, too, or have someone else there from the LAPD undercover and immediately available.

"You're always provoking people," Dante finished. "That's a good thing if those people are abusing animals, of course, and I applaud it. I can't fault you for solving murders, either, if that's your hobby."

I felt stung. It was definitely not my hobby. "Like your Kendra's, you mean?"

He laughed. "Don't let her hear you say that."

"I don't like it any more than she does."

"Okay. Forget it. But I'll see you later at the studio."

Sure enough, just after I showed my ID and stepped through the gate I spotted Dante standing in the street in front of the nearest building, talking to Mick Paramus and Morton Lesque.

Not wanting to interrupt anything despite my raging curiosity about their conversation, I dodged a few slow cars and headed down the busy studio avenue to the building where the animals were kenneled. No one was around. They had to already be on the set.

I went there next, in time to watch another scene being rehearsed under the direction of R. G. — a fairly bland scene where the dogs were all in a large room together, communicating.

I knew that when this scene was shown in the final movie the dogs would be conversing by telepathy in English, talking over whether they should stay in this place or run away. The Sheba dog would already have bonded with the Millie character, and all the dogs now had a roof over their heads and enough food to eat — plus they had shelter volunteers giving them a lot of attention. In the script, they wondered why things had suddenly gotten so good for them. They didn't trust it.

None of them but Sheba, who told the others to give this new situation more of a chance.

I could hardly wait to see the final product.

Meanwhile, I watched the rehearsal scene, with Cowan giving hand signals to the dogs. He'd brought a couple of assistants whom I'd seen before. The choreography of the scene was a little tricky considering that all the dogs had to act right on cue, but, surprisingly, it started to come together. The animal handlers, including Jerry Amalon, were at the far side of the set. So were Dr. Cyd and Grant.

I had a sense of isolation, as if I was quarantined from the other animal people. Or being avoided by them. I shrugged it off. Loneliness isn't my style. Besides, I'd come in late. That was all.

I joined the others as soon as the scene had played out. Everyone was friendly and acted as if they were glad to see me. I smiled, chatted — and watched Jerry as he hurried to check on the dogs along with Winna, Elena, and the other handlers.

He wasn't avoiding me more than any of the others.

Dante and those he'd been conversing with eventually came in, too, and Dante made his pronouncement. Gathering up the same animal people, he took them, and me, off to one side. "You know, as much as I've loved seeing how you all treat the dogs here, and how your shelter set looks, I want to make sure you're aware of how real shelter dogs are treated. I've talked it over with Director Paramus." And the head of the studio, although he didn't say that. He didn't have to. He had walked in with both of them. "I've also talked it over with Lauren." He looked at me, and I nodded.

I saw Grant's double take. Did the American Humane rep think he should have been consulted, too? What did he anticipate Dante would be saying?

"You're all invited to tour HotRescues tomorrow. You'll be shown the best of the best." He looked at Winna, who stood near me. "I definitely want all the handlers to attend." When Dante said he definitely wanted something, everyone listened. I wasn't surprised when Winna nodded, then turned to her assistants as if to make certain they got the message.

"Should be fun," Jerry said. Was he just trying to cover himself?

One of the handlers said she already had plans for the next day, which was Sunday. The others all seemed eager to go.

I could hardly wait until tomorrow.

CHAPTER 27

Tomorrow did arrive, as always, right on time. I got to HotRescues early — not unusual when I didn't have something else interrupting me.

Dante had requested that the dog handlers appear there around ten A.M., which was fine with me. That was after the shelter opened for potential adopters to come and meet our residents. Not that we often had a crowd lined up waiting to get in, but this timing would let us prepare for our expected visitors.

At the moment, I sat at the table beneath the window in our welcome area. Nina sat across from me. "Do you really think this is a good idea?" she asked. Her frown drew additional lines on her forehead and at the sides of her eyes. She was younger than me, but always used to look frazzled because of what her abusive marriage had done to her. Now, she didn't look frazzled very often, but the wrinkles hadn't completely gone away.

"Don't know," I admitted. "But if that kid Jerry was our intruder, he'll have a hard time pretending he's never been here before."

"Maybe, but if it was him I'm sure he's already thought of a way to disclaim or explain it. He's certainly had time to consider what to do."

"Thanks for your perspective," I said, meaning it. "He could be an actor like everyone involved with the movie. If so, he's a good one. He appears too nice to be a menace who threatened to poison our dogs. And whoever it was probably had no motive to be here if he wasn't involved in Hans's death — unless it had something to do with Hope and Councilman Randell instead. So . . ."

"So, we'll just have to see," Nina finished, smiling. "You're in the right profession, Lauren."

I frowned at her, puzzled. "What do you mean?"

"You're always so dogged about anything you get involved with."

I grinned. "Punning becomes you." Standing, I looked at my watch. Yes, I still wore one of those old-fashioned gadgets on my wrist, even though my young adult kids considered me woefully ancient in my worldview — and my failure to use my smartphone for every waking need.

It was nine fifteen. The *Sheba's Story* folks would start arriving soon, but I was already itching to get them here to start my observation.

"Come on, Zoey." She'd risen to her feet in anticipation as soon as I got up, and looked at me expectantly. "It's time to go visit everyone again."

"The dogs and kitties could hardly have forgotten your last visit," Nina said, "since you just got back here ten minutes ago."

True, but I figured that checking out everything again would take just enough time.

I hadn't counted on receiving a call, though. That smartphone I'd ignored when I checked the time rang in my pocket. I pulled it out.

"Hi, Carlie," I said. Zoey and I still walked down the hall toward the door to the shelter area. "How are you today?" I was being either mean or overprotective. Or both. But I hadn't told Carlie what I was up to today, or why.

"I'm okay," she said. "I'm working on editing a *Pet Fitness* show — one that has

314

nothing to do with the film industry. It's about how pets do after surviving a life-threatening disease. I've interviewed families of some of our clinic's patients for their perspective, and I wondered whether we could talk to Miracle and you on camera about how she got over parvo a while ago."

"Absolutely," I said. "She's been here long enough." The sweet Basset-Lab had been here for quite a few months. "Maybe the exposure will help her find a new home. When would you like to do it?"

"Sometime this morning?"

"Let's make it late this afternoon." I hoped she wouldn't ask why this morning wouldn't work. I wasn't really sure of my availability this afternoon either, but I could get someone else to show off Miracle. I didn't want Carlie here this morning, especially with a camera crew, while I laid my potential trap for the HotRescues intruder.

"Okay." We talked a little more about timing. Carlie said, "I'd imagine that if you were working on any more ideas about catching whoever killed Hans, you'd let me know." It wasn't a question. We were good enough friends that she certainly made that assumption.

Even though at the moment it wasn't true.

315

"You know I'd keep you in the loop if there was anything important going on," I responded, sidestepping a direct answer.

But she did know me well. "Then there's something that's not important going on?"

I didn't want to lie to her, even if I didn't want to tell her the whole truth. "Honestly? I'm spending more time trying to catch the person who broke into HotRescues the other night. If that person turns out to be Hans's killer, I hope to figure that out, too. Either way, soon as that's resolved I'll concentrate more on your situation, Carlie. I promise."

By then, Zoey and I were outside. The dogs in the first kennels we passed had had volunteers inside with them, but the next group were alone and started barking — a behavior I normally discouraged, but it gave me a good excuse to end my conversation with Carlie. We could no longer hear each other as well.

I then asked all the volunteers to join me outside the kennels, in front of the storage building at the rear. Our handyman, Pete, too. I couldn't help smiling at Hope as we walked by. The poodle-cocker mix looked at me quizzically but stayed silent.

I checked my watch again. Nine thirty, closer to the time the film personnel would

316

arrive. I looked at the group of volunteers, who included Bev and Mamie, some high school kids doing community service for credit, young ladies Sally and Ricki, and others whom I also wouldn't want to endanger. Including Pete and the rest of our staff.

Heck, I didn't want to endanger anyone, including our resident pets. But what was about to happen here was just for observation. No reason for anyone to get hurt.

I told this group we were about to have visitors and asked the volunteers to act as tour guides, showing off our dogs and cats to these people. They wouldn't necessarily be interested in adopting but were involved in a film production that could really help draw attention to shelter animals.

Everyone seemed excited. I certainly was.

That was when I heard a page from Nina. "Lauren, to the front, please."

Let the games begin.

The first arrivals were, fortunately, those we'd intended to bring in and hide — Antonio and Brooke. I caught up with them just outside the door to the main building near the first group of kennels.

"I just talked to the operative on duty from EverySecurity," Brooke told me quietly. "They've checked out the cameras

317

remotely, and all seem to be working fine."

The three of us turned to look toward the cameras mounted on poles outside the kennel runs. The one on the right just to this side of the center building had caught the view of Jerry wandering through Hot-Rescues a few nights ago. We knew that one worked well, but it hadn't given us enough information to get our intruder arrested.

Not yet, at least.

We briefly discussed what I'd told the volunteers to do. "I sure hope we get something useful after all this," I said fervently.

"Amen," Antonio agreed.

"I didn't get a chance to talk to Pete, though, about what we expect of him."

"We'll do it," Brooke assured me.

I heard a low murmur of voices from inside. "I think they're starting to arrive."

"Antonio and I will go sit at the monitors after we talk to Pete," Brooke said. "Good luck."

"Thanks. I'll join you soon."

At the moment, though, I had people to greet. Zoey and I headed inside toward the welcome area.

I was surprised to find so many people from Sheba's Story there. I'd thought it would just be Winna with her assistants. But Grant Jefferly was there, too, in his American Humane vest, and so was Cowan in his standard all-black outfit, and even Millie Roland — rather, her real counterpart, Lyanne Shroeder, wearing a lot of makeup but not as much as when she was about to be filmed. They were all crammed into the relatively small welcome area. So were Mick Paramus and R.G. Nina was passing around a sign-in sheet. That might not be necessary since I knew these people. On the other hand, it would be good to have an official record in case we needed to verify later who'd attended.

"Good to see you all," I said. "Go ahead and sign in, and then I'll take you into the kennel area." I paused, slowly sucked in my breath, then asked, "Have any of you been here before?"

I looked directly at Winna but could see Jerry out of the corner of my eye. He was shaking his head. So were others.

Maybe they hadn't. Maybe I was all wet in suspecting Jerry on the basis of that one small gesture.

On the other hand, how many other people wrapped an arm around their head like that?

I did a quick, obvious scan of all of them so it wouldn't appear strange for my gaze to include Jerry. "You're in for a treat," I said, "one that Hans Marford experienced since he'd wanted to see what a well-run animal shelter looked like."

He had come with Niall and Dante, neither of whom was here today. Of those two, I still kept Niall on my suspect list but didn't believe he'd been our intruder. Nor did I envision the poised writer and assistant producer making that odd, distinctive gesture. Even so, I'd try to keep an open mind.

Could I be certain that the person who had broken in the other night was in this group?

Maybe not, but my bet was on Jerry.

"This should be fun," Elena said. "You know how we love animals." She looked toward Jerry and Winna for their confirmation, and both nodded. "We've heard such great things about HotRescues." The young handler smiled.

Maybe she was laying it on too thick, but I smiled back. "All of it is true." I saw Grant hand the clipboard back to Nina, who gave a half-salute to show that everyone had signed in. "And now you can see for yourself." I gestured toward the hall to the kennel area. "You all head that way and I'll meet you outside. I want to leave Zoey with Nina."

And to get Nina's initial impression. But,

as she shepherded Zoey into the area behind the welcome desk, she just gave a tiny shrug. She had no insight for me, at least not yet.

I'd already talked things over with Antonio and Brooke. They'd be watching the security camera in real time, as would the Every-Security operative, wherever he was.

I would watch in real time, too, to see Jerry's reaction as he went into the shelter area.

And we were going to do something I absolutely never did.

Time to go see how it worked out.

"They're really cute," Winna said as she peered into the first kennels on the left in our initial shelter area. A couple of the dogs were barking. Others were sitting behind their glass doors as if regally awaiting the notice of their subjects so they would be given the petting and other attention they deserved. "I see what you mean about a great shelter. Everything is clean, and they all look so well cared for."

"That's for sure," said Mamie Spelling, who had come to greet the *Sheba's Story* folks along with the other volunteers I'd spoken with earlier. She sounded so proud it made me grin — both in affirmation of what she said, and because I remained glad that this former hoarder now helped so well around here.

I remained behind the visitors, observing Jerry but also trying to keep close watch on them all.

They all gushed over our highly deserving residents, but none gave any indication of having been here before.

I admit that I'd really hoped it would be that simple. But I'm no fool. It had been a long shot.

And that long shot appeared to be missing its mark.

On impulse, I maneuvered around some of them to stand between Bev and Mamie. "I'd like to introduce you to some of the junior handlers on the set," I told them. "This is Elena, and this is Jerry. And the senior handler there, that is Winna. This is the first time any of them have come to HotRescues."

Okay, I was being repetitious, but I was still watching for any change in attitude, anything at all to indicate that Jerry was hiding something.

"Are you interested in becoming volunteers here?" Mamie asked.

Good question. One that could possibly elicit some kind of helpful reaction.

"Maybe," Elena said. "I'm really impressed with it all." She waved her hand dramatically around in a smooth, model's gesture, as if attempting to encompass everything she saw.

"Me, too," Jerry said. "I can see now why some of the shelter scenes are being shot the way they are. I know Mr. DeFrancisco would want us to make a good impression on our film audience, and keeping things looking like HotRescues should do that."

Sounded as if they were trying to outdo one another so word would get back to Dante. It never hurt to have a wealthy producer on one's side.

But that wasn't helping me.

I herded the crowd through the rows of kennels. Pete came out of the ground floor of the center building. He looked at me quizzically.

Brooke must have just spoken with him. I nodded.

This group continued forward, at least one person pausing in front of each kennel to talk to the dog or two inside.

That left the dogs in the kennels we passed alone once more.

But not exactly.

I turned slightly and nodded to Pete. He, in turn, did as Brooke had undoubtedly told him.

Starting with the kennel nearest the entrance to the building, he first tested its door, which stayed shut. Then he started opening the kennel gates. Not all of them, but only those of dogs we already knew got along together.

I'd already checked the gates nearest the rear of the shelter, around the storage building, and felt confident that everything was secure.

Everything except the states of mind, I hoped, of our visitors — or at least one of them.

In moments, the place looked as it had the night our intruder had been there, with dogs running all over the place.

"Hey!" Grant Jefferly called out in alarm. Obviously he wouldn't be able to verify that no animals around here were being endangered — not that he had to.

"What's happening?" Winna was the next one to apparently freak out. Her subordinate handlers looked dazed, then upset. "Cowan," she shouted, "how do we get these dogs under control?"

Pete and the rest of our kennel staff and volunteers were suddenly in the midst of things, snapping leashes on the eight or nine dogs that were dashing around.

Mick Paramus and R. G. looked shocked, but they did attempt to grab some of the

324

dogs' collars to catch them, too.

"Sit," Cowan said to Shazam, the Doberman who'd run up to him. Of course well-behaved Shazam obeyed.

Not so all the other dogs, though. But once they were leashed, they were all okay.

I'd been worried about all the animals, but I also trusted my staff and volunteers, who'd been let in on what was about to happen and given instructions on how to help.

I'd been watching the dogs carefully anyway, in case we had any real problems, which we didn't.

But neither did we have anyone make the gesture we'd seen on the security footage the night of the break-in.

Not even Jerry Amalon.

CHAPTER 28

I wasn't happy.

Never mind that the killers in the murders I'd previously solved didn't just appear on computer monitors waving at me or making strange gestures. I'd wanted an easy answer this time.

Not that I'd have had foolproof evidence of Jerry's guilt in killing Hans, even if he'd stared at the running dogs and gotten discombobulated enough again to make that odd motion. But at least it would have given the authorities reason to interrogate him for the break-in here and ask why he'd chosen HotRescues — like, if he had a grudge against me for asking if he was guilty of Hans's murder. Or because I'd asked a lot of people that . . . and got them thinking more about who else could be guilty.

For now, I calmly helped our staff round up the dogs and return them to their kennels.

"Everything all right around here, Lauren?" asked Grant. I'd just returned Hope to her enclosure and took an extra minute to stay near the poor, sweet thing who watched me soulfully, as if she accepted without question this additional oddity in her life.

"You mean, are all the animals okay?" I responded. "Yes, they're fine. We just had a bit of a miscommunication." That was my overt excuse.

"You know," he said pensively, "I've heard so many good things about HotRescues' reputation as one of the best pet shelters around. I'd never have thought a mistake like that could be made."

I looked into his narrowed blue eyes. I had the uncomfortable feeling that he was attempting to read my thoughts.

"Not usually," I said with a rueful shrug. I wanted to make it clear that my facility was every bit as good as what he'd heard. Even better. Instead, I continued, "We're all just a little flustered over that break-in. I'll be talking to our people about taking extra care. You can be sure of that."

"But I noticed . . ."

"What?" I prompted.

"I thought you'd be a lot angrier over something like those dogs getting loose. It was almost as if you expected — wanted — it."

I'd be upset if I believed that Grant had been our intruder and had analyzed me so correctly. Right or wrong, I believed I could trust the American Humane representative. Maybe that was because of how much he clearly cared about animal welfare.

Even so . . . "Of course not," I said, although my tone remained light. I wasn't admitting anything.

Neither did I show any anger at what amounted to an accusation from him. Not when he was right.

"Well . . ." He smiled, revealing his white teeth. "Keep me informed." He turned and followed the group of *Sheba's Story* folks being shown into the newer area of our shelter on a continuation of their tour.

I didn't ask what he meant, but I sort of admired Grant for his intelligent grasp of what I hadn't said. I also didn't like it.

What if he was more involved than I'd thought?

Folding my arms, I followed Grant.

One group of our visitors had already turned the corner into the kennel area within the newest part of HotRescues. Grant caught up and followed Mamie into the building where our smaller dogs and puppies were housed downstairs, with offices above. Cowan was with them. Mamie was so short that I could barely see her, despite Cowan's not being much taller.

Bev and our other volunteers remained with the rest of the visitors. I stayed far enough back that I couldn't hear what she was saying, but everyone seemed to be separating into smaller groups to look in the nearest kennels.

Unsurprisingly, each group was comprised of the people who worked most closely together. Mick and R. G. stayed close to Bev, who showed off the enclosures back here, which were of a different design but equal quality to the ones in the front. The gates here were chain link instead of glass.

All the animal handlers except Winna were as youthful as Sally and Ricki, who acted as their tour guides. This group stayed in the courtyard. Sally pointed out our picnic area, where people interested in adopting could visit and bond with the dog they wanted to get to know better.

Jerry looked interested, as if he were seeing this all for the first time. That could in fact be true for this part of HotRescues, since he'd been seen only in our older area.

But I wished I could hear what he was saying. What they all were saying.

I knew I'd be told if any of the *Sheba's Story* people happened to mention anything looking familiar. Our volunteers had been primed to listen for that.

But I wanted more.

Watching from this distance didn't do me any good. I decided to go inside with Brooke and Antonio. Our security cameras didn't have sound, but they could zoom in on an area.

Would that help me learn something useful? Or was today just a total waste?

No, it couldn't be. If nothing else, we had a lot of new visitors to HotRescues who were involved with a movie where rescued dogs were stars. That could only help publicize us and our inhabitants who needed new homes.

Although word could also get out that our staff was careless, and I was indifferent, and —

Damn! I had to stop this!

I turned abruptly and started walking back toward our older shelter area — and nearly ran into Pete, who was hurrying toward me. We both stopped without colliding.

"Everything okay, Lauren?" The expression on the handyman's face looked guilty, as if he anticipated that I was about to

chew him out for letting the dogs loose —
despite my telling him to do so in the first
place.

"Everything's fine," I told him. "You did
the right thing." I hesitated. "Everything is
okay, isn't it? I mean, all the dogs are back
where they belong?"

"Sure. I checked. And then I checked
again. But you looked so upset that I was
worried."

I made myself give a quick laugh. "Then
you're always worried," I joked. "Don't I
always look upset?"

He laughed a little, too. "If you say so.
Mostly, I'd say you almost always look
stern, like you take everything around here
seriously. That's the right way to be."

I wanted to hug him. Instead, I shot him
a genuine smile. "You looking for a raise,
Engersol?"

"You giving me one, Vancouver?"

"Tell you what. Be my extra set of eyes
there, where our volunteers are still giving
tours. I'll be back outside soon."

I edged around him, then turned to see
Pete approaching the nearest group, the
animal handlers.

He had helped my mood, at least a little.
But I still wanted another perspective on
this crowd.

Maybe, somehow, I'd still get the view I wanted.

"So how are the cameras working?"

Brooke and Antonio sat side by side on chairs, arms touching, at the small desk in the downstairs security office, watching a computer screen. I felt a bit like an interloper as I joined them. But I had only caught them doing security work, nothing racy. Besides, they knew I was coming.

I took a position behind them, peering over Brooke's shoulder at the black-and-white pictures. The controls allowed the observer to choose which camera to monitor, or even post several of the videos on the screen at one time. That's what they had going now — the pictures from both cameras panning over the newer area of Hot-Rescues.

"They're doing a good job," Brooke said. "We watched the dogs get loose, with Pete's help. If he hadn't been under orders to do that, we'd have been on his case pretty much instantaneously."

"Great. He seems worried now, so give him a pat on the back when you see him." I leaned over to look more closely at the screen. "Nothing looks much different from when I left."

Brooke looked up with her smiling amber eyes. "You expect all hell to break loose when you walk away?"

"No. I was just hoping that a certain visitor would look up toward the camera and shout that not only had he been here before, but he'd let the dogs loose last time. And then confess to murder."

Antonio laughed. "Good thing cops don't have your kind of expectations, Lauren, or we'd all be nuts in no time."

"Isn't that a given — to become a cop, you have to be nuts?"

We all shared a laugh, but only momentarily. I'd noticed something and bent over Brooke's shoulder, staring at the screen.

"Did you see that?" I all but gasped.

"Well, hell. You may not be getting your entire wish, Lauren," Antonio said, "but looks like at least part of it's coming true."

Jerry Amalon was standing beside Elena, right outside the last kennel run before the cat house. Inside was Fletcher, a Lab mix we'd recently rescued from a high-kill shelter.

Jerry wasn't looking at Fletcher.

I wasn't sure what he was looking at. Maybe nothing.

But he'd just looped his arm over his head in the same gesture I'd seen him make at

Solario Studios.

The same one, too, that our intruder had made on our security tape a couple of nights ago.

CHAPTER 29

We all stood at once.

Antonio shot a glare back at Brooke and me. "Let me handle this."

That was all right with me. He was a cop. He knew the drill as far as approaching a suspect and arresting him.

But wasn't that premature?

Antonio didn't look official that day. He wasn't wearing any kind of uniform, not even a suit. But his T-shirt and jeans could work as an undercover uniform, couldn't they?

Besides, I was sure he had his badge with him. Wouldn't he always? That would make him official enough.

I followed the others out of the apartment and down the stairs, then toward the area where Jerry had been captured on the security video.

Antonio's long legs caused his stride to be a lot faster than either Brooke's or mine.

He was also agile in the way he maneuvered among the *Sheba's Story* visitors and the HotRescues volunteers. Soon, Antonio reached the kennel housing Fletcher. Jerry still stood there with Elena. They were so involved in a heated conversation that they didn't seem aware of either the nearest dog — or the arms of justice that were about to embrace Jerry.

"Hi, folks," Antonio said, interrupting them. He planted himself so close that they couldn't avoid being aware of his presence. "You're with that *Sheba's Story* production, aren't you?"

"That's right." Elena's expression looked quizzical. "Do you work here at Hot-Rescues?"

"No," Antonio said. "I'm with the Los Angeles Police Department." He pulled the badge I knew he'd have with him from his jeans pocket and flashed it. "Are you Jerry Amalon?"

Jerry's complexion, reddened by whatever Elena and he had been talking about, suddenly faded to blizzard white — an even starker contrast with his black Solario Studios T-shirt. "Yes," he croaked. Then, more strongly, he asked, "How do you know my name?"

"Why don't we go somewhere private to

336

discuss that?" Antonio reached to grasp Jerry's arm.

"What's this about?" Jerry looked frantically toward me as he resisted Antonio.

"It's about the last time you were at HotRescues," I answered coldly, getting an angry glare from Antonio. I suppose he would have preferred that I said nothing. Since I had, Jerry might now have a little more time to come up with some flimsy excuse.

But Jerry undoubtedly knew just what this was about, so he'd already had plenty of time to come up with whatever story he thought would work.

"Like I told everyone before, this is my first time at HotRescues." His words ended on a sob, and I noticed he had tears in his eyes.

As much as I like to pride myself on my expertise in reading people, I was taken aback. He sounded, and looked, really genuine.

On the other hand, he was in the film industry. I hadn't originally thought him to be a wannabe actor, but my opinion had wavered. Even so, he was putting on one heck of a convincing act.

"Why do you think he was here before?" Elena had taken a step forward as if she wanted to protect her coworker. I'd already figured there was something more between them than handling animals together.

Antonio shot me a fierce glare. So did Brooke, who stood behind him. They must have thought I was going to say something about that tell-all gesture.

I knew better.

"That's something I need to discuss with him," Antonio said to Elena. Then, directed at Jerry, "Will you please come with me?"

Before he responded, two guys in suits strode up from around the rear corner of the shelter. They were followed by Nina, who looked relieved to see me. She joined me as the two men started talking to Brooke.

That told me who they were.

I moved away from the crowd, whose members from the studio mostly looked bewildered — and curious. I didn't want them to know what was going on.

"These two men," Nina whispered to me when we stood near the cat house entry. "They showed me their IDs. They're from EverySecurity and said they saw something on the monitor they were watching that required a visit."

I nodded. "They're right, but Antonio's in charge, not them."

Together, we approached where Brooke spoke with the two guys. They, too, had distanced themselves from the crowd. "Thanks for coming, gentlemen," I said, "but as I'm sure Brooke has told you we have things under control, thanks to the presence of an LAPD detective."

"But no one —" one of the suits began.

"I'm Lauren Vancouver, head administrator of HotRescues. If you'd like to wait in my office till we see how things go here, that will be fine."

In fact, I told them I'd walk them there. I'd already suggested that Antonio take Jerry upstairs to the security apartment.

First, though, I looked around at our *Sheba's Story* visitors. "Excuse us, gang," I said. "I'll be back with you in a few minutes, but for now our volunteers will take you to see anything else at HotRescues that you think may be helpful for the rest of the filming. Okay?" I didn't wait to find out if it was okay but started walking the EverySecurity guys toward the front of my shelter.

Once we were out of earshot, I learned from them that they had indeed been watching the monitors in real time, as directed by Brooke. Though that gesture Jerry made when he broke in here had been kept secret from the *Sheba's Story* crew and the media, our security company personnel were well aware of it.

They also knew that our security director Brooke had a direct in with the cops.

"So you see," I said as we reached the ground floor of the main building, "I'm not sure what you can do right now to help. But I'll make sure Antonio knows that you stand ready to do whatever the police need from you."

The two men looked irritated, but they apparently knew when they weren't wanted.

"All right," said the older one with the least amount of gray hair. "But you'll let Mr. DeFrancisco know that EverySecurity was here?"

"Sure," I said. I met Nina's eye. She had followed us in here. "Please show these gentlemen out."

"Of course." She inserted herself between them. "You know, you're welcome back here anytime. We appreciate your monitoring HotRescues so well these days." That was a dig about the old days when they had screwed up. "And anytime you or any of your friends or family are interested in adopting a dog or cat, please come and meet some of the best available pets around."

With that, she opened the door. With a last glower, both men left.

"Thanks," I told her.

"Is Dante going to be okay with this?" she asked, looking worried.

"Sure," I said. "His instructions were that I should be sure Antonio knew what I wanted to try by inviting the Sheba's Story gang, so he could either be here or send other cops. Antonio is questioning Jerry even as we speak." I filled Nina in on Jerry's telling gesture. "Both Brooke and Antonio, and the EverySecurity folks, saw it on their security camera monitors. Having EverySecurity involved was another of Dante's requests. I'm sure they'll follow up to make sure that Dante is happy with their reaction."

"Okay. Did Dante say anything else?"

"Only that I had to be careful." I didn't mention that I was supposed to keep myself surrounded by other people. She was with me now. I'd make sure I didn't put myself in harm's way, but how could I now, with our suspect being interrogated by the police?

"You will be careful, won't you, Lauren?" Nina stood straight, clutching the side of the welcome desk with one hand as if supporting herself in case my answer was negative.

But it was positive. "Of course I will. I'm always careful."

I stopped in my office to get Zoey as I passed by. Her company would be more gratifying than any of the visitors'. I liked Grant well enough and definitely valued his protective attitude about animals. I hadn't developed much of an opinion about Mick Paramus, and I wasn't wild about R. G. I thought Cowan a bit too chilly to be the best animal trainer. And I was a lot less fond now of Winna and her assistant handlers. That probably wasn't fair. They weren't all responsible for what one of their number did.

Rather than joining them all outside again, I decided to do a little eavesdropping. Fortunately, Zoey was a quiet dog unless there was something for her to bark about. She and I both entered the downstairs security office in the center building. Upstairs was Brooke's apartment, and I heard voices coming from there.

I quickly led Zoey into the security room, hoping that the insulation was bad enough to let me hear what was being said. Unfortunately, it wasn't.

For a moment, I pondered trying to sneak unobtrusively upstairs. First, I had an urge to view once more what had given rise to my mixed feelings of vindication and anger against Jerry.

His stupid gesture.

Stupid in more ways than one. It looked nerdy and dumb. He'd also used it twice in condemning circumstances.

On impulse, I sat at the desk and clicked on the monitor, then scrolled back through the camera footage until I found it — Jerry standing beside Elena, right outside Fletcher's kennel, apparently engrossed in a discussion.

Jerry looked flummoxed — enough that a nervous gesture like the one he'd made hadn't been out of line.

Elena, who usually appeared airy and excited to me, looked emotional, although I couldn't read what emotion it was. Anger? She seemed to be sidling up close to Jerry. He'd move back, and she'd do it again.

And then that gesture.

I'd watched this before, of course. Seen it in person while outside.

Then, my eyes had been on Jerry. But this time . . . I looked at Elena. There was just a touch of a smile on her face that immediately evaporated. Like the emotion of their conversation, I wasn't really able to read it.

But it looked a lot like triumph to me before it disappeared.

Suddenly, I had another thought. A wonderment.

All the animal handlers must spend a lot of time together ensuring that the animals were walked, fed, and watered as much as needed. They might get to know each other well — especially those who seemed to have an additional relationship of some kind. They could learn each other's pleasures and boiling points.

And gestures.

I sat very still for a moment. From upstairs, I heard Antonio's voice raised and a squeal that could have been Jerry crying.

Where was Brooke? Probably right outside the room, since she couldn't be present if this was an official police interrogation.

I wished I could hear them.

I wished I could call to tell Antonio to slip in a few additional questions that had just popped into my mind.

But I couldn't.

There was one thing I could do, though.

"Come on, Zoey." I snapped on the leash I'd stuffed into my pocket. Then I led her out of the building and around toward the back loop, which would take us to where our visitors were still being shown around.

Only, on our way there, most of those visitors, and the volunteers acting as tour guides, slipped by on their way back toward the HotRescues exit.

344

"Thanks," called R. G. Mick Paramus saluted his appreciation. With them were Cowan and Grant and Winna and her crew.

But not all of them.

I almost started to panic. I counted all of our volunteers, too, and Pete Engersol. There was someone I didn't see, though.

Elena.

I thought of Dante's instructions that I wasn't to do anything alone. Well, I wasn't alone. Zoey was with me.

Besides, even if I was right, Elena wouldn't do anything here and now. It would be too obvious. And she loved animals. She wouldn't harm any . . . would she?

I hurried to the back area. Okay, I wasn't really being stupid. I made a quick call to Brooke, told her there might be something wrong and asked her to join me.

As I hung up, my phone vibrated again. Matt.

"Can't talk now," I said. "I think I was wrong. I think it may be one of the other animal handlers, and she's here right now."

"I'm here at HotRescues, too," he said. "Where are you? Wait for me, and I'll come with you."

"I'm in our new area but I don't see her. Come on back."

"Wait!"

But I'd hung up.

I didn't see Elena. But I heard a whole lot of noisy yaps from the building containing our smaller dogs.

Zoey and I quickly ducked inside.

"Oh, hi, Lauren," said the sweet, enthusiastic voice I expected to hear. "This has been such a great visit. I know it's time to leave, but I'm waiting for Jerry. I guess he's gone to the rest room. I can't find him. Which may be a good thing, since there were a couple of little dogs here that I wanted to see again."

Elena stood in front of one of the kennels that contained two small dogs, Pint-Size and Tiny, both Pomeranian mixes who'd been here for a while.

"They are cute, aren't they?" I approached, keeping Zoey at heel. "Are you interested in adopting?"

"I'm thinking about one of the Sheba poodles, but these are so sweet." So was she, all adorable in her Solario Studios T-shirt contrasting beautifully with her soft brown hair, her green eyes glowing as she smiled widely at me. So cute. So pretty.

So vile.

"Yes, they are," I agreed. "But you know," I went on conversationally, "I'm intending to take in the Sheba dogs once the filming is over. We do pretty thorough background checks and are very selective in our adoption process. We like actresses, of course, but people who put on an act to hurt our animals, or who try to frame other people for their crimes — well, I really don't consider them appropriate new moms for our dogs."

"What do you mean?" Her face still glowed with her smile, but that glow had turned more fiery. Her tone was less cheerful, too.

"Well, I suspect you're very much aware of the nervous gestures of your friends like Jerry. That you might even study them to use if you ever get acting roles — or to protect yourself. It's you who was our trespasser here at HotRescues, isn't it, Elena?"

Before I realized what she was doing, she had yanked a leash from her own pocket and swirled it around my throat.

As I gagged, she said, "If that's true, just what do you think you're going to do about it, Lauren?"

She pulled the leash tighter.

CHAPTER 30

I screamed. Or at least I tried to. It came out as a croak, since Elena tightened the leash even more.

I turned slightly, wanting to face her fully but unable to move very far. Even so, I could see that she looked furious. Evil. Triumphant. And I was even more determined to survive so I could kick her right in her nasty face.

My mind raced even as I feared I was losing consciousness. The small dogs yipped and barked around us, but much louder and more sinister was the loud rumble in my brain. Instead of coming up with a solution, I remembered Matt's order to wait for him, along with Dante's prior instructions. I was supposed to be careful. I wasn't supposed to be alone.

Then I remembered again, even as Elena screamed and toppled over, dragging me with her. I wasn't alone.

That rumble had been my dear Zoey, growling. She had leaped on Elena.

That distraction, as she fell over with Zoey still making that loud snarling noise and standing on her chest, was enough for me to tear the leash from around my neck, gagging but alive.

Just as the door crashed open.

I expected Matt, but got a three-fer instead: Matt, plus Antonio and Brooke.

Matt looked furious. At me, for not listening to him? Or, more logically, at Elena for attacking me?

I couldn't ask him. I had to help gently guide Zoey away from the woman she'd attacked to save me. I sat on the floor, hugging her and praising her in my cracked voice, coughing nearly between every word.

Antonio took control.

"What's Antonio doing here?" I asked Brooke as she knelt on the floor near me, or at least I tried to ask that before my next round of coughing. "Thought . . . he was . . . with Jerry," I finished.

"We're convinced that Elena used him," she said quietly as Antonio read Elena her rights. "He told us that he made that gesture when he was nervous, and the few times he'd made it lately was when Elena had been with him, goading him about how he'd never be more than an assistant animal handler, and how she was going to be a famous film star someday, that kind of thing."

"Today?" I managed to croak out.

"Yeah, she was going through that scenario right here at HotRescues, pointing out some of Jerry's permanent 'fans,' the dogs, since he'd never be anything better. He'd argued with her, then started to cave in to her goading — and made that gesture."

I recalled that Elena was with us the first time I had seen him hold his head that way, too. "Who was disguised . . . and broke in . . . at HotRescues?" I asked.

"Elena," Brooke said with a decisive nod, as Matt bent down and put his arms around me. At first, he had stayed in front of the door. I assumed he was acting as Antonio's backup in case Elena tried to run.

"Are you okay, Lauren?"

I tried nodding, which just made me cough again. I looked away, even as I felt somewhat comforted by Matt's holding me close. When the coughing subsided, I tucked my head against his firm chest, still catching my breath.

When I felt a little better, I sighed.

"Can you stand?"

Without answering Matt, I began to pull

my legs up under me. He helped me to rise.

Where I got a really great view of Antonio pushing Elena, her wrists handcuffed behind her back, out the door of the small dog building.

I wanted to clap and cheer.

Instead, I again leaned against Matt. Zoey stood on her hind legs, her front paws on my side. I reached down and patted her soft, furry head. "Good girl," I said.

Matt insisted on taking me to the nearest hospital's emergency room. I was sore but alive. That was what the doctor who examined me confirmed.

Matt was really quiet while all this was going on. Was it because I couldn't easily talk back?

I wasn't sure, but I didn't feel well enough to ask him.

I did, however, insist on his taking me back to HotRescues rather than going home. He stayed with me there, sweet man that he is, and I mostly hung out in the welcome area with Zoey, sort of holding court with our staff and volunteers, assuring them that I was fine before they all left for the day. And, yes, I acknowledged, this wasn't the first time I'd been attacked at HotRescues, but I certainly hoped it was

351

the last.

Maybe it was a good thing I couldn't talk well, though. I couldn't really answer their questions about Elena.

I was surprised at first to see that Carlie was at HotRescues when we returned. So was her film crew. I only recalled then that she had gotten my okay to film our Doberman Miracle that day for her *Fittest Pet* show because he had survived Parvo.

"Oh, Lauren." She raced up to me as I entered our welcome area. She was dressed for filming in her white veterinary jacket over black slacks, her blond hair styled immaculately around her face. Her expression was concerned, her violet eyes wide. "Are you okay? Nina told me what happened."

"Are you all right, Lauren?" Nina echoed. She had just appeared in the kitchen door.

"It's late. You should be out of here by now." I directed those words to Nina. My voice was getting stronger, though it still rasped. "And, yes, I'm fine."

Matt stood behind me, and I heard a noise from back there that sounded almost like a disgusted snort. When I turned, though, his expression was bland.

I figured I'd imagined it — although he still hadn't said much to me.

"You can go home now," I told Nina.

Carlie took me aside. "I think we'll come back sometime later this week to film Miracle. Too much going on now, and it's getting late. But you're sure you're okay?"

"Yes," I said, feeling both warmed by her caring and exasperated that she was asking again. "I'm fine."

"Then tell me — is that Elena the person who killed Hans? Am I no longer a suspect now?"

I laughed despite my growing annoyance. "I don't know, not yet. All I can feel fairly confident of at the moment is that Elena's the one who broke into HotRescues."

"Okay. Fill me in when you know more." She left with her crew a few minutes later.

"Are you ready to go home yet?" Matt asked when we were alone in the office. Nina had left, too.

"Maybe. Let me talk to Brooke."

I assumed our security director was back checking on our residents again. Before I had a chance to call her, she appeared in the welcome room from the hallway leading to the kennel area.

"Antonio contacted me," she said. "He's booked Elena. I asked him a bunch of questions, and he figures we'll all want to hear the answers — at least what he knows so far. We're to meet him for a quick dinner."

■ ■ ■ ■

We gathered around a small table with a checkered tablecloth in a family restaurant not far from the Devonshire station. Matt and I had taken Zoey home first.

Antonio arrived shortly after the rest of us. He still wore his casual outfit. He looked tired, but his smile was huge as he kissed Brooke and greeted Matt and me.

We all ordered quickly, then looked toward Antonio. "We don't have all the answers yet," he said, "but here's where things stand."

Elena was now being questioned by the detectives assigned to investigate the murder of Hans Marford. "A public defender is on the way to represent her. She isn't talking much now, but she did tell me a bit before the others got there. She knew how to get Jerry nervous enough to make that strange gesture. She didn't exactly admit to having broken into HotRescues but she didn't deny it strongly either."

"And what about Hans Marford? Did she kill him?" For Carlie's sake — and to satisfy my own curiosity — I had to ask.

"That's why I wanted to get together with you briefly now. You've got to keep this quiet, of course, since we don't want anything to screw up our ability to convict her if the evidence does point her way. But till she realized she was bragging too much and stopped talking, she gave me enough to continue a murder investigation involving her as the prime suspect."

"What?" I asked when he stopped to take a drink from his water glass.

I noticed that Brooke and Matt, too, were leaning over the table in anticipation and almost laughed — but that might have delayed what Antonio had to say.

He ran his fingers through his dark hair as if in bewilderment. His scowl from beneath his jutting brow also looked perplexed. "I don't know why she said so much. She didn't seem stupid to me. Maybe she thinks that even having what she said recorded — and I did show her that my smartphone was recording it — she can somehow withdraw or deny it. But she said that Mick Paramus had promised her she would get a starring role in his next film, whatever it was. After she seduced him. She said she hoped he knew that directors who make those kinds of promises to her after sex but renege — like Hans Marford — don't survive very long."

"Then she admitted to seducing Marford

to get an acting role in *Sheba's Story* and ran over him when he didn't follow through?" That was Matt talking. The expression on his handsome face was more angry than confused — and that confused me.

"She wasn't quite as clear about it as that, but, yes." Antonio took another swig of water, obviously wishing it was something stronger. He had to return to the station as soon as we were done eating, though, so drinking alcohol wasn't on his current agenda. "The thing she seemed most clear about was that she was going to be a huge star someday and would do anything it took to get there. She kept talking — ranting, really. Acted crazy by saying so much, but not nuts enough to get off on an insanity plea."

"And you believed all she admitted?" Matt demanded. His scowl grew deeper, as if he was filled with doubt. I wondered why.

"No reason not to," Antonio said. "She had as much access to those cars owned by the studio as anyone else in the film crew, and she knew where they usually hid the keys. The driver of the murder vehicle wore gloves, and she'd worn even more of a disguise when she broke into HotRescues. Plus, she knew about Carlie Stellan's prior relationship with the director. She's the one who told the detectives about it when they questioned her. So, yes, I believe it was her. Why wouldn't I?"

Unlike Antonio, Matt had no reason not to have a drink with dinner. He drank a hefty swig of beer, then looked at Antonio.

"Because some women . . ." Matt answered, but didn't finish.

I wasn't sure what that had been about, but his glance toward me suggested he had something else on his mind.

The rest of our conversation, while we hurriedly ate to let Antonio return to the station, was filled with speculation about how the rest of the investigation would be conducted.

And how easily assistant animal handler — and would-be actor — Elena Derger would be convicted of the murder of director Hans Marford.

CHAPTER 31

Monday that week was almost boringly normal. I spent the day at HotRescues. I did handle two adoptions, though, so calling the day "boring" was actually inappropriate. In fact, that part was fun. Maybe I should just have left the word "boringly" out and called the day "normal."

That isn't exactly appropriate, either. A normal day isn't one during which I tell my staff, volunteers, and friends over and over, ad infinitum, about how I was okay after being attacked right here at HotRescues by a possible murderer who nearly choked me to death with a leash.

Yes, I'd heard from Antonio, by way of Brooke, that Elena had indeed been placed under arrest for murder. Apparently the cops thought they had enough evidence to convict her. At least somewhat thanks to me, and her nearly killing me, but I didn't ask for any particulars.

I also talked to Dante. I'd spoken briefly with him on Sunday to let him know all that had happened. He called again on Monday to let me know he was visiting HotRescues on Tuesday morning around ten A.M. "I'll have someone with me, too," he said but didn't elaborate.

I hoped it was someone interested in adopting a pet.

Tuesday started off normally, too. Zoey and I arrived at HotRescues early, as usual, in time to help Pete feed the animals. I left it to him and some of our volunteers to do the usual cleaning of all of our kennels and the grounds. I visited all of our enclosures and greeted our inhabitants. Zoey accompanied me.

Still relatively normal.

So why did I feel as if I was waiting for the next shoe to drop?

I was in my office when Dante arrived, and Nina called for me to come out.

When Zoey and I got to the welcome room, there was Dante, wearing a nice white shirt and dark slacks, obviously dressed for business.

And no wonder. With him was someone who looked familiar, even though I hadn't ever met him: Councilman Guy Randell.

He was of moderate height, not as tall as

Dante. His hair was dark with silver running through it in a manner that gave him a look of maturity instead of age. I wondered if he had it painted in. He'd clearly shaved well that morning, although a hint of a black beard appeared beneath his pale skin. No time for sitting out in the sun — or in tanning salons, I supposed.

In person, he looked pretty much the way he did in TV interviews, not bad looking but not especially handsome. He pasted a huge smile on his face as Dante introduced him.

I was predisposed not to trust him, thanks to his possible mistreatment of the dog we called Hope. But since Dante had brought him to HotRescues, I at least had to hear him out.

"I'd like to visit the dog in question," the councilman told me. "There has been some confusion about her, and I want to straighten it out."

The confusion, I thought, *was in the way you dumped your poor canine best friend on the streets and then disowned her.* But I acted cordial — again because Dante was involved. And also because I hadn't decided how much I could trust Katrina/Cathy, our volunteer who was apparently this man's ex-girlfriend.

I preceded the two men down the hall and out into our kennel area. Guy Randell seemed charmed by our facility, and by the first dogs we saw. They all greeted him with barks.

And then we got to Hope's kennel. Guy stopped and stared. "That's her," he said. "May I visit with her?"

I exchanged glances with Dante, who nodded. I wasn't going to argue. I let Hope out and put her on a leash so she'd stay near us. The councilman knelt, patted her, then stood.

"I know what you've heard from Katrina," he told me. "For your information, I dumped her — Katrina, that is — but not this dog. Ginger — Hope — was hers, but only for a short while. Let's go somewhere private, and I'll tell you about it." The privacy request was because some of our volunteers were around and had obviously recognized him. They were pointing and chattering.

"My office is available," I said.

Once we were settled there, both Hope and Zoey at our feet, I listened to the politico's story. Turned out that the whole thing, at least according to him, was devised by his former lover for revenge. She wanted him to look like a nasty animal abuser and set things up so she could make him appear to have abandoned Ginger while she talked to the media about him.

He claimed that she must have given his contact information to the microchip company and that he had never been contacted by them to confirm it. Since the publicity against him was heating up, he'd gotten his legal staff involved with the media — and to contact Katrina for a retraction.

True? I wasn't sure. But I'd gotten Katrina/Cathy's claim in writing that the dog wasn't hers but the councilman's. She'd also said that, to the extent she saved Hope and became her owner, she was relinquishing Hope to our care.

Although abandoning the pup on the street, if she was the one who'd done it, wasn't a good sign that she'd ever saved Hope in the first place.

Councilman Randell, too, agreed to sign relinquishment papers — not that he admitted to owning Ginger/Hope either.

One way or another, she was now definitely and officially relinquished. To the extent I'd had any questions before, she was now available for HotRescues to rehome. And we had a really good match just waiting for her.

"Thanks," I said to both men as they left.

I looked down at the dog whose leash I held. "And Hope thanks you, too."

Before Dante left, he took me aside for a minute. "Morton told me to let you know that, once things are settled down, he wants to have a talk with you."

"If it's about doing a screenplay based on what happened," I said, watching Dante grin, "count me out."

I went to Solario Studios shortly afterward to check in and see how things were going. The cast and crew of *Sheba's Story* had had a day to get used to what appeared to be the real story of who'd killed Hans. Did they know why yet?

The guard at the gate let me in, and, not seeing any obvious filming activity on the lot, I hurried to the building where the She-bas were housed.

Most everyone I wanted to see was there. Mick Paramus was talking to the actors about the scene that would be shot later that afternoon. Cowan was demonstrating some of the moves that Stellar would make on camera. The more nervous Sheba looka-like was going to cower when someone abusing her yelled — until the Millie character played by Lyanne yelled right back at him and took possession of the dog.

I stood off to the side and listened for a while, but then Grant spotted me. He came over, as always wearing his American Humane vest, and whispered, "Is what I heard true?"

I noticed then that Winna, who stood with Jerry and some of her other handlers, was staring at us. Jerry's eyes widened as he saw me and he glared, as if he was angry that I could have believed he'd done the things that his counterpart Elena was allegedly guilty of.

Mick apparently noticed the distraction. He handed his clipboard to R. G. and approached me.

"I heard some pretty nasty things happened at HotRescues when we left," he said. "Are they true?"

"I —" I saw that a lot of people were starting to crowd around us, so I asked, "Is it okay if I give a brief announcement about it?"

He nodded.

I stepped back to face everyone. "I figure that most of you have heard about Elena. I'm not going to accuse her of anything here, but what I can tell you is that she and I had a bit of an altercation, and the result seemed to indicate that she might have been the person who broke into HotRescues last week."

"Did she kill Hans?" That was Lyanne, and she looked excited, as if she enjoyed the idea of something sleazy to talk about. She must love the paparazzi who interviewed her.

"I don't know," I said. "There have been some allegations along those lines that I understand are being investigated by the police." That sounded vanilla enough to me that even Kendra Ballantyne would probably approve of it. I figured the media would eventually pick up on Elena's arrest and give more details than I felt comfortable talking about.

I answered a few more questions just as generally. The crowd seemed disappointed that there wasn't something even juicier for me to report.

When I was done, I thanked Mick, but before I could get away he said, "The cops have asked me some questions. I was aware that Hans . . . well, let's just say that he and Elena seemed to have something going for a while. And then, once he was gone and I was the new director, she seemed to be interested in me for more than telling which scene the dogs would appear in next. I didn't buy into it, and she seemed to accept it. That's why I didn't really suspect her. But then I heard she had set her sights on Erskine Blainer, who's directing *A Matter of Death and Life,* the next film Hans was in the running for."

The director who'd fought with Hans, whom I'd considered a primary suspect . . . before. Just in case the detectives interrogating Elena weren't aware of her contacting Blainer, I silently vowed to let Antonio know. Maybe there'd be more evidence against her available there.

Before I left, I joined up with Grant again. "I gather that the filming didn't slow down because of the new twist in the murder investigation," I said.

"No, and in fact it's going well. I anticipate that the actual filming will be over within a week or three."

"And assuming things go as they have been, you'll be able to give your certification?"

He nodded. " 'No Animals Were Harmed.' "

I smiled and to my own surprise, and his, too, I expect, I gave him a quick hug. "That's just the way it should be," I said.

"Not only that, but the poodles and other dogs that aren't otherwise being taken in by members of the cast and crew should be available for HotRescues to rehome in about a month. You up for that?"

"I sure am!"

I returned to HotRescues. It was fairly late in the day by then. Even so, I wanted to give an update on everything to Matt.

"I'm on my way there now," he told me.

"Great," I said. "We can grab some dinner."

When he showed up a while later, Nina had already left for the day, and Brooke had arrived and was making her initial security rounds. Of course I made sure they were as up to date as I was on everything — especially Hope.

I was a little surprised that Matt had Rex along when I unlocked the door to let them into the welcome area now that HotRescues was officially closed for the day. He must have taken time to go home to get his sweet dog, but the evening was still young. "Hi," I said to both of them. When I moved to give Matt a kiss, Rex must have pulled on his leash since Matt was suddenly turned at an angle that preempted any embrace.

"Where shall we go for dinner?" I asked, kneeling to hug Rex instead as Matt patted Zoey's head.

"Not sure I have the time . . . Look, Lauren, can we talk for a minute?"

I froze. His tone was so serious, and when I looked up at him so was his expression. I refused to allow myself to start anticipating what he wanted to say. Instead, I just said lightly, "Sure. Have a seat." I pointed to the small table along the wall, and we each planted ourselves in the chairs facing one another.

My heart was racing, but I stayed placid, at least on the outside. "So what's up?" I asked.

He pursed his lips, then began, "The other day, when I got to HotRescues and you called for help, and then Antonio and I got there after that woman had attacked you, I —"

He hesitated. Was he about to declare how upset he had been? How worried for me?

How he hated to see that the woman he loved had been nearly killed?

Was he about to propose?

Hell, I hated when my mind went off on tangents like that. But if so, what would I say? My last marriage had been such an awful mistake. But the first one . . .

"You didn't listen to me," he finished. "Again."

I blinked at him. That wasn't what I'd anticipated. He was upset because I didn't obey his orders?

"This wasn't the first time I wasn't happy about your getting involved in a murder investigation. You're not a cop, or private eye, or anything like that. I'm much more of a law enforcement type than you, and not even I try to solve homicides."

"You try to protect animals," I said, keeping my tone as light as I could. "That's even more important. To me, at least."

I looked down at Zoey and Rex, who now lay at our feet on the tile floor. That was better than looking at Matt's face. Was he chewing me out? I was still alive.

Was he telling me I had to follow his orders to stay in whatever relationship we had?

I never took orders from anyone. My ex-husband had tried that — and it was one of the things that had caused me to boot him out.

On the other hand, this time Matt had been right. If I'd done as he commanded and waited for him — only a short while, since he was already at HotRescues — I might not have been hurt, and Elena would still have been caught.

"That's one thing I really like about you," he said more gently. "We do share a love of animals. But . . . Lauren, I've been think-

369

ing. I care about you a lot — and that's why I don't like worrying about you. Not the way I do, anyway. About your safety."

"You don't need to," I replied, but I was touched by his caring look.

"No," he said, "I don't. Will you promise me something?"

With that soulful expression in his eyes, I'd have considered promising him anything. But of course I wouldn't. Not without knowing what he wanted. "What's that?" I asked, trying not to let suspicion enter my tone.

"That this is the last time you'll put yourself in harm's way by poking your nose into a murder investigation."

"I didn't plan to get involved in any of them," I reminded him, trying to keep the chill out of my voice. But I didn't like the way he'd said that. I wasn't poking my nose anywhere. I was helping myself, or my friends.

"I know. But will you promise?" He took me into his arms as if to bribe me with his closeness.

"I can promise I won't go looking for trouble," I muttered against his chest.

"Would you say you'd gone looking for it in any of these instances?" he asked.

I pulled back. "What do you think?"

His laugh sounded rueful. "I know that you've convinced yourself that you haven't." He held up his hand as I opened my mouth to yell at him. "And maybe you're right. Tell you what."

"What?" I asked suspiciously.

"Next time you even think about trying to solve a murder — and I really hope there isn't such a next time — you'll tell me right away and we'll discuss it. And you'll try to pay attention when I tell you to back off. Or you'll at least wait before jumping into danger till I can get there to help you."

He'd scolded me before, and I appreciated his caring. In fact, instead of wanting to yell at him I found myself smiling. "If I can," I said. "And I appreciate it. But you really don't have to worry about me, Matt. I have no intention of getting involved in another murder case."

"Okay. That's good enough — for now."

"Great. Are we having dinner together tonight?"

"Sure, if you're hungry."

I was. And I might even be hungry for more than food. His caring about me that way warmed me deep inside.

"Give me a few minutes, though," I told him. "I have a couple of phone calls to make."

He and Rex went outside into the kennel area, taking Zoey with them. That way the dogs could do what nature demanded, if they wanted, while I finished up in here. Of course I made sure that Matt had biodegradable poop bags with him.

I hurried down the hall into my office and moved the mouse so my computer woke up from sleep mode. Then I looked up a name and phone number. The Barancas. I'd have to call Kevin later to tell him that I'd called his girlfriend Mindi's home, and what I'd been able to tell her parents.

I dialed their number. Judy Baranca answered.

"Hello, Judy," I said. "It's Lauren Vancouver — Kevin's mom? I'm here at Hot-Rescues and have some great news for you. Hope is now definitely available for adoption. When can Joseph and you come in and fill out the paperwork — and pick her up?"

Judy screamed in delight. And called her husband to the phone.

They promised to come in the next day to adopt Hope.

One more call to make: Carlie. "Hey," I said. "I've got some more news both about the Hans Marford murder and some other stuff I'd like to talk to you about."

"Great! Are you available for dinner tonight?"

"If you'd like to join Matt and me. You can bring Liam, too."

That worked for all of us.

We had a great evening, especially since Carlie promised to feature the dogs from *Sheba's Story* who needed a new home on an upcoming episode of *Pet Fitness*. I was sure that, for the first time, we were likely to have people lined up at the door of HotRescues ready to adopt a new pet.

Later, Matt and I, and our dogs, headed to my house and closed the door behind us.

I couldn't help wondering, as I got ready to join him in bed, what he'd really do if I happened to get stuck trying to investigate another murder someday.

I hoped I wouldn't have to find out — although I couldn't help giving myself a virtual pat on the back for having solved my fourth — fourth! — case.

ABOUT THE AUTHOR

Linda O. Johnston is a lawyer and a writer of mysteries, paranormal romance, and romantic suspense. She lives in the hills overlooking the San Fernando Valley with her husband, Fred, and two Cavalier King Charles spaniels, Lexie and Mystie. Visit her website at www.LindaOJohnston.com.

CPSIA information can be obtained
at www.ICGtesting.com
Printed in the USA
FFOW04n2030291013
2226FF

9 781410 461858